Shoot
the Moon

Billie Letts

GRAND CENTRAL
PUBLISHING

NEW YORK   BOSTON

Grateful acknowledgment is made to quote from the following:

"This Place" music and lyrics by Shawn Letts. Copyright © 1992. All rights reserved. Used by permission.

"Love Poem" reprinted by permission of Bonnie Nims from *The Iron Pastoral*, William Sloane Associates, 1947.

Excerpt from "Welcome Home," from *The Awful Rowing Toward God* by Anne Sexton. Copyright © 1975 by Loring Conant, Jr., Executor of the Estate of Anne Sexton. Reprinted by permission of Houghton Mifflin Company. All rights reserved.

Grand Central Publishing
Hachette Book Group USA
237 Park Avenue
New York, NY 10017
Visit our Web site at www.HachetteBookGroupUSA.com

Grand Central Publishing is a division of Hachette Book Group USA, Inc. The Grand Central Publishing name and logo is a trademark of Hachette Book Group USA.

Printed in the United States of America

Originally published in hardcover by Hachette Book Group USA
First Trade Edition: July 2005
First Mass Market Edition: August 2008

10 9 8 7 6 5 4 3 2 1

PRAISE FOR *SHOOT THE MOON* AND BILLIE LETTS

"[An] exciting, heartwarming, and poignant thriller."
—*Midwest Book Review*

"A story of discovery with some mystery and romance thrown in the mix . . . Billie Letts is a marvelous storyteller who fills SHOOT THE MOON with colorful locals."
—*Memphis Commercial Appeal*

"A tender yarn."
—*Entertainment Weekly*

"Evokes the closeness of small-town life . . . Perfect for the beach."
—*Kirkus Reviews*

"It's no wonder Letts has received numerous awards for her writing. She has a gift for expressing heartfelt emotion—pain, sorrow, and especially love. This novel is a definite keeper."
—*Anniston Star (AL)*

"Letts's characters are well-developed as she gradually reveals their hidden secrets and personalities. The encompassing nature of this novel, complete with humor, pathos, and mystery, showcases Letts's superlative writing."
—*Romantic Times BOOKclub Magazine*
(Top Pick, 4½ stars)

more . . .

"Letts's third novel is another juicy story . . . Letts says she would categorize her novels as 'slice of life' . . . SHOOT THE MOON is a rich and generous slice."

—*Winston-Salem Journal* (NC)

"An absorbing read . . . Billie Letts has written another amazing novel to follow *Where the Heart Is*. Her ability to create vivid and realistic characters shines through and makes this novel a pleasure to read."

—TheCelebrityCafe.com

"This entirely gripping and charming read is southern mystery at its finest . . . suspenseful and enthralling."

—NewMysteryReader.com

"I thought it would be impossible for Billie Letts to better her two previous books, *Where the Heart Is* and *The Honk and Holler Opening Soon*. I was wrong. The author is a master at characterization and storytelling . . . This story does shoot the moon . . . Highly recommended."

—ReviewingtheEvidence.com

"More than a mystery . . . an exciting, heartwarming, and poignant thriller."

—*I Love a Mystery*

"Letts at her very best . . . SHOOT THE MOON is not only a wild and woolly mystery, but holds a love story that is as tender as it is surprising. Brava to Billie Letts for yet another slice of Americana that goes straight to the heart."

—BusinessKnowHow.com

"An excellent . . . mesmerizing novel . . . This is one that you will find hard to put down . . . Unforgettable. Don't pass on this one."

—BestsellersWorld.com

ALSO BY BILLIE LETTS

Where the Heart Is
The Honk and Holler Opening Soon
Made in the U.S.A.

This one is for my sons, Shawn and Tracy, who bring me joy—even on the darkest days.

Acknowledgments

GRATEFUL APPRECIATION GOES TO:

Elaine Markson, my agent, who found me three books ago wandering around a writers' conference hoping someone would look at my work; Jamie Raab, my editor, who must feel much like a midwife after helping me deliver this one; Lisa Callamaro, who gave me the gift of seeing my first story on the big screen; also double thanks to Ben Greenberg for going beyond the call of duty;

Robert W. Allen, Ph.D., Harold Battenfield, D.O., Glen Burke, Katrina Farr, Shari Finik, George Haralson, Chief Deputy, and Wesley E. Johnson, J.D., for their technical advice;

Wilma Shires, whose extraordinary patience and expertise wrestled all these words onto a computer disk;

Mary Battenfield, Brad Cushman, Molly Griffis, Arlene Johnson, Teresa Miller and Georgann "Sister" Vineyard, a great group of friends who kept me going;

Dana Letts, my stepson, who found information for me when I couldn't;

And Dennis, my husband, lover, friend . . . my first reader, my toughest critic and my biggest fan.

I thank you all!

Shoot
the Moon

Prologue

Back when it happened, back in 1972, there wasn't an adult in the county who didn't know every detail of the crime.

Lige Haney, editor of the *DeClare Democrat*, kept the story on the front page for months. Of course, other news made the headlines now and then—a spring flood washed out the Post Road Bridge; two local boys, the Standingdeer brothers, were wounded in Vietnam on the same day; and a fire downtown gutted TenPenny Hardware and the Hungry Hawk Café.

But none of the news had the staying power of murder and abduction—a young mother stabbed to death, her ten-month-old son missing—the worst crime ever committed in DeClare, Oklahoma.

Television news teams came in from all over the state, their trucks and vans lining the town square, where most of the reporters used the courthouse as a backdrop for their broadcasts.

Lantana Mitchell, a twenty-one-year-old rookie with KWTV in Tulsa, wasn't the brightest of the bunch, but she was the most eager and certainly the best looking, which gave her an edge over the older, more experienced reporters. At least with Oliver Boyd Daniels.

Daniels, deputy sheriff of DeClare, was a mean drunk; a tough-talking, tough-looking guy; a man's man who appealed to women despite missing part of one ear and three teeth, the gap in his mouth covered by an ill-fitting bridge. He was also husband to a wife much younger than him; and father of an eight-year-old boy with Down syndrome. He lost the teeth and the piece of ear in a bar fight in Baton Rouge. He found the wife, his third, when she was leading cheers at a DeClare High School football game.

But Lantana Mitchell was looking for her big break in the news business, so she welcomed the deputy into her room at the Riverfront Motel every night for the ten days she was in town covering the story.

Daniels promised to feed her inside information about the crime; she promised him she wouldn't use his nickname, "O Boy," on the air.

In the end, they both lied . . . he because Lantana wouldn't do everything he wanted her to do in bed; she because Daniels didn't tell her about the missing boy's pajama bottoms he found on the bank of Willow Creek.

Instead, he leaked that news to Arthur McFadden, his half-brother, in exchange for a used bass boat. Because they had different fathers, their likeness was not striking; Arthur was shorter, thinner and less robust than O Boy.

But both had inherited the cold blue eyes of their mother, eyes that could veil all emotions except one—anger. And like her, drunk or sober, they could be intimidating and cruel. The major difference in the brothers' personalities, though, was that Arthur could come across as charming when a situation demanded it, an ability O Boy neither possessed nor understood.

Arthur owned and operated the local daytime radio station, KSET, which was on the air from sunup until sundown, seven days a week.

Arthur loved the station, rarely regretting the sacrifices he'd made to own it, even though his work was never-ending. He read the news, weather and farm reports; prerecorded all the commercials; conducted live interviews regarding every event in the county; read the public service announcements; did all the billing and bookkeeping; answered the phone; paid the bills; and hosted *Swap Shop*, a local favorite on which listeners called in to buy, sell or trade fresh eggs, car parts, hunting dogs, baby beds, hand-stitched quilts, lawn mowers and junk of all descriptions—new or used.

The only other person involved in the day-to-day operation of KSET was Kyle Leander, Arthur's twenty-five-year-old stepson. Kyle, who had discovered psychedelic drugs the year he flunked out of Yale, deejayed an afternoon show he called *Catharsis*, during which he played acid rock, read excerpts from Carlos Castaneda and quoted Timothy Leary.

Arthur hated *Catharsis* just a little more than he hated Kyle, but it was Kyle's mother, Anne, a wealthy widow from Atlanta and Arthur's current wife, who had put up the money to buy KSET. And Kyle's job, which paid him twenty-five hundred a month, was part of the bargain.

But Arthur didn't have to deal with Kyle on the day he broke the news of the discovery of the kidnapped child's pajama bottoms because Kyle was in rehab, shipped off to a high-dollar clinic called Restoration in North Carolina to dry out again. And that suited Arthur just fine.

He had the station all to himself and filled the *Catharsis* time slot with a live interview with O Boy Daniels, who predicted the case would be solved within days, if not within hours.

Until then, there'd been no real break in the crime—no fingerprints or tire tracks, no murder weapon, no strangers in town that anyone could remember. No clues at all as to who had killed the young woman and taken her little boy.

But now, with something to go on—a pair of blue pajama pants with yellow ducks—the community roared into action.

Hap Duchamp, president of the First National Bank, offered a reward for information leading to a conviction. Of course, no one ever claimed the money because the man arrested and jailed on suspicion never made it to the courtroom.

Most folks, though, especially the locals, were less interested in the money than they were in helping to find the missing child.

Matthew Donaldson, the fire chief, put out a call for volunteers, and for the next ten days, firemen, policemen and too many civilians poured into DeClare from all over the country. Four major search teams were formed, and by the end of the week, the hunt was going on twenty-four hours a day.

Swanson's Funeral Home provided a tent under which the DeClare Ladies' Auxiliary set up tables, where they made sure food and drinks were always available to those involved in the search. Teeve Harjo, whose husband, Navy, owned the local pool hall and booked sports bets, put herself in charge, making sure the ham sandwiches were fresh and the coffeepot was never empty.

The DAR, not to be outdone by the Auxiliary, whom they regarded as a rough bunch lacking social grace and breeding, contributed enough Purina Dog Chow to feed all the tracking dogs being brought in by their handlers. The suggestion came from Martha Bernard Duchamp, the club historian, whose great-grandfather had been killed at Gettysburg; whose grandfather had made a fortune in cotton; whose father had started the First National Bank; whose son was now its president.

John Majors, owner of Majors' Office Supply, printed a thousand flyers with the missing boy's picture, which the Boy Scouts tacked to every telephone pole in town and taped in the windows of all the businesses on Main Street.

The Young Democrats bought several hundred yards of yellow ribbon, which the high school choir kids cut up and tied to every tree in DeClare except for the half-dozen Chinese elms in Raymond Cruddup's front lawn.

Raymond claimed that the trees were too delicate to be disturbed. Raymond Cruddup was the town grump.

The churches of DeClare organized round-the-clock prayer circles, where prayers were offered up for the little boy's safe return. Many of the circles continued their supplications for weeks, long after most doubted there would be a return—safe or not.

Even so, preachers used the tragedy of the crime as the theme for Sunday sermons, and for months afterward baptizings increased, as did church memberships, especially at Goodwill Baptist, the largest church in town.

Patti Frazier, the organist at Goodwill Baptist, wrote a song about the kidnapping, a tune she called "Gone Missing." Encouraged by the response of the congregation when she sang her composition at a Wednesday night service, Patti recorded "Gone Missing" on her tape recorder and gave a copy to Arthur McFadden, who played it every hour on KSET.

But 1972, the year little Nicky Jack Harjo disappeared, was a long time ago. Over a quarter of a century. And much had changed since then.

TenPenny Hardware was rebuilt soon after the fire that destroyed it, but business fell off after Wal-Mart came to town, and the TenPenny closed its doors in 1984.

The Hungry Hawk Café, razed in the same blaze that took the hardware store, was never rebuilt, but six years later a McDonald's opened on the same site.

Lige Haney continued to edit the *Democrat* until diabetes began to rob him of his sight. Finally, in 1986, he sold the paper to a news conglomerate buying up small-town weeklies all over the country, and he and his wife, Clara, retired to Florida. Four years later, having endured two hurricanes, they gave up on the Sunshine State and returned to DeClare. But just two weeks after they'd moved back, a tornado swept through the eastern edge of town, destroying their new home. Fortunately, Lige, Clara and Phantom, Lige's Seeing Eye Dog, a sturdy blond Lab, survived unharmed in their basement.

Soon after rebuilding, Lige went back to the work he had always loved by writing a weekly column called "Statecraft" that he dictated to Clara, who typed the pieces on Lige's old Smith-Corona. "Statecraft" focused on Oklahoma politics and reflected Lige's "yellow dog" Democratic viewpoints, which did not set well with the Republican ownership but was a favorite with locals.

Television news teams returned to DeClare occasionally in the intervening years, but only twice for major stories. They came back when an ice storm on the interstate caused a pileup of thirteen cars that killed four teenagers on their way to a basketball game; then again to cover a triple homicide on Bois D'Arc Road, the result of a drug deal gone bad.

But neither event brought Lantana Mitchell back to the community. After the O Boy Daniels fiasco, which left her with a pregnancy she terminated with an abortion in Kansas City, she learned to use her looks and ambition with more discretion.

Two years following her stint in DeClare, she attended a media convention in Chicago, where she met and charmed an executive with ABC—a man with both ears, all his teeth and no wife. After Lantana nudged him into marriage, he made her anchor of the evening news in Los Angeles.

The marriage didn't last, nor did the job, but a hefty divorce settlement allowed her to return to Tulsa, where she wrote four nonfiction crime books, one of which was published.

O Boy Daniels hit a rough patch in the early eighties when he nearly beat to death a county prisoner suspected by many in the community to be a pedophile but who was most certainly going to get out of a conviction because of a legal technicality.

O Boy claimed the prisoner was trying to escape, but the jury, even though they believed the child molester deserved a good beating, couldn't buy the lie because of the restrictions placed on them by the presiding judge.

After serving two years at the state penitentiary, O Boy returned to DeClare, opened a bait shop near the river and moved back in with his wife, Carrie, the former cheerleader, and their disabled son, Kippy.

Five years later, O Boy ran for sheriff and won, even though the law prohibited him, a convicted felon, from carrying a firearm. Apparently, the voters of DeClare figured O Boy was tough enough that he didn't need a weapon.

Arthur McFadden continued to operate the radio station after his wife divorced him and moved back to Atlanta. Arthur's only regret about the split was that the terms of the divorce left him stuck with Kyle Leander for as long as Kyle wanted to keep his job at the station. And Kyle had no intention of leaving.

Hap Duchamp served as president of the First National Bank until 1980, when rumors began to circulate that he was a homosexual. He resigned before he was removed by the board of directors, and with the law degree he'd earned from Tulsa University twenty years earlier, he started his own small practice. Then, relieved of the pretense of being straight, he and his lover, Matthew Donaldson, former fire chief, moved in together in an elegant A-frame they built in a wooded area near the river.

Teeve Harjo was still active in the Ladies' Auxiliary but had less time to devote to the organization than she had years earlier. Her husband, Navy, had sneaked out of town one night, taking his new Buick, on which he'd made only three payments, and over twenty thousand dollars he'd taken in wagers on a Cowboys' game. In addition to Teeve, he left behind his young daughter, a second mortgage on the house and a lot of angry gamblers.

But the pool hall was paid for, so, with no other income and limited job skills, Teeve took over the operation the day after Navy left. Instead of being the disaster that most predicted, Teeve turned out to have a good head for business. She added a couple of video games, stopped booking bets and selling beer so teenagers could come in to play and turned the storage area into a tiny lunchroom, where she served sandwiches and her popular peanut-butter pies made from a secret family recipe. Five years after Navy left, Teeve's Place was thriving.

Martha Bernard Duchamp, DAR historian, took up drinking soon after her son's "coming out." In the beginning, she was able to conceal her newly acquired taste, but by the time she fell and broke her hip in 1985, everyone in DeClare knew she had her Jack Daniel's delivered by the case from Ritzy's Liquor Store.

Raymond Cruddup died in 1987, his Chinese elms in an ice storm the following winter.

Patti Frazier's song "Gone Missing" was recorded by a gospel quartet on an album titled "In God's Hands." When the album did well on the Christian music charts, Patti sold three more of her songs and made enough money to buy the Riverfront Motel when the owner put it on the market.

By 1999, the population of DeClare, Oklahoma, had risen to seven thousand, about a thousand more than what it was in 1972. The business district downtown had spilled over from Main Street to State Street three blocks away, and two small industries had relocated to the county.

Crime across the country had grown to such frightening levels that TV and newspaper accounts of mass murders, school killings, rape and child abuse had become routine.

But the old-timers, the ones who had lived through

the murder of Gaylene Harjo and the abduction of her son, would occasionally rehash the crime as if it had happened only the day before.

Now, twenty-seven years after the boy's disappearance, the hundreds of yellow ribbons tied to trees by the high school choir had rotted and dropped away. And the flyers posted everywhere the Boy Scouts could make them stick were gone.

All except one.

Yellowed and brittled with age, a flyer with the little boy's picture was still taped to the window of Teeve's Place.

Chapter One

His early morning flight from Los Angeles had been delayed for nearly two hours because of fog. Plenty of time for him to back out, just let it all go. Once he even grabbed his bag and left the terminal, but he changed his mind. Again.

After boarding, he found himself seated next to an elderly woman who was weeping quietly. She was still crying when, twenty minutes later, she offered a whispered apology, but he pretended sleep. Whatever her problem was, he didn't want to hear it. He had no interest in hearing people whine.

When she left her seat to go to the lavatory, he slipped from the first-class cabin and found an empty row near the back of the plane.

For a while he tried to read but gave it up when he felt a headache coming on. He hadn't slept at all the night before, hadn't even gone to bed. Instead, he'd spent the hours sitting on his balcony, trying to persuade himself not to make this trip.

Then, just before five that morning, he'd phoned to

make his flight reservation, left a vague message on his receptionist's answering machine and pulled a suitcase from his closet.

Now, with his stomach churning from too much airport coffee, his knees wedged against the seat in front of him, his body heavy with fatigue, he decided that when the plane landed, he'd give this up. Take the next available flight back to L.A.

But he didn't.

After he picked up his rental, a Mitsubishi Eclipse, and a map at Tulsa International Airport, he headed east.

The Avis blue-chip car, the only convertible available, wouldn't have been his first choice; he drove a Jaguar XK8 in L.A. But even before he drove out of the city, he realized he'd underestimated the Oklahoma heat, well over a hundred, with humidity so high that his shirt was plastered to his back despite the hot wind.

The two-hour drive took him through mostly empty country, the highway skirting towns called Coweta, Tullahassee, Oktaha—names that conjured scenes of Gene Autry movies.

He arrived in DeClare before dark, then checked into the Riverfront Motel, which looked just a little more inviting than the White Buffalo Inn at the edge of town or a decrepit hotel called the Saddletree a few blocks away.

His room was about what he expected. Drab and cramped, smaller even than the dorm room he'd lived in at Tufts for five years. Behind the drapes he found sliding glass doors leading to a balcony that overlooked a river backed by woods of towering pines.

He didn't bother to unpack, but he hadn't brought much anyway. He wasn't planning to stick around long.

The motel restaurant was crowded, according to his waitress, because it was Thursday.

"Catfish night," she explained, managing to turn "night" into a three-syllable word. "All you can eat for six ninety-five."

"Is it baked?" he asked, a question she thought was hilarious.

"You're not an Okie, are you? Only one way to fix catfish, and that's to fry it. You want baked fish, be here for the Sunday buffet. We have baked cod then. But come before noon, 'cause when the churches let out, this place is packed."

"I'll be gone before Sunday."

"Not staying long, huh?"

Though he'd already framed the lie, he hesitated. Another chance to back out.

"I'm here to look up some old friends of my parents."

"Who's that?"

He felt his heart quicken, his breath come short. But he was in it now.

"A family named Harjo."

"Which one? We got Harjos scattered all over this part of the country. They're all related, one way or another. Ben was the oldest, I think."

"Where can I find him?"

"He's dead, but his wife, Enid, lives way the hell out in the boonies. Can't tell you how to get there. Your best bet is Teeve. She was married to a Harjo. He took off years ago, but she's still close to the family. She runs the pool hall on Main Street."

After his dinner, and with enough fat in his system to grease axle rods, he walked to the center of town. Four depressing blocks scarred by struggle and failure.

Buildings of crumbling native stone, many of them empty; a boarded-up movie theater, its marquee advertising a citywide garage sale; a bank wearing a new facade, the centerpiece a massive clock running an hour late.

Business owners battling the Wal-Mart east of town had tried to lure customers back by installing canvas awnings, camouflaging peeling paint with cheap brick veneer, placing wrought-iron benches on the corner of every block. But the awnings were tattered and fading, the veneer was flaking paint and the benches were covered with pigeon droppings.

The pool hall, closed by the time he got there, didn't look as if it were faring any better than other businesses he'd passed along the way. The sign reading TEEVE'S PLACE hung crookedly over the door, and the plate glass window fronting the building bore a foot-long crack patched with caulk and masking tape.

Inside, a fluorescent bulb blinked in a tin ceiling pitted with rust. The long, narrow room was crowded with a makeshift counter, pool tables from another era, video games, vending machines and a game table with four mismatched chairs.

As he turned and started back toward the motel, a mud-splattered pickup drove by, a rifle mounted in the back window, a Confederate flag strapped across the grille, two pit bull pups chained in the truck bed.

If he'd been back home just then, he might have been cussing the traffic clogging the 405 or complaining of the heavy brown air dimming the sun or fighting the panic he felt when a tremor hit.

But at that moment, Los Angeles seemed like paradise.

Chapter Two

Teeve Harjo unlocked the front door of the pool hall while balancing four pie boxes against her chest. As soon as she took those back to the lunchroom, she returned to her car for the others.

Ordinarily, she baked only four and always sold out by two o'clock, her peanut-butter pies still the best dessert in town and the recipe still a secret. But Hap Duchamp had phoned yesterday to order three, as he and Matthew Donaldson were having weekend guests.

Always an early riser, Teeve liked to have her pies in the oven by six, then sit on her patio drinking coffee while she watched the birds at the feeders in her backyard. But her morning routine had changed since her daughter, Ivy, had come home.

She'd just flipped on the lights in the lunchroom when she heard the screen door out front slam shut, a signal that the "domino boys" had arrived.

The oldest of this foursome was Ron John O'Reily, who at eighty-two was developing Alzheimer's; the grumpiest but undisputed leader of the pack was Lonnie

Cruddup, who in temperament was much like his deceased sibling, Raymond. Johnny and Jackson Standingdeer, Cherokee brothers in their late fifties, rounded out the group.

Because they'd always considered the pool hall to be a man's refuge, they had pouted when Navy took off and Teeve took over. Then, when she'd stopped booking bets and quit selling beer, they'd fumed. But when she'd added the lunchroom and changed the sign out front to TEEVE'S POOL HALL AND TEA ROOM, they'd jumped ship.

Luring them back had not been easy, but Teeve was both inventive and determined. Not because of the few dollars she collected from their games, but because dominoes was an institution in Oklahoma pool halls and she'd be damned if she'd let four old coots depart from history.

So she had delivered a freshly baked peanut-butter pie to Lonnie Cruddup along with the promise of a new domino table to replace the shaky one he'd complained about for almost thirty years. But Lonnie was not appeased. He said his gang would be the butt of jokes for the rest of their lives—which, given their advancing years, was likely not a long time—if they were seen going into a tea room.

After an hour of nearly failed negotiations, a compromise was reached, and a week later, Lonnie had led his boys back into the pool hall, passing beneath a newly painted sign that read, quite simply, TEEVE'S PLACE.

Lige Haney was the first in for lunch, as he was every Friday, the day he delivered his column to the newspaper office.

"You give those Republicans what-for this week, Lige?"

"It was both my duty and my pleasure to do so, Teeve," he said as Phantom led him to his table. "Did you by any chance watch the news last night? Channel twelve?"

"I was beat. Went to bed before nine."

"Oh, you missed an insightful interview with our esteemed senator Jackson Langley, who spoke eloquently and with perfect balance—an amazing achievement given the difficulty of standing on one foot while the other was crammed toe-to-heel in his mouth. But this phenomenon is not uncommon among the ranks of the GOP. One does not have to be blind to see that.

"Anyway, he was asked to comment on the efforts of animal rights activists to outlaw cockfighting in our fair state. Langley, vigorously indignant, said the first thing Communists do when they take over a country is to outlaw cockfighting."

"Well, everyone knows those damned Commies are just faunching at the bit to invade Oklahoma," Teeve said.

"I laughed so hard, Phantom got out of bed to check on me."

Phantom, on hearing her name, raised her head from her paws for a few seconds, then, assured she was not being summoned, settled once again beneath the table.

"Morning, Teeve. Lige."

"Hey, Hap."

Hap Duchamp had given up Versace suits and Armani ties the day he walked away from the bank, preferring instead jeans from Kmart, shirts from Sears and shoes from Payless. He got bad eight-dollar haircuts at the Corner Barbershop, still drove his ten-year-old Chrysler and seemed entirely comfortable with who he was.

"Lige, I see you're cheating on Clara again, taking a younger girl to lunch." Hap knelt to give Phantom a pat, then took a seat at Lige's table.

"Well, this one's not as pretty as Clara, but she treats me better."

"Hap," Teeve said, "you come to eat or to pick up your pies?"

"I couldn't eat a bite, Teeve. I had half of a leftover pizza for breakfast."

"Pizza for breakfast?"

"Matthew's come up with the notion that gay men are supposed to cook like Julia Child. He made beef bourguignon for dinner last night, but it was a disaster, so I had pizza delivered. This morning he fixed quiche Lorraine. Another dismal failure. The fact is, the man can't cook a lick, but he won't admit it."

"How's your mother, Hap?" Lige asked.

"Oh, you know Martha Bernard. She thinks a day without drama is a wasted day. If her housekeeper's not swiping the silver or her accountant isn't siphoning off her money, then someone's taking her mail or poisoning her azaleas. Last night, though, she got a little closer to the real thing."

"How's that?"

"Someone smashed a window, broke into the guesthouse. Took a couple of silver candlesticks, a deer rifle that hadn't been fired since Dad died. An old black-and-white TV. Not much of a haul."

"All the same," Lige said, "Martha must have been pretty shook up."

"Aw, she loved it. Police cars, sirens. She was pissed that O Boy doesn't have a SWAT team, but all in all, she had a good night. Enough excitement that she downed a few more bedtime toddies than the one she admits to."

While she was putting together Lige's lunch, Teeve glanced into the pool hall, where she saw a man standing near the door, watching her.

He was young—thirtyish, she guessed, good-looking and dressed like money walking. Gold at his throat and wrist, linen slacks, Italian loafers and silk shirt, the left sleeve cuffed up to accommodate a thick bandage on his forearm.

She figured him for a salesman from Billiard Supply, though most of their sales reps didn't look as prosperous as this one.

"Here you go, Lige," she said as she placed his plate in front of him. "Sandwich at two o'clock, potato salad at nine."

"Did you forget my dill pickle?"

"It's straight up noon."

"Thanks."

Teeve marveled at the way Lige managed to eat without a mishap, never spilling his drink or knocking his fork off the table, no mustard smeared in the corners of his mouth, no food stuck to the front of his shirt. He was neater than most sighted people she served.

"Teeve, I'd better grab those pies and get out of here," Hap said as he pulled bills from his wallet. "I've got to go by the IGA on my way home. Matthew's fixing something called salicornia for dinner tonight."

"That sounds like an eye disease."

"Now you know why I'm going to the store. Lay in a supply of bologna and cheese just in case."

Teeve had forgotten about the stranger in the pool hall until she saw him walk out just after Hap left. He seemed vaguely familiar to her, but she couldn't recall seeing him before. Still, something about his eyes reminded her of someone she knew.

April 21, 1966

Dear Diary,

Today was the best birthday of my life because I am finally a teenager! My very best present was from Mom. A bra! I've been asking for one since Row got hers last summer but Mom said I didn't need one. Guess she changed her mind when she saw that my breasts are getting bigger. Its a double A cup but after I put it on she said it was to big. I think it fits just fine.

My brother Navy sent me a Ship 'n Shore blouse with a Peter Pan collor but I think Mom bought it and put his name on the card because he's on a ship in the Indian ocean. (Not our kind of Indian. The other kind.) James and Josie sent me a book Where the Red Fern Grows. *They live in California and haven't seen me since I was ten or eleven so I guess they think I'm still a little girl. Anyway, I already read it.*

Row got me a music box with a teeny ballerina that turns when I open the lid. Martha Sue Crow whose in my Sunday school class gave me a bottle of Evening in Paris perfume. Martha Sues supposed to be my secret pal but she can't keep anything secret. Mr.

Duchamp whose Moms boss at the bank gave me some charcoal pencils for my drawings.

Daddy gave me a pair of school shoes. Their way to big but he says I'll grow into them and no sence wasting money on shoes that will be to tight before I get any wear out of them. He calls them sensible. I call them ugly.

I bet I'll outgrow my bra before I outgrow the shoes.

Spider Woman

Chapter Three

He spent the early morning in his motel room calling Harjos listed in the DeClare phone book. Two of his calls were answered, but each time he heard a voice on the other end of the line, he hung up.

While he had coffee in the dining room downstairs, he took a look at the local newspaper, which gave ample coverage to a benefit chili supper at the fire station, three overnight burglaries, an accident involving a pickup and a cow, and an outbreak of pink-eye at the grade school.

When he went back to his room, he made his plane reservation for the next night, a seven-thirty flight from Tulsa.

He intended to have this business behind him as soon as he could, but he'd been to the pool hall three times and still hadn't talked to the Harjo woman. The first time he went was the night before, his first night in town. But he'd arrived too late. She'd already closed. He'd gone again earlier this morning, but she was busy in the back where she had a café the size of a closet and about as appealing. Then, when he'd returned at noon, the place was swarming with kids.

Now, while waiting to catch her alone, he sat on a bench across the street and used his cell phone to call the clinic.

"Albright Animal Hospital."

"Hi, Charlene."

"Dr. Albright. Are you okay? Your message sounded—"

"Something came up at the last minute. Everything all right there?"

"Well, Mr. Carletti's cat didn't make it. You know, I got worried that maybe your arm got worse and you—"

"What about the borzoi?"

"His temp's down, but he's still wheezing."

"I need to talk to David."

"He's in surgery. Mr. Leno's Dalmatian has a bowel obstruction. You want me to have Dr. Cushman call you back?"

"No. I'll reach him later."

"You had a call from Oakhaven Cemetery. Some question about the monument."

"I'll deal with that when I get back. Anything else?"

"Mrs. Lee has called for you several times. Her poodle is stressed again."

"Tell David to take care of it."

"Do you know when you'll be back?"

"Tomorrow night."

"Is there a number where I can reach you? I've called your cell phone, but—"

"I've had it switched off."

"Is there another number in case—"

"I've got to go. I'll see you Monday."

He knew his sudden and unexplained departure would be added to Charlene's growing list of concerns. She'd been hovering for the past three weeks, uneasy about his weight loss, troubled by changes in his routine.

She had reprimanded him gently for not eating "right," for failing to keep his dental appointment, for forgetting a meeting with his financial adviser. Unusual lapses, she said, for a man who fills out his day calendar a year in advance.

Charlene had been at the clinic since the day his father opened it in 1960, and though she was dependable and efficient, her intrusiveness was beginning to get on his nerves. It might be, he thought, time for her retirement, something he intended to take care of before long.

If something didn't change, she would be packing his lunch, reminding him to brush his teeth, buying his socks and underwear. And right now, the last thing he needed was another mother.

Chapter Four

Teeve was so busy with the lunch crowd in the café, she didn't even look up when the first wave of teenagers hit the pool hall at eleven-thirty. After she'd stopped selling beer, her place was no longer off-limits to the high school students, who were free to leave the campus for lunch.

They were a noisy and messy bunch, spilling their drinks, littering the floor with their chips and candy wrappers while they wrangled over the jukebox and video games. But now, with Ivy helping out an hour or so each day, Teeve didn't spend as much time refereeing as she used to.

"Okay, you fireballs. Let's flip a coin," Ivy said when she jumped into the middle of a shoving match between two boys, each claiming it was his turn at one of the video games.

Ivy was naturally pretty but did nothing to enhance her looks. She had fair skin, a complexion so light she looked pale, but she refused to wear makeup. She wore her long, honey-colored hair pulled back in a braid exactly as she had since she was a girl, and no amount of cajoling by her mother had persuaded her to change it.

At thirty, she still had the athletic frame and posture she'd had as a teenager, but her shape had changed considerably over the past few weeks.

When she came home back in May and said she'd quit her job in Chicago, Teeve wasn't much surprised at the news. Ivy had never been much of a "stayer." She'd quit piano lessons when she was eight, dropped out of Girl Scouts at eleven and attended only three meetings of the Honor Society before she stopped going.

But when Ivy said she'd come home "to stay for a while," her tomcat, Bernie, in tow, Teeve knew something was going on. The girl had hated DeClare, had been so anxious to get out that instead of attending her high school graduation, she had headed for Amsterdam to join the Greenpeace fleet in protesting the killing of whales in the North Sea.

But now, the shock of Ivy's return a few weeks earlier had begun to wear off when Teeve remarked that Ivy looked like she'd lost weight.

"Well, that's fixing to change, Mom."

"How's that?"

"I'm pregnant," Ivy said, then asked, "do you have any blue thread?"

Two weeks passed without another word from Ivy about her situation. Finally, Teeve couldn't stand it any longer. Trying to sound unrehearsed, she said, "Honey, why don't we sit down, have a cup of coffee and—"

"Have one of those mother-daughter talks?"

"Oh, no. Nothing like that. I thought we might . . . you know, just visit."

"Okay. I got pregnant by a guy I slept with three

times. Well, four, I guess, since we did it twice in one night. I'm not going to marry him, I don't even like him much. I was on the pill, but apparently he had some mighty powerful sperm.

"I've seen a doctor who declared me 'healthy as a horse,' a cliché I didn't care for. I bought a book called *What Every Pregnant Woman Needs to Know*, my bowels move regularly, I do not crave strange foods and I throw up every morning.

"I'm going to have this baby in six months, more or less, and I don't really know how I feel about that yet, but I suppose I'll figure it out as I go. Any questions?"

"No," Teeve said. "I guess that about covers it."

"Good. I'm glad we had this talk, Mom. Morning paper come yet?"

Now, three months later, Teeve didn't know any more than she did when Ivy had first told her of her pregnancy. But she knew her daughter, knew that pushing her wouldn't do a damn bit of good.

"Psst."

Teeve, preparing a takeout order of Reubens, glanced up to see Ivy motioning to her from the lunchroom door.

"You know that guy out there?" she whispered.

Looking over Ivy's shoulder, Teeve saw that the man with the bandaged arm had returned.

"He came in ten, fifteen minutes ago," Ivy said. "Just stands there and watches the kids. I tried to make conversation with him, but he doesn't say much. I think he's up to something."

"Like what?"

"I don't know, but he's creepy. Might be a pedophile."

"Well, watch him."

Teeve stayed busy for the next half hour, but she took

a break when the kids cleared out for their one o'clock classes.

"What happened to that guy who was hanging around?" Teeve asked.

"He wandered out a little while ago."

"Did you ever find out what he wanted?"

"I couldn't get anything out of him. Seemed like a weird one to me, but I don't trust any man who wears a necklace. I've gotta run. Got an appointment with Doc Bruton in a few minutes."

"Okay. See you later."

After she closed the lunchroom at two, Teeve swept out, wiped down the tables and took the trash out to the Dumpster. Then she went into the pool hall, where two regulars who worked the early shift at the toy factory were shooting eight ball.

As she passed the front door, she was disturbed to see the man Ivy called "creepy" standing on the porch, watching her through the screen. She went behind the counter, where she feigned interest in yesterday's paper, holding it in such a way that she could see him peripherally as he opened the door and stepped inside.

When she lowered the paper, he was standing on the other side of the narrow counter, staring at her.

He was even better looking up close than he was from a distance. He had radiant brown eyes, and bronzed skin that did not, she guessed, come from a tanning bed, and his dark hair, shiny and thick, fell softly across his forehead.

"If you came in for lunch, you're too late."

He looked the room over, taking it all in as if he hadn't seen it before.

"Lunchroom's closed," she said.

His eyes came to rest on a framed print of five nattily dressed dogs playing poker.

"There's a café in the next block. The Pantry. You can't miss it."

"I'm not interested in eating," he said.

Teeve had a notion that he might be another agent from the OSBI. One of the state boys showed up every couple of years or so, trying to catch someone making a wager, a holdover from Navy's bookie days.

"What are you interested in?"

"Change for a dollar."

He pulled a bill from his pocket and pushed it across the counter with his bandaged arm.

"Looks like you had an accident."

He shrugged, a kind of "it happens" gesture. After she dropped four quarters onto his palm, he got a Coke from the vending machine, then wandered toward the eight-ball players and watched their game until they finished.

As they walked out, Teeve remembered reading about a robbery that took place over in Wagoner a few weeks back, a woman held up at the Git-N-Go where she worked.

"You know, I was just getting ready to close up and—"

"Sign in the window says you're open until six."

"Usually I am, but I have a meeting to go to."

"Will you be back?"

"What?"

"Are you going to open up again after your meeting?"

Teeve was tempted to tell him it was none of his business, but she didn't.

"Why? Are you planning to come back?"

"I might."

She'd had enough then, didn't give a damn if he was the law or just some thug hoping to clean out the cash register. She was tired of the game.

"Look. If you want to shoot pool, fine. If you want to play videos, that's fine, too. But if you've got something else on your mind, then—"

"I'm trying to locate someone. I think she might be related to you."

"Who's that?"

"Gaylene Harjo."

Teeve tensed, threw him a look of warning. "Who the hell are you?"

"I'm not quite sure," he said. "But I think I might be her son."

Chapter Five

Teeve didn't buy it. Not at first.

She was certainly not swayed by the letter he showed her, a letter from a California attorney who had arranged an adoption in 1972. She didn't trust much of anything coming out of California and had no use for lawyers at all.

And when he produced a birth certificate for Nicodemus Jack Harjo, she dismissed it. Documents, she knew, could be had for a price.

But then an old memory stirred . . . a lamp crashing to the floor, a baby screaming in pain.

Little Nicky Jack had crawled beneath a table in her living room, entangled himself in an electric cord and toppled a heavy ceramic lamp. She had helped Gaylene hold him down while the emergency room doctor pulled loose flaps of skin together and put fourteen stitches into his head.

Now, reaching across the counter, she used her fingertips to brush his hair back from his face. And there it was. Running from his widow's peak into his hairline. A thick, jagged scar.

Teeve thought briefly about slipping next door to the liquor store for a bottle of bourbon. She hadn't had a drink in years, not since the day Navy left her, but she could use one now.

Instead, she turned out the lights in the pool hall, locked the door and put the CLOSED sign in the window.

Seated at a table in the lunchroom, they suffered through several uncomfortable moments until both spoke at once.

"This must seem—"

"I don't know how to—"

"Sorry."

"Go ahead."

While she took off her glasses to examine an imaginary spot on the lens, he studied a stain on the tabletop.

Finally he asked, "Are you related to her?"

"Gaylene? I was married to her brother."

Following another uneasy silence, Teeve said, "Everybody thought you were dead."

"Dead? Why would—"

When someone began knocking on the door of the pool hall, Teeve put a finger to her lips.

"If you need to get that—"

"I don't."

They waited until the knocking stopped, then Teeve said, "How about a cup of coffee?"

"Okay."

They didn't try conversation again until she returned to the table with two cups and a carafe.

"Would you like a slice of pie?"

"No, thanks."

"Peanut butter."

"I beg your pardon?"

"I make peanut-butter pies." The only sound in the room was the clinking of her spoon as she stirred sugar into her coffee. "I guess I should say welcome back or something like that, but I don't suppose this seems much like home. You were only ten months old when . . ."

The unfinished sentence hung between them for a few seconds.

"When what?"

Teeve studied his face. "You don't have a clue, do you."

"That's why I'm here."

When the phone in the pool hall started ringing, Teeve shook her head, an indication that she didn't intend to answer it. But when it became obvious that the caller wasn't going to give up, she went to the front and picked up the receiver.

Teeve's visitor overheard little of her whispered conversation, but uncomfortable with the thought that she might think he was eavesdropping, he went to the sink, poured out his coffee and rinsed out his cup, making a noisy job of it.

"My daughter," Teeve said when she came back. "She was at the door earlier. Thought something had happened to me."

"Did you tell her . . . about me?"

"No."

"I'd like to keep this quiet."

"That might be hard to do. DeClare's a small town."

He nodded. "I looked around after I got here last night."

"Where did you stay?"

"The Riverfront Motel."

"If you checked in as Nick Harjo, everyone in town will hear about it."

"I used my own name. Well, I used my other name."

"And what's that?"

"Mark Albright."

"Mark Albright," she said, testing the sound. "Tell me, Mark Albright, where have you been all these years?"

"California. I've lived there all my life." He twisted his lips into a wry smile. "At least I thought I had."

"You mean you didn't know . . ."

"That I wasn't who I thought I was? No. I learned three weeks ago that I was adopted."

"Adopted." Her voice had an edge to it. "How did you find out?"

"My mother died two years ago, Dad . . . earlier this month. I found the decree of adoption and birth certificate in their safety-deposit box."

"You have any idea why they never told you?"

"I've thought about little else for the past three weeks. My father . . . well, he was a very private man. Quiet. Thoughtful. Stayed in the background. But my mother was extremely well-known. Enjoyed the spotlight, but maybe she didn't want the press to pick up the story, start digging around."

Teeve looked puzzled.

"We lived in Los Angeles; my mother was in the movie business. Everything's a story in Hollywood."

"Was she an actress?"

"For a while, but she gave that up years ago. Became an agent. A pretty powerful agent."

"You ever think maybe there was something strange about the way they got you?" Teeve asked.

"Like what?"

"Something they were trying to hide about the circumstances of your adoption?"

"What? Why would I think that?" He was beginning to look and sound agitated, angry. "Lots of people don't tell their children the truth about their adoption. And if you're trying to blame my parents, then you—"

"But you don't have all the facts. You don't know the truth of what went on here."

"That's why I came here. I want Gaylene Harjo to tell me her side of the truth."

"She can't do that."

"She can't? Or she won't?"

Teeve leaned forward, reached across the table and put her hand on top of his, but he pulled free of her touch.

"Gaylene's dead."

She waited for some response, watched for a reaction, but could see nothing more than the muscles clenching in his jaw.

"She was murdered. The same night you disappeared."

September 7, 1966

Dear Diary,

Yipee! I'm a freshman at last. Freshman is a really cool word because when your in the eighth grade theres no one word to describe what you are. You have to say I'm an eighth grader or I'm in the eighth grade but when you get to be in the ninth grade, you can just say I'm a freshman. That word says it all.

Me and Row have all the same classes except for last period, she's taking home ec and I'm in auto mechanics. I think I'll be alot better off knowing how to change spark plugs than learning how to fix sponge cake or make an apron. Besides I don't want to be a housewife, not ever. I can't see how a woman can be happy if all she gets to do is cook and sew.

I don't even know for sure that I want to get married but sometimes I think wearing an engagement ring would be neat.

Spider Woman

September 26, 1966

Dear Diary,
I won a red ribbon today at the county fair for my watercolor of the tiger lillies in Mom's garden. To celebrate Daddy took Mom, me and Row to the Dairy Queen for milk shakes. I felt like a celebrity.

My art teacher says she's surprised to find a girl as young as me knows so much about art and artists. I told her about how Mr. Duchamp had gotten me interested when I was just a little kid.

I can't wait to tell him tomorrow about my red ribbon.

Spider Woman

Chapter Six

He left the pool hall abruptly, loaded down by the weight of what he'd just learned.

All his life he'd had other people taking care of him—nannies, drivers, cooks, secretaries, accountants, lawyers, a father, a mother . . . or two. Most had served him for money, a few for love. But now he was on his own. Neither money nor love could provide him with what he needed—someone else to deal with this mess.

He didn't doubt that a killing and abduction had taken place here, could think of no reason for the woman to lie. But he needed more than a scar on his forehead to prove he was that stolen child.

At the newspaper office he spent nearly two hours looking at microfilm, reading about the discovery of the girl's body and the stab wounds it bore, the weeks-long search for the missing baby, the suicide of a man arrested for the crime.

He saw grainy black-and-white photographs of Gaylene Harjo at eighteen and found in her features his own high cheekbones, broad nose and deep-set eyes. And he studied a picture of Nicky Jack Harjo at ten months, staring into the same face he'd seen in pictures of himself taken on his first birthday.

Suddenly the room seemed to grow smaller, the walls pulling in on him. He tried to draw a deep breath, but his lungs wouldn't allow it. Gulping for air, he bolted from the building.

Outside, he squinted against the sunlight, pain shuddering behind his eyes. He started for the motel but had gone less than a block when the first wave of nausea washed over him. Tasting bile, he turned into a narrow alley and vomited.

In front of a hardware store, he stumbled and fell to one knee. When he got back on his feet, he braced himself against a windowpane, trying to clear his head. But a man gesturing at him through the glass sent him shuffling away.

On the lawn of the library, he was sick again. He thought about going inside to rest, but he knew he would never make it up the front steps, so willed himself to move on down the block.

He was light-headed now, so dizzy that he pitched into a brick storefront, scraping his cheek.

"Hey, mister. Are you okay?"

The voice, a woman's, came from somewhere behind him, but looking back would have cost him energy he didn't have. His legs, quivering with the strain of each step, felt rubbery, and the sidewalk beneath his feet seemed to be rolling.

By the time he reached the motel, he looked like a wild-eyed drunk on the back end of a hard binge. He had a tear in the knee of his grass-stained slacks, his shirt—tail flapping—was ringed with sweat; his cheek was bruised and bloody, and his hair looked like matted fur on a wet dog.

Later, he wouldn't recall the motel housekeeper helping him to his room, wouldn't remember falling inside the door or crawling to the bed. But he would have no trouble calling back the face of the girl he dreamed of, the face that would return to him in sleep again and again.

Teeve, in robe and house shoes, was waiting on her front porch when Mark's car pulled into the drive just before eleven that night. She doubted the doorbell would wake Ivy, but she didn't want to take the chance.

"Sorry about calling so late," he said.

"Come on in."

She ushered him inside, then through the living room to a den at the back of the house, a room both cluttered and comfortable.

"You look like hell," she said, motioning him to a chair across from the one where she sat.

Though he had showered and changed, he couldn't hide his bruised cheek or his puffy eyes or the weakness that showed in the way he moved.

"Are you all right?" she asked.

"I'm fine."

"Would you rather sit on the couch?"

"Look, I owe you an apology for this afternoon, the way I ran out."

"I threw a lot at you. Too much, I suppose."

Mark propped his elbows on the arms of his chair, knit his fingers together and lowered his chin onto his hands.

"Can I get you something?" Teeve asked. "I could make some coffee."

He shook his head. "Tell me about the man who killed Gaylene Harjo."

Unable to hide her surprise, Teeve shot him a questioning look.

"I spent some time in the newspaper office today," he explained.

She let out a sigh. "Joe Dawson was arrested on suspicion. That doesn't mean he was guilty."

"You don't think he was?"

"Anyone needed help, black or white, could count on Joe. He worked with kids who got in trouble, took some of them in. When there was a fire . . . a flood, he was the first one there with food, clothes, money. Whatever he had, he shared. No, Joe didn't have a damn thing to do with what happened to you and Gaylene. I'll go to my grave believing that."

"Then why did he kill himself?"

"Some figured he wanted to save his family the grief and humiliation of a trial."

"You don't sound convinced."

"Joe wasn't a quitter, never gave up on anything. He had lung cancer. Inoperable. But he'd just started another round of chemo even though his doctor said his chances weren't good."

"So what happened in that jail?"

"One of the deputies said he found Joe dead three hours or so after he was locked up. Wrists slashed with his own pocket knife. Supposedly the same knife that had killed Gaylene."

Mark went to his empty shirt pocket for a cigarette,

vestige of the habit he'd given up four years earlier. "Is that deputy still around?" he asked.

"Yeah. He's the sheriff now. O Boy Daniels."

"I'd like to talk to him."

"Well, if you're still hoping nobody will find out who you are, I wouldn't go down to his office. He has a bait shop out on highway forty. Near the Post Oak Bridge. If you do talk to him, don't call him O Boy. That sets him off. His name's Oliver Boyd Daniels."

Mark pushed out of his chair, went to sliding glass doors that opened onto a patio and stared into the night.

"What was she like?"

Teeve hesitated because of something she heard in his voice. The whisper soft sound of sadness.

"Gaylene Harjo," he said. "What was she like?"

"Sweet, pretty. Smart. Real smart. She had two or three scholarships to go to college, but she got pregnant and . . ."

He turned, shoved his hands into his pants pockets and fixed Teeve with his eyes.

"Who was it?"

"She wouldn't say. Some thought it was Kyle Leander, a guy works at the radio station, but she denied it."

"Do you know who her friends were? How she spent her time?"

"Well, her best friend was Rowena Whitekiller."

Mark shot Teeve a quizzical look. "Did you say 'Whitekiller'?"

"Oh, we're so used to Cherokee names around here; to us, they're as common as Jones or Smith. Anyway, Gaylene and Rowena ran together from grade school to high school.

"They were good kids, not wild, but they had some good times, I guess. 'Course, most teenagers go through a phase, party too much, drink too much.

"But after Gaylene found out she was pregnant, she pretty much stayed to herself. Learned to cook, checked out a bunch of books from the library on child care. Even had me teach her to crochet. Made you a pair of blue booties about this long"—Teeve held her thumb and forefinger about two inches apart—"and made you a cap to match. She was so proud because she made them herself."

Teeve's eyes teared up.

"Was she still living at home?" Mark asked.

"No. She and Ben, her daddy, had a falling-out. A real bad one, so she rented a trailer from Arthur McFadden. He runs the radio station, owns some land way back of the river. I asked her once if she was scared to be so isolated—not many folks lived out there then—but Gaylene didn't seem to be afraid of much of anything. Besides, she'd grown up way out in the country, so—"

Teeve froze when an orange tomcat curled around her ankles. Bernie. That could only mean that Ivy wasn't far away.

She was standing in the kitchen doorway, eating mayonnaise from a jar, unconcerned that her Sierra Club T-shirt, taut across her bulging belly, didn't quite cover her baggy cotton underpants.

"Ivy!" Teeve jumped out of her chair, looked like she wanted to run. "What are you doing up?"

"I had to pee."

"Honey, this is . . . uh, he was in the pool hall today. I think you saw him, and, well, he's trying to sell me an insurance policy."

"Isn't it kind of late to be making house calls?" Ivy asked as Bernie bounded onto Mark's lap, unusual behavior for a cat that had no use for strangers.

"Yes. I mean no. I asked him to come by tonight. Late tonight. So we could go over a few things."

"Uh-huh."

"I've been thinking about this for a while now. Time to face the fact that I'm not going to live forever. Right?"

The only sound in the room was the clinking of Ivy's spoon as she dipped up another bite of mayonnaise.

"I mean, fifty-six isn't old, but I've reached the age of . . . insurance."

Teeve looked to Mark for help but got none.

"This young man has made me realize that I don't have anything much to leave you except for the pool hall, which isn't worth more than a few thousand dollars. Of course, there's this house, but you wouldn't live in it. And if you sold it . . . well."

Teeve turned her palms up to indicate that the outcome was obvious.

"Oh, I didn't introduce you two, did I?" Teeve tapped the side of her head to underscore her forgetfulness. "Don't know what I was thinking. Honey, this is Mark Albright. And this is my daughter, Ivy."

"How do you do," Mark said.

"Hi, Nicky Jack." Ivy licked mayonnaise from her upper lip, then smiled. "Welcome home."

January 9, 1967

Dear Diary,

   I'm the best basketball player in my gym class. Coach Dougless said if I keep practicing she might let me play on the varsity team next year. I'd like that because Danny Pittman, the cutest boy in school is always at the games. His girlfriend Becky Allan plays forward.

   I don't know what is worse, watching her lead cheers at the football games when she flips up her skirt to show off her legs or when she runs down the basketball court and her breasts jiggle. I've watched Danny watching her and he can't take his eyes off her boobs.

   I'm still wearing a double A bra. I saw an add in a magazine at the bank for bust cream. I'd like to send off for it but Daddy would probably find out because he picks up our mail in town at the post office and he'd kill me if he knew I even thought about my breasts.

   Spider Woman

Chapter Seven

After a few fitful hours of bizarre dreams, Mark got up early, skipped breakfast and left the motel before eight the next morning.

Following the directions Teeve had given him last night, he got on highway 40 and headed north. He was nine or ten miles out of town, an eighteen-wheeler riding his bumper when he rounded a sharp curve and saw the bait shop on the left-hand side of the highway. Too late to turn in, he drove on, slowing as the road straightened. When the truck passed, he made a U-turn and went back.

"Hook 'Em," read a hand-lettered sign hung over the door of a cinder-block building. Fifty yards back of that was an undistinguished house with gray siding. Off to the side, a thin woman wearing a loose denim dress was hanging sheets on a clothesline.

As Mark got out of his car, he saw a thick-bodied boy dipping dead minnows from a tank in front of the shop.

"My name's Kippy," he said, smiling. "I'm working."

He wasn't a boy, as Mark had supposed, but a man of indeterminate age with the broad, flat facial features and slow, awkward movements of Down syndrome.

"You want some dead minnows?" he asked.

"Not today."

"Catfish like dead minnows. I caught a catfish this big." He held up his arms, hands three feet apart. "You want to see it?" he said with enthusiasm.

"Sure."

The shop, rank with the smell of fish and stink bait, was neat and well organized—rods in racks along one wall; cane poles leaning in the corners; tables lined with boxes of jigs, sinkers, spinners; shelves crowded with lanterns, fuel, cookstoves; rafters hung with hats, caps, waders; glass cases filled with expensive lures and knives.

Smiling proudly, Kippy pointed to a catfish mounted above a window, then repeated—verbatim—the words printed on the mounting board.

"'Twenty-two pound flathead caught by Kippy Daniels, June 2, 1988.'"

"That's a fine catch," Mark said.

"I caught him all by myself. But my mama took the hook out 'cause catfish have real sharp teeth."

"Is your daddy here?"

"Huh-uh." Kippy went to a refrigerated case, took out a small plastic container and removed the lid. "You know what these are?" He dug his fingers into peat moss and pulled out a tangle of worms. "Night crawlers. They can't bite you 'cause they don't have any teeth."

The woman Mark had seen outside came in the back door carrying a laundry basket and a bag of clothespins.

"Kippy, put the worms back."

Carrie Daniels spoke with a slow Oklahoma drawl. Mark could tell she'd once been a beauty, but time had coarsened her skin, years of disappointment had dulled her eyes and someone had left welts on her upper arm and a yellowing bruise on her jaw.

"Can I help you?" she asked.

"I'm looking for Oliver Daniels."

"Mama, can I have a bottle of root beer?" Kippy asked. "Can I? Please."

"I guess so." Then to Mark she said, "Oliver went over to Muskogee to pick up a generator."

"You know when he'll be back?"

She shook her head.

"Well, if he's not going to be gone too long, I think I'll wait."

"Be best if you come back later. He's liable to be—"

When a bottle crashed on the concrete floor, Kippy said, "Uh-oh," then watched his root beer river its way toward the door.

"It broke, Mama."

"It's okay, honey," she said with practiced patience. "Just an accident." But when she heard a vehicle pulling onto the graveled drive out front, a look of alarm crossed her face.

"I'll pick it up," Kippy said.

"No! You'll cut yourself."

"Let me get that for you," Mark said, moving toward Kippy.

Carrie, pushing her way past him, said, "I'll take care of it. Kippy, I want you to go—"

Stopped in midsentence when the front door swung open, she involuntarily threw up one hand as if to shield her eyes from a harsh light.

O Boy Daniels, in razor-creased jeans, a stiff western shirt and snakeskin boots, looked like he'd never backed away from a fight. An old scar zigzagged across his chin, another cut a path through a tangle of eyebrow and a lump of puckered flesh sat on the side of his head where the missing part of his left ear should have been.

Though he was a few years past sixty, his body was still hard, his hands powerful, his eyes wary and dangerous . . . a man who could break a horse or a woman without caring about the difference.

"What's going on?" he asked, scowling at the dark liquid puddling around his boots.

"We . . . uh, had a little accident," Carrie said, her voice pinched with tension.

"Daddy, a bottle—"

"Just slipped through my fingers," Mark cut in.

O Boy studied the three faces turned toward him, then said, "Carrie, clean up this mess."

After he stomped out, Mark watched him from the doorway as he wrestled a heavy generator from the bed of his pickup.

"Kippy, go on up to the house and change your jeans. You've got root beer splattered all over the legs. And hurry."

"Okay, Mama."

Mark pulled a Coke from the cooler, then dug in his pocket for change.

"It's on the house," Carrie said. She gave him a tired smile, then grabbed a roll of paper towels and began sopping up the spill.

Mark found O Boy at a workbench at the side of the building, where he was bent over the generator.

"Mr. Daniels, I wonder if I could have a few minutes of your time?"

"For what?"

"Some information about Gaylene Harjo's son."

O Boy picked up a grease cloth and wiped his hands, but he never took his eyes off Mark.

"Since you investigated her murder, I thought you might be able to help me out."

"You a cop . . . or a reporter?" he asked, then spit in the dirt. "I got no use for either one."

"Then I guess I'm in luck. I'm an attorney."

O Boy snorted. "I wouldn't call that luck."

"Name's Albright. Mark Albright."

"So what's your business with me?"

"I'm trying to locate Nick Harjo."

"That right?"

"I'm handling an estate, he's the heir."

"Don't see as how it's gonna do him much good."

"Why?"

"He's dead."

Mark could feel his pulse quicken. "I was told his body was never found."

"It don't take a genius to hide a body, Albright. But sometimes you have to be damn lucky to find one. We musta dug up an acre of land on Joe Dawson's place. Come up empty, but that don't mean—"

"You're convinced Dawson was responsible?"

"Gaylene was killed with his knife. Same knife he used to slice hisself up. I can put two and two together."

"And he was your only suspect?"

"Oh, I looked at a few others. Some of the punks Gaylene partied with. But I had my eye on Dawson from the beginning. When the medical examiner matched Dawson's knife to her wounds, that was that."

Mark leaned his hips against the workbench, crossed his arms, then gazed out over the river. "Well," he said, "I've got a piece of property in Arkansas appraised at twenty-five thousand dollars that was left to Gaylene Harjo. Since she's deceased, and from what you say, her only child's dead, too, I need to find out who fathered him."

"Who the hell would leave her some property in Arkansas?"

"I'm not at liberty to say."

"So what you're telling me is that whoever knocked her up . . ."

"Will inherit. Yes." Mark tried not to sound overly anxious when he asked, "Do you have any idea who it was?"

"Nope."

"Did you try to find out?"

O Boy's eyes flashed with anger. "What are you trying to say?"

"I'm just wondering if—"

"I did my goddamn job, Albright."

"What about Kyle Leander?"

"What about him?"

"I've heard he spent time with her."

"Hell, who didn't? Let me tell you what you *don't* know about Gaylene. She couldn't keep her pants on.

Slept with half the men in this county. Anyone who wanted her. And there was a lot of hard-dick old boys around here wanted her."

"Did that include Joe Dawson?"

"Gaylene Harjo was a slut. Pure and simple. And I've never known a slut who culled."

Mark couldn't control the tightening of the muscles in his jaw or the heat of anger coloring his skin, but the changes were too subtle for O Boy to notice.

"Not much of a surprise she ended up the way she did," O Boy said. "But that kid of hers . . . he deserved better."

The front office of KSET, small and spare, was deserted when Mark arrived. A metal desk in the corner of the room looked unused, its surface covered with a fine layer of dust. Between two plastic patio chairs, a chrome table held a stack of *Radio Journals*, the most recent three years old. The walls were bare except for a framed certificate dated 1972 that named Arthur McFadden "Oklahoma Broadcaster of the Year."

When a phone rang somewhere in the back of the building, Mark followed the sound down a hallway to an opened door. The call went unanswered even though the bearded man sitting beside it could have picked up the receiver without doing more than bending his elbow.

He wore faded jeans and a grateful dead T-shirt. His feet, shod in ratty sandals, rested on a littered desk. His ears were covered with headphones, his eyes closed, his head nodding to a percussion beat Mark could hear from across the room.

This office, unlike the one at the front, was anything

but bare. The walls, painted black, were covered with posters—Jimi Hendrix, Jefferson Airplane, Janis Joplin, Joe Cocker. A bedraggled American flag was tacked above one window, a lava lamp stood atop a stack of old LPs, and a floor-to-ceiling bookcase held a jumble of memorabilia, most of it from an earlier era.

Mark studied a framed photograph of a teenage boy—barefoot and shirtless, dark hair haloed in an Afro, one hand holding a water pipe, the other flashing a peace sign at the camera—a younger version of the bearded man across the room.

While the rest of the world was moving toward the new millennium, Kyle Leander was stuck in the sixties.

When the phone stopped ringing, Mark faked a cough, then, getting no response, tapped one of the ragged sandals, causing its wearer to jerk into action.

"Hey, man."

Kyle jumped up, yanked off his headphones. "I didn't hear you come in." He pumped Mark's hand and propelled him to a recliner covered with cat hair.

"Well, I heard your phone ringing and—"

"Phones. That's all they're good for, huh?"

"Is this a bad time for you? When I called, you said . . ."

"You ever read *Einstein's Dreams*? That book says all that needs to be said about time. You know what I'm saying?"

Mark nodded to show his agreement—to what, he wasn't sure.

"You want something to drink? Herbal tea? Mineral water? I don't do coffee." Kyle tapped a finger against his temple. "Caffeine messes with my mind." He blinked rapidly, as if to demonstrate one of the damaging effects of ingesting caffeine. "I don't put petroleum products on my body, either."

Mark let that one go without reply.

"So," Kyle said, "let's hear that tape."

"What?"

"Your tape. On the phone you said you were bringing me a tape."

"Uh, I think you've confused me with someone else. I'm Mark Albright."

"Oh, man. Forgive me. I thought you were with Groan, this band out of Memphis. Guy called, asked me if I'd give him some airtime." Kyle, thoughtful, cupped his chin in his hand and stared into space.

When a scruffy gray cat jumped onto the arm of the recliner, Kyle said, "That's Brown Buffalo. If I die before he does, he inherits all this." He made a sweeping gesture to indicate the vastness of his estate, which Mark assumed would include the lava lamp and flag.

"I wanted to see you—"

"Yeah, I remember now. You're trying to get some information on someone I used to know. Right?"

"Gaylene Harjo."

Kyle Leander's reaction on hearing the name was physical. His head jerked as if he were dodging wasps, his eyes darting around the room before fixing again on Mark. And then he began to sing.

> *I hear a soft rain on the windowpane*
> *Like so many evenings before*
> *But there's one sound missing*
> *in this time, in this place*
> *I don't hear your voice anymore*

He stopped as suddenly as he'd started, his chest heaving as he sobbed.

"I'm sorry," Mark said.

Kyle snuffled, wiped his face dry with the arm of his shirt. "Man, do you know what it's like to love a woman so much that just watching her breathe stops time?"

Mark, his discomfort obvious, said nothing. But Kyle pushed for a response.

"Well, do you?"

"No. I'm afraid I don't."

"Makes you feel like you'll live forever, man. Fucking forever."

Kyle began pacing the length of the room, agitated, arms fluttering, like a child imitating flight.

"That only comes along once, you know. And when it's gone, it's like a piece of you's been cut out." He ran a finger down the center of his chest. "Bzzzzzt. Gone. A missing heart. Now you tell me how you live without a heart. Huh?"

"I . . . uh . . ."

"Exactly!" He made a flying leap across the room. "So what do you do? Fill up that hole with bubble wrap? Stuff it full of newspapers? Dead leaves?"

Mark wondered if he was supposed to pick the best possible answer, but Kyle drifted away for a while, a brief visit to his past. When he returned, he was calmer.

"We used to go to the river together to watch the sun come up. She said each morning was like a new breath." He stopped, folded his arms across his chest and closed his eyes. "A new breath," he whispered.

The sound of a door slamming somewhere in the

building got him moving again, traipsing in a small, tight circle.

"Gaylene loved life. Couldn't stand to see anything die. Once when she was driving me home, she ran over a squirrel and . . . God, I miss her."

Suddenly spent, he dropped onto a bench, his head resting against the wall behind him, hands limp on his lap.

"Tell me about her son," Mark said.

"Nicky Jack." Kyle cracked a smile. "Man, she loved that little guy. You should have seen her with him. He was the center of the world for her."

"Kyle . . ." Mark hesitated, creating an uneasy silence. Though he had already formed the question, he wasn't sure he was ready to hear the answer. "Were you his father?"

"Oh, no, man. Ours was a spiritual love. Oh, I won't deny that I wanted her, wanted her more than anything. But that never happened." Kyle's eyes filled with tears. "I used to pretend he was mine, made believe I was the one. But I wasn't."

"Do you know who was?"

"Didn't ask her, didn't care who she'd been with. That didn't matter to me." Weeping again, he buried his face in his hands.

"Kyle!"

Arthur McFadden, a cigar clamped between his teeth, was closing in on seventy. He was painfully thin and slightly stooped, but he had a powerful voice, the voice of a man accustomed to having his way. He dismissed Mark with little more than a glance, then zeroed in on Kyle, seemingly oblivious to his former stepson's distress.

"I want you to take care of a problem in the control room."

Choking back sobs, Kyle said, "I . . . I can't."

"Yes, you can. The automation unit is screwing up again. Fix it." Arthur shot him a look of disgust, then wheeled and walked away.

Mark waited until Kyle had regained some control before he asked, "Do you have any idea who killed Gaylene Harjo?"

"I wish I did. I swear I'd shoot the bastard did that to her and Nicky Jack."

"You think whoever killed her, killed the boy, too?"

"I won't let myself believe he's dead. 'Cause if he's alive, she's alive, too. In him." Kyle wiped a hand across his face. "He's out there somewhere."

March 7, 1967

Dear Diary,

School today was so-so. We had a spelling test in English class. I think I failed because I didn't study. Row always makes the best grades, but I think spelling is borring.

I sent off for the bust cream today. Row said I could send it to her house and even if Mrs. Whitekiller sees it, she won't say anything. I should be so lucky!

Mom had to work late at the bank so we didn't get home until almost seven. Daddy wasn't too happy that we had tuna fish sandwiches for dinner, but Mom said she didn't have time to cook the roast she thawed out. Sometimes I think he doesn't realize how hard she has to work at her job, keep house, can stuff from the garden and help him with the chickens and goats. I think women work alot harder than men. If I get to heaven I want to be a man.

Me and Daddy watched television tonight. We saw Gun-smoke *and* The Andy Griffith Show *because those are his favorites, but on the news we saw a big crowd of black people in Washington protesting the war in Vietnam. I told Daddy that I would like to go to Washington and march with them, but he said that was colored people's business not ours.*

Guess he has not noticed that we're colored too.

Spider Woman

Chapter Eight

He's convinced that Joe Dawson buried the body some-where on his land," Mark said.

Ivy laughed, momentarily drawing the attention of the domino boys. Lowering her voice, she said, "I'd like to have seen the look on his face when you told him who you are."

"I didn't. I said I was an attorney handling an estate Nick Harjo would inherit. If I could find him."

"And he bought that?" Teeve asked.

"He seemed to."

"Well, don't underestimate O Boy Daniels. He might come across like a yokel, but he's nobody's fool. You ever watch that old TV show, detective acted like he didn't have a clue? Can't think of his name. Always chomped on a cigar, wore a wrinkled raincoat?"

"Columbo," Lonnie Cruddup yelled from the domino corner. "His name was Columbo. Damn good show."

"Right." Then to Mark and Ivy, she whispered, "Let's go outside. Lonnie's turned up his hearing aid."

When they were assembled on the sidewalk, Teeve said, "What did O Boy say about Gaylene?"

"Not much." Mark hoped his face didn't betray the lie.

"That's a switch. Never known him to pass up a chance to dish some dirt."

"Did you see Kippy while you were there?" Ivy asked.

"Oh, yes."

"He was a few years older than me, but he was in some of my classes at school. His mom went to all his classes with him, sat in a little desk beside his. Helped him with his work, made sure he passed from one grade to the next. When he walked across the stage at graduation, everyone stood up and cheered. He didn't get a diploma, but he got a certificate."

"They should have given Carrie a diploma," Teeve said. "She was devoted to him. Still is. Didn't get a bit of help from O Boy, but she—"

Teeve stopped in midsentence as a white Impala drove by, the driver staring at the trio gathered in front of the pool hall.

"Arthur McFadden," she said. "The guy I told you about who owned Gaylene's trailer."

"I saw him this morning," Mark said.

Teeve looked puzzled. "Where?"

"At the radio station. I talked to Kyle Leander."

"You've been busy, haven't you."

"I was curious to see what he had to say."

"Guess you could tell he's burned out a few circuits. But all in all, Kyle's not a bad guy, though Arthur doesn't see it that way."

"I got the feeling they're not overly fond of each other."

"Arthur's ex-wife was loaded, just what he was looking for. And Anne needed someone to help her deal with Kyle after his father died. Left her with a ton of money and a real messed-up son."

"Did she live here?" Mark asked.

"She was from Atlanta. She met Arthur when she came here for her aunt's funeral. Came for the funeral one week, married Arthur the next week, then moved here the week after that. Well, sort of moved."

"What does that mean?"

"She kept her big house in Atlanta, bought a smaller one here, not her kind of place, from what I heard. But see, I don't think she ever intended to stay. Doubt she planned to celebrate many wedding anniversaries with Arthur."

"Then why did she marry him?"

"Kyle. She wanted to get him out of the city, believed he wouldn't have access to drugs in a little town like this. Of course, that didn't stop him, didn't even slow him down. But Kyle loved music almost as much as he loved drugs, said he wanted to be a DJ.

"So when Anne met Arthur, found out he worked at the radio station and dreamed of owning it, she bought it. Actually, the station wasn't for sale, but she had the money.

"Six months later, she was gone. Back to Atlanta. Arthur got to keep the station, but according to their divorce settlement, he had to keep Kyle, too, so they're pretty much stuck with each other. Seems like—"

Teeve was interrupted by Lonnie rapping on the window, holding his coffee cup so she could see it was empty.

"If those old bastards don't die soon, I'm gonna have to shoot them," she said as she went back inside.

"Look, I know you're busy," Mark said to Ivy, "so I'm going to get out of your way."

"Nah. Kids have other places to go on Saturday. What've you got in mind, Nicky Jack?"

"Thought I'd take a drive."

"Where?"

"I'd like to see where she lived."

"You mean the trailer where Aunt Gaylene—"

"Yes."

"I'll drive you."

"You don't need to."

"I don't mind. Besides, it'll be easier to take you than to tell you how to get there. Come on."

Mark followed her across the street to her old Ford Aerostar. The van was a patchwork of bumper stickers, their messages a plea to save everything from the Key Largo cotton mouse to humpback whales. Inside, it looked like home to a nation of pack rats.

Floorboards were inches deep in running shoes, bird-seed, mildewed towels, newspapers, tools and telephone books. The back held cardboard boxes filled with corn shucks and tree bark, empty wire cages and bulging garbage bags. The front seat was a jumble of books, binoculars, unopened mail, dog biscuits, maps, a canteen and a tangle of animal leashes.

Ivy dug out the books, handed them to Mark. "Hold these," she said, then swept the rest of the mess onto the floor.

While she watched her rearview mirror, waiting for a break in the traffic, Mark glanced at the titles of the books in his lap: *How to Grow Fresh Air*, *The Natural*

Habitat Garden, *Sacred Depths of Nature* and *Drum of the Earth*.

Ivy gave a thank-you wave to the driver who let her pull out of the parking space, then squeezed the van into the line of vehicles waiting for the light to change at the corner.

"Everyone still comes to town on Saturday. They spend their money at Wal-Mart, have burgers at McDonald's, then drag Main."

"Have you lived here all your life, Ivy?"

"Hell, no! Left as soon as I could. Swore I'd never live in this town again. But I came back after I started growing this kid."

"Where were you before?"

"I've moved around. Spent two years in Honduras with the Peace Corps, worked in California with the Forestry Department. Did a stint as a river guide in Wyoming. Taught organic gardening at a community college in Vermont. Managed an animal shelter in Chicago. Guess I haven't found where I fit yet. What about you?"

"I'm a veterinarian. I have a clinic in Beverly Hills."

"Ah, physician to the stars' pets."

"Pretty much."

"What's that like?"

"Well, the animals are a lot like their owners . . . primped, pampered and shivering, terrified that somebody might not be paying attention to them."

When Ivy turned off Main, they lost most of the traffic, the two-lane road winding through the edge of town.

"You married?" Ivy asked.

"No."

"Neither am I, but I was in love for a few hours one day when I was in the fifth grade. I have a short attention span, Nicky Jack."

"Would you mind very much not calling me Nicky Jack?"

Ivy grinned. "I guess Nicky Jack does sound like one of those names little kids give to their imaginary friends. I called mine Fluty Marie."

"Mine was Wallace."

"Wallace?" Ivy made a face. "Sounds like some disapproving old man."

"Wallace wore a gray three-piece suit, dark tie. Very conservative. And he didn't like me much."

"Nick! The whole point of a make-believe friend is to create someone who is . . . well, a friend, someone who's always on your side."

"Guess I had a better sense of fashion than fantasy."

Ivy laughed. "You know, I'll never forget something that happened when you were a baby, maybe five or six months old, so I would've been, oh, three or four.

"You were asleep on Mom's bed; she was in the kitchen with Aunt Gaylene. Now I'd watched them change you, and I'd seen that equipment between your legs and wondered why I didn't have what you had. I thought maybe there was something wrong with me.

"I'd asked about it, but I suppose Mom had dodged the question, so I sneaked into the bedroom and took off your diaper to try to figure things out for myself.

"You woke up, but didn't cry. As a matter of fact, I think you enjoyed the examination. But then you started to pee. That little job popped up, sprayed like a damned fountain. I clamped my hand over it, but it was like one of those cartoons where a hose gets loose, squirting water all over the place.

"You peed in my face, on my hair, the bed, the floor. And I started to cry, which, of course, brought Mom and Aunt Gaylene running.

"Mom was furious, ready to paddle my butt, but Aunt Gaylene wouldn't let her. She thought it was funny. Threw her head back and howled while she hugged me. And that's the way I remember her. Laughing."

Mark gave Ivy a weak smile, then turned to look out his window.

"Nick, does it bother you when I talk about Aunt Gaylene? Because if it does . . ."

"I really wish you wouldn't call me that," Mark said.

"What?"

"Nick."

"Oh, I thought you meant for me not to call you Nicky Jack because it sounds, well, childish."

"It does."

"So you're not going by the name Nick, either?"

"No."

"Guess I misunderstood. I thought—"

"Please. Call me Mark."

"Okay," Ivy said.

For the next several miles, neither spoke. Not until a red pickup with teenage girls blew past the van, a McDonald's box sailing out one window, a Styrofoam cup from the other. Ivy hit her horn, yelled, "You dumb shits!" then swerved onto the shoulder. She left the motor running while she retrieved the litter from beside the road.

When she slid back under the steering wheel, she tossed the trash into the backseat, then pulled a notepad and pen from over her visor. Mark watched as she wrote down the pickup's tag number.

"Was that a '97 Chevy or a '98?" she asked.

"I'm afraid I don't know much about trucks."

"I think it was a '98."

"What do you do with that information?" he asked.

"Turn it in to O Boy. He probably throws it in the wastebasket as soon as I walk out. If it was up to me, I'd stick the bastards in jail."

Ivy made two more stops on the way to the trailer— one to bag up more roadside trash, another to pick up a half-starved hound, which she fed, then put into one of the cages in the back.

When she slid into the driver's seat again, Mark said, "Are you going to keep him?"

"No, Mom can hardly put up with Bernie, my cat. DeClare has a no-kill shelter. I'll take him there."

Mark had never known a woman like Ivy, a woman who wanted to improve the environment and rescue the strays of the world but seemed barely able to manage her own life. She was in her early thirties, he guessed, unmarried, but pregnant; driving a vehicle filled with trash; and by her own admission, unable to keep a job. She was, no doubt, one of those people who had little order in her life. A woman who was living without a plan.

He kept his own car immaculate, had it detailed once a month, had never been foolish enough to father a child, owned a thriving animal clinic and checked his day planner each night before he went to bed.

"Here we are," she said, when she came to a barbed-wire fence posted with PRIVATE PROPERTY and NO TRES-PASSING signs.

She turned in at a break in the fence, easing the van

across a rocky gully. A hundred yards beyond that, she parked, turned off the ignition.

"We'll have to walk the rest of the way."

"How far is it?"

"Not too far. Maybe a quarter of a mile. Used to be able to drive right up to the trailer, but not anymore."

After they got out, Ivy went to the back, opened the hatch and scrounged around in the debris, emerging with a pair of worn western boots, a garbage bag and a can of insect repellent. Leaning against the van, she slid her feet out of the black rubber thongs and pulled on the boots.

"You want to watch where you walk. This place is crawling with snakes." She sprayed her legs and arms with the repellent, then offered the container to Mark.

"Chiggers and mosquitoes will eat you alive without this."

"You make it sound like a safari. But I'll be fine."

"Okay, then. Let's go."

Ivy struck out on a trail soon disappearing into pines, blackjacks, pin oaks and bois d'arcs. Boulders and waist-high weeds made slow going for Mark, but Ivy moved at a steady clip. Even as she stopped now and then to stuff litter into the garbage bag, he still fell behind.

"Look," she said, pointing to a shallow ravine where two does and a fawn skittered into a grove of cedars.

Midway up a steep incline, Mark flushed a covey of quail, their sudden flight causing him to lose his footing. When he landed, he felt the sting of nettles through the seat of his linen slacks.

Ivy, waiting for him at the top, pretended not to see him fall, kneeling to examine the shell of a blue jay egg. When he finally struggled to the crest, he was panting, slapping at mosquitoes, welts already rising on his face and arms.

"You okay?"

"Sure," he said, gulping for air.

She slowed her pace as they descended the hill to a small pond shaded by willows. As they skirted the bank, a stubby black water moccasin slithered into the edge of the water.

Just beyond the pond, the trailer, sheathed in trumpet vines and Virginia creeper, was shadowed by pines, banked by redwoods and azaleas. A weathered wooden porch tilted beneath the front door, which had been sprayed with graffiti.

"Kids," Ivy said. "I don't know how they find this place, but they do."

Then Mark noticed the containers—coffee cans, plastic buckets, tin tubs—arranged around the porch. Filled with a variety of plants and flowers, all dead.

"Grandma Enid," Ivy explained. "Mom brings her out because she doesn't see well enough to drive anymore, but that doesn't stop her from coming here every year. January thirtieth."

"The day Gaylene died," he said, his voice flat, giving away nothing. When he noticed Ivy's questioning look, he added, "I read everything I could find about her at the library yesterday. I know when she was born, when she died, how many times she was stabbed, where she—"

"Lord, that must have been hard."

"It wasn't easy."

"I suppose it helps you to distance yourself from what happened to her if you call yourself Mark and call her Gaylene."

"What should I call her? Mother? Mom? Ivy, I've

been Mark Albright for as long as I can remember," he said, impatience beginning to creep into his voice. "And I'm not sure I can make the leap to having people call me Nick or saying 'Mother' when I'm talking about her."

"Yeah, I can see that."

"No, I don't think you can. How could you? You grew up knowing your family. Aunts, uncles, cousins, grandparents. Right?

"You spent most of your life with them. Birthdays, holidays. You've seen their pictures, listened to their stories, held their babies, cried at their funerals."

Ivy nodded.

"But they're not the people of *my* history. My father's name was Morris, my mother was Helen. They were wonderful parents. I was my dad's best buddy; my mother adored me. And they made sure I knew I was loved.

"They took me to New York when I was seven, to Paris when I was ten. And I skied Aspen every winter. I lived a life most people only dream of."

"Then what are you doing here?"

"Right now," he said, his eyes shifting to the old trailer, the pond downhill, the cans of flowers nearby, "I'm not really sure. I came to meet Gaylene Harjo, see what she had to say, then get out. I didn't come to establish a relationship with her if that's what you're thinking."

"What I'm thinking is that you must feel awfully alone right now."

"How the hell would you know how I must feel, huh?" His anger, an emotion he had been taught to suppress, was just below the surface now. "All of this meant nothing to me until a few weeks ago. So I show up here, meet you, and now, twelve, fourteen hours later, you're going to tell me how I should feel?"

"Mark, I know you're upset, and you have every right to be bitter, but maybe . . ."

"You know? You don't know a damn thing about me, not a goddamn thing, so don't try to fit me into your notion of what I should be, what I should feel. Don't try to cast me in the role of the long-lost son mourning the loss of a mother he never knew, because that's not going to happen. But here *is* what's going to happen. I'm going to take a quick look at this trailer, go back to town, pick up my car and drive to the airport in Tulsa. About three hours after I board a plane, I'll be back in Los Angeles, where I live. My home. Then I'll see my shrink, who'll tell me to try to 'fit this into my life experience,' and in time, my trip to DeClare, Oklahoma, will seem like nothing more than a bad dream."

He pulled back then, confused by this anger, mystified by this voice that seemed not to be his.

Embarrassed, he stepped up on the porch to open the door. As an afterthought, he turned back, prepared to offer Ivy a hand up, but she shook her head.

Dank and dark, the trailer smelled of mildew, like the locked trunks he had discovered in his parents' attic.

The living room held an overturned canvas camp stool and an aluminum lawn chair, the plastic webbing torn loose from the frame. The linoleum was littered with cigarette butts, burned candles, pecan shells and ruined cassettes, their tapes curled and spooled across the floor.

The kitchen had been gutted—stove and refrigerator gone, cabinet doors and faucets missing. A dead bird lay in the rusted sink, an empty Spam can and bottle opener on the countertop.

The toilet had been wrenched from the bathroom, leaving a gaping hole in the floor. "Shit Happins" was scrawled in lipstick on the tile over the tub, the medicine cabinet yanked from the wall, the mirror smashed.

A filthy blanket covered with rat droppings was piled in one corner of the bedroom, a pair of yellowed men's briefs and a used condom in the other.

He tried to imagine how this room might have looked when she lived here, tried to see it with bright curtains at the windows, a baby bed and rocking chair, a shelf holding teddy bears and a wooden Pinocchio doll. But those images were blurred, the pictures dark and distorted.

As he started back down the hallway, he noticed a closet, the door hanging by only one hinge. The floor was strewn with wire hangers, a broken broomstick, lightbulbs and curtain rods.

But there was something else, something half-hidden beneath the crumpled page of a magazine. A bootie crocheted of blue thread, a white silk ribbon laced around the top. The shoe, no bigger than his thumb, was covered with dust, and the ribbon was frayed at one end. But as he turned it between his fingers, studying the intricate stitches, he knew it was a connection. An unexpected gift from her.

"Where in the world have you two been?" Teeve asked when Mark and Ivy walked into the café. "I couldn't for the life of me figure out what happened to you. I looked up and you were gone."

"We went out to Aunt Gaylene's trailer," Ivy said. She and Mark hadn't spoken since his flare-up at the trailer, not even when she stopped briefly at the shelter to drop off the stray dog. And the silent ride back to town had only increased their discomfort with each other.

Teeve looked unsure of how she should react, knowing her nephew had just been to the place where his mother had been killed. "Well, I guess you had lunch."

"I'm not hungry," Ivy said.

"How about you, Nicky Jack? I've got some roast beef left," she offered, thinking food might provide some solace.

"No, thanks."

"He doesn't want us to call him that, Mom."

"Well, I guess it sounds kind of babyish, doesn't it?"

"His name is Mark. Mark Albright. Besides, he doesn't have time to eat. He's got to get to Tulsa."

"Tulsa? Why?"

"I've decided—"

"He's flying back to Los Angeles this evening."

"No," he said, trying again to break into the conversation, "I've—"

"But you just got here," Teeve said. "I thought you'd want to meet Enid, your grandmother."

"Yes, I do," he said.

Ivy looked mystified.

"I'm not leaving, Ivy. At least not for a while."

"But you told me—"

"I changed my mind."

May 2, 1967

Dear Diary,

  I got my period while I was in math class! My stomach was acheing all morning, but I thought it was gas. Boy was I wrong. When I felt something wet in my pants I was pretty sure I knew what was happening. I went to the bathroom to check and sure enough there was blood. Not a lot, thank goodness, because I had on a pair of tan corduroy pants so it could have been a disaster.

  The school nurse gave me a sanitary napkin then signed a note so I could leave early. When I got to the bank and told Mom I'd started, she left work and took me home. She fixed me a cup of maidenhair tea which is an old recipe for Cherokee girls when they start they're periods. I didn't like it much, but I drank it anyway. I'm glad I finally got my period though. Row's been menistrating since she was twelve and I think all the girls on our basketball team do too.

  I guess I am a woman now.

Spider Woman

Chapter Nine

Did you hear what I said?" Ivy asked.

She and Mark had the café all to themselves, as it was well past lunchtime, but the pool hall was anything but quiet. Lonnie Cruddup and Ron John O'Reily were yelling at each other over the domino table, Teeve was trying to break up an argument between two girls at the video machines and three pool players were razzing a fourth who'd just missed an easy shot.

Ivy tried again. "I asked you why you decided to stay. What changed your mind?"

Mark ran a hand through his hair, glanced into the pool hall to make sure no one was watching, then reached in his pocket and pulled out the blue bootie. As he placed it in the center of the table, he said, "I found this in the trailer. In the corner of a closet."

Ivy picked up the bootie, pinched a piece of lint from the heel and said, "So you think—"

"She made this for me."

"Aunt Gaylene?"

"Yes."

"Mark, a lot of people have been in that trailer since you and Aunt Gaylene lived there. Lots of kids. And some homeless folks, more than likely. Maybe families.

"This"—she handed the bootie back—"could have been left by any number of women, or girls, with babies. After all, the place has been empty for years."

"No," he said, closing his fingers around the tiny shoe. "It was mine."

"How can you be so sure?"

"Ivy, when I saw this, when I picked it up, I knew. Before then, I'd been distanced from all this, like it was happening to someone else. None of it had anything to do with me until that moment."

They were quiet for a while, the only sounds coming from up front.

Finally Ivy said, "So how long will you be here?"

"As long as it takes."

"For what?"

"To know her," Mark said as he stuffed the bootie back in his pocket. "Don't you see, Ivy? I can't figure out who I am until I know who she was."

"Mark, I'm so glad you've decided to stay for a while longer," Teeve said, keeping her voice low so the domino boys couldn't hear. "Your grandma is going to be thrilled to death to see you."

"We're going to her place now."

"Unless you need me here, Mom," Ivy said.

"Honey, you all go on. Nothing here I can't handle."

"We'll be going by Wal-Mart. Anything you need?" Ivy asked.

"Yeah, you might ought to pick up a case of . . ."

When the door opened behind him, Mark could tell

from the look on Teeve's face and the shift in her posture that whoever was coming in had put her on alert.

"Afternoon, O Boy," she said.

Mark had an uneasy feeling when he saw the sheriff, dressed now in his uniform, a badge on his pocket. And he remembered Teeve's warning: *Don't underestimate O Boy Daniels. He might come across like a yokel, but he's nobody's fool.*

"You're a little late for lunch," Teeve said.

"I didn't come for lunch. I came to talk to Mr. Albright here." He inclined his head toward Mark.

"Well, my feelings are hurt," she said, trying her best to sound natural.

Then, when she noticed that O Boy's arrival had gotten the attention of the domino boys, she said, "Why don't we go in the back and—"

"I can take care of my business right here."

"No reason for us to stand when we can sit back there, have a cup of coffee."

"What brings you to DeClare, Mr. Albright?"

"Insurance," Teeve offered too quickly. Then, remembering that Mark had told O Boy he was an attorney, she added, "And he's a lawyer, too."

"Trying to settle an estate. Isn't that your story, Albright?"

"Yes, but—"

"Now, that's interesting. Real interesting. You say you're a lawyer. But when you checked into the Riverfront, I believe you told Patti Frazier you were in real estate. And now you've got Teeve believing you peddle insurance." He leaned against the counter and crossed his arms. "Either you're confused, fella, or you have your hands in a lot of pots."

"Well, I—"

"You got to town night before last. Is that right?"

"Yes."

"Patti said you checked in at six."

"Six, six-thirty. I'm not sure."

"What did you do when you got here?" O Boy asked.

"Drove around for a while."

"Why?"

"Just taking a look at the town," Mark said.

"Yeah, that's what I figured."

"I'd like to know why you're asking me these questions. If I'm in some kind of trouble . . ."

"What happened there?" O Boy asked, gesturing toward Mark's bandaged arm.

"I was bitten by a dog."

"Tell me how that happened."

"I'm a veterinarian. I was treating a keeshond in my clinic and—"

"Hold on here. You were a lawyer, then an attorney, and now you're a vet?"

"I can explain all that," Mark said.

"You're damn right you can. And you will."

"When I came to town—"

"So, you got bit by a Keystone, whatever the hell that is, and you—"

"Keeshond. It's a dog."

"Did you need stitches?" O Boy asked. "Go to a doctor?"

"No, I took care of it myself."

"Sure you did."

"What's this about, O Boy?" Teeve asked.

"Haven't you been reading your paper, Teeve? We've

had five break-ins the last two nights. They started when your friend here hit town."

"Well, that doesn't mean—"

"And whoever tried to get into Dewey Gentry's workshop tangled with his German shepherd."

"Are you accusing me?"

"I think we'd better talk about this in my office."

"O Boy," Teeve said, "you're making a mistake."

"How's that?"

"He's not . . . well . . ."

"He's not what, Teeve?"

"He's not who you think he is. You don't know the truth about what's going on here."

"Then maybe you'd better tell me."

"This is Nicky Jack."

O Boy looked as if he'd just had the wind knocked out of him. Not only did he seem to be having trouble drawing breath, his skin paled to the color of corkwood.

"Nicky Harjo," Teeve said. "Gaylene's son."

Chapter Ten

"Then I had dinner in the motel."

"Yeah." O Boy grinned, an expression intended to convey contempt, not humor. "I hear you don't care for fried catfish."

"Is that a felony here? Or just a misdemeanor."

"I'd call it bad judgment."

The phone on the desk rang only once before O Boy picked it up, holding the receiver to his good ear. "Daniels," he said, grabbing for a pen and notepad, brushing aside the soiled bandage Mark had removed from his arm.

The wound the sheriff had insisted on seeing was five days old now, the purple bruising beginning to yellow. The dog's teeth had punctured the skin in two places, but the deepest lesion, where the flesh had been ripped away, was held together by six stitches, healing but still tender.

"Okay. Let me know when you find out," O Boy said to his caller.

As he cradled the phone, he turned his attention back

to Mark. "So what did you do after you had your supper?"

"I walked to the pool hall, but it was closed. I didn't see Teeve until the next day. That's when she told me what happened to Gaylene Harjo and her son."

"And that's you. Right?"

"As far as I know."

"Then what?"

"Went to the newspaper office, looked at some microfilm, went back to the motel."

"But you took a little detour, didn't you. Stopped in for a few drinks somewhere along the way."

"No, I—"

"I got two witnesses who saw you staggering down Main Street yesterday afternoon."

"I was sick."

"You had to have help to get to your room."

"I don't remember that."

"One of the dangers of drink, I'm told. So let's say, for the sake of argument, that you passed out in your room. You stay there all night?"

"No, I slept for several hours, woke up around ten-thirty, then went to Teeve's house."

"How long were you there?"

"An hour or so."

"Anyone see you when you got back to the motel?"

"Not sure. The lobby was empty."

"No one on the desk?"

"I . . . I can't remember."

"Seems to me there's a lot that you don't remember. Hell, you probably don't remember coming out to my place this morning with that bullshit story about you being a lawyer."

"If I'd told you the truth, you'd have thought I was crazy."

"You wanna know what I think? I think you got to town Thursday night, saw that old flyer in the window of the pool hall, got the idea to pass yourself off as Nick Harjo and—"

"Why would I do that?"

"Gives you a story to explain why you're here. Just a coincidence that the break-ins start up on the same night you hit town. Only problem was, you got chewed up by some guy's watchdog while you—"

"I told you—"

"Yeah, yeah. You got bit by a Keystone."

"Keeshond. Look at the teeth marks. They don't look anything like the bite of a German shepherd. Call my clinic in Los Angeles. They'll tell you that I—"

"Oh, I'll be making some calls. You can count on it. But while I do that, let me find you a comfortable place to wait. Quiet spot where you can relax a while. That sound like a good idea to you?"

As he was being led from O Boy's office to the jail at the back of the building, Mark had envisioned sharing a cell with drunks, junkies and maybe a maniac or two. As it turned out, he was the lone occupant of his cell, the only bonus he could determine in being locked up.

At first, he read the graffiti scrawled on the walls. His favorite was "Do'nt blame Marybeth for what I done cause it ain't her fawlt," signed "Fred," a line that set Mark's imagination spinning as he constructed a history for Marybeth and Fred.

For the next hour, Mark paced from the bars across the front of the cell to the concrete windowless wall at the back, a distance of some twelve feet according to his calculations.

During the second hour, he overcame his reluctance to lie down on the stained ticking mattress, which was probably infested with all manner of bugs naked to the human eye. But sleep, he figured, offered him, at present, his only means of escape.

At first, he scratched at imagined bugs setting up housekeeping in his hair, bugs slipping down the collar of his shirt and creeping up inside the legs of his trousers. But when he heard snoring coming from one of the other cells, he finally dozed, lulled by the regularity of the sound.

"Hey, buddy. Nap time's over."

Mark was jerked from sleep by the same deputy who had locked him up two hours earlier.

"Come on," he said, growing impatient. "Your lawyer got you sprung."

"I don't have a lawyer."

"Well, you don't have *much* of a lawyer, but you got one."

Mark trailed the deputy, retracing the path he'd followed earlier, entering a hallway, then passing the room where the sheriff had questioned him before he'd been led to the jail.

At the end of the hallway, the deputy unlocked a door to a narrow room with an area that looked like a bank teller's cage, where a uniformed woman was working at a computer. She got up when they entered, obviously expecting them.

"Step over here," she said, her voice and manner stiff and officious. "Reclaim your property."

She emptied a large manila envelope onto the counter

in front of her and called out items as she shoved them beneath the bars to Mark.

"Wallet. Cash—two hundred forty-three dollars, sixteen cents. Car keys. Motel key. Gold chain. Nail clippers. Wristwatch. Plastic comb. And one blue baby bootie."

After he signed the release form, she handed him a copy and said, "Have a nice evening."

In a public office at the front of the building, Ivy was waiting with a man Mark had seen on his first visit to the pool hall.

"Are you okay?" Ivy asked as soon as Mark stepped through the door.

"Yeah."

"This is Hap Duchamp," she said. "I hope you don't mind that I called him, but I thought you needed a lawyer."

Hap extended his hand. "Nick? Or Mark?"

"Mark, please."

"Sorry it took so long to get you released," Hap said.

"I'm just glad you got me out when you did. I was beginning to think I'd be in that cell all night."

"Let's talk outside." Hap gestured toward a desk where a secretary was watching them with interest. He held the door for Ivy and Mark, then followed them out to the sidewalk.

"So, is this finished?" Mark asked.

"I think so," Ivy said.

"O Boy didn't have any evidence to link you to those burglaries," Hap said. "He had nothing at all."

"Then why did he put me in jail?"

"I'm guessing it's because you told him you're Nick Harjo."

"That's a crime?"

"No, but I think he wanted to keep you until he could check you out."

"What do you mean, 'check me out'?"

"I believe he's afraid you really might be who you claim to be. And if you are, it wouldn't look good for him."

"Why?"

"O Boy worked real hard to convince folks around here that Joe Dawson killed Gaylene and her son. And after he matched Joe's knife to her wounds, he pretty much thought he had wrapped it up. But if you really are Nick Harjo, then his theory's shot all to hell. Might even cost him the next election. Still enough people in the county who believe Joe was innocent."

"Then why did he let me go?"

"Well, for one thing, he didn't have a reason to charge you. But if I had to guess, I'd say he discovered something to make him believe you *might* be the Harjo boy, so he probably couldn't wait to let you go. More than likely he's hoping you'll hightail it out of here."

"You mean he wants me out of town so he can save his political ass."

"Yeah. That's the way I see it."

"Then I think I'm going to need your help."

"Sure. What can I do?"

"Help me prove I'm Gaylene Harjo's son."

In the four hours since Mark had ridden in Ivy's van, she had managed to fill the passenger seat with an interesting mix—a package of crackers, a stack of old *National Geographic*s and two boxes of baking soda.

She moved the magazines and crackers, then handed

Mark the baking soda while he was fastening his seat belt. "Here," she said, "this is for you."

"What's it for?"

"Chiggers, mosquito bites. Remember our hike to the trailer?"

"What makes you think I've got bites?"

Without missing a beat, she said, "Sprinkle it in your bathwater. You'll still itch, but it'll help."

As she pulled away from the courthouse, Mark surreptitiously scratched at a welt on his upper arm.

"Would you like to get something to eat?"

"No, just drop me at the motel if you don't mind. I need to wash the smell of jail off me."

"It's distinctive. *Parfum de prison*."

"Tell me about Hap Duchamp."

"He comes from the oldest and wealthiest family in town, maybe the whole state. But he's a decent guy. Hap's not impressed by his family or their money."

"Is he a good lawyer?"

"I think so. But I can't speak from personal experience. He's never had to get me out of jail." She laughed as she pulled into the motel.

"I'm glad to know you're sensitive to my situation. Now, would you like to come in? Watch my chiggers drown?"

"Why, you have a sense of humor after all."

"Yeah, I'm a riot," he said as he got out. "Oh, since it looks like I'm going to be around here for a while, I'm going to need to buy some clothes. Any suggestions?"

"Wal-Mart."

"I thought they sold shovels and Crock-Pots. Batteries. Stuff like that."

"You've never been in a Wal-Mart?"

"No."

"Welcome to the real world, Nick Harjo," she said with a teasing smile as she waved and drove away.

As he entered the lobby, two women behind the reception desk suspended their conversation when they saw him; a man seated in the waiting area looked up from his newspaper to gape as he walked by; two teenage girls going into the dining room stepped back to avoid getting too near him.

He knew he looked like he'd been held captive and tortured, his body bearing stitches, scratches, bruises and bites . . . both he and his clothes having suffered through an afternoon in the woods, an evening in jail.

When he unlocked the door to his room and switched on the light, he was stunned by what he saw—drawers hanging open, phone receiver off the hook, his suitcase upended on the bed, the clothes in his closet pulled from their hangers and piled in a heap on the floor.

And he knew without looking that the adoption decree and birth certificate were gone.

July 19, 1967

Dear Diary,

Tonight at prayer meeting I won a plastic rose for memorizing more scriptures than anyone else in my class. I am good at memorizing, but a lot of times I don't understand what the scripture means. Like this one in Ezra. "Now because we have maintenance from the king's palace, and it was not meet for us to see the king's dishonour, therefore have we sent and certified the king." Now what does that mean? Well, I usually just memorize short verses like "For the body is not one member, but many." I don't know what that one means either, but its short.

I wish Danny Pittman went to our church, but I don't think that's ever going to happen. Once we had a white couple who came one Sunday, but they never came back. Might be because we sang "Amazing Grace" in Cherokee and they felt embarrassed. We always sing one hymn in Cherokee, but "Amazing Grace" is the only one I know.

Spider Woman

Chapter Eleven

After Mark phoned Hap Duchamp to tell him about the missing documents, he started to call Charlene at home but hung up before he finished dialing.

If the sheriff had already spoken to her, told her Mark Albright was suspected of a series of burglaries in Oklahoma, she would be hysterical. And he couldn't deal with Charlene's hysteria. Not now.

He took a long baking soda bath, during which he removed two ticks from his groin and one from behind his knee, counted twenty-four chigger bites around his midsection and nineteen on his ankles.

While he soaked in the tub, he tried to make sense of the last forty-eight hours, reconstructing the events, putting them in order.

Until the past few weeks, almost everything in his life had gone according to plan. His plan. A sort of paint-by-numbers for living.

He had mapped out his future when he was sixteen, the result of a questionnaire prepared by his guidance counselor, the form asking, "Where do you see yourself in five years? Ten years? Twenty-five?"

Most of his classmates had responded by filling in the blanks. But not Mark Albright. He had spent days and nights composing his answers, finally turning in a ten-page blueprint for his life.

His plan included a bachelor's degree from UCLA and a DVM from Tufts. Marriage at thirty; a beautiful wife. Professional success in his own Beverly Hills clinic. A healthy investment portfolio that would provide a home in Malibu and another in Palm Springs, two vintage Jaguars, and membership in the Bel-Air Country Club. Trips abroad. All part of Mark Albright's Life-by-Design.

Becoming Nick Harjo had not been in his plan.

When he finally pulled the plug on the tub and watched the water swirling down the drain, it seemed a metaphor for what had happened to that other life.

After he shaved and rebandaged his arm, he picked through his clothes. Not that he had much to look at— two pairs of slacks and two shirts, the total of what he'd brought with him. Twenty-five hundred dollars' worth of Versace, Fendi and Valentino, some beyond salvage now.

He decided to wear the least torn, stained and smelly of the bunch, put aside his favorite shirt to see if the cleaners could resurrect it, then tossed the rest in the wastebasket.

He used a wet towel to clean his loafers, a pair of Guccis he'd bought in Milan, but they didn't look much better when he finished. The leather looked like it had been clawed, and one shoe was missing a tassel. But he supposed Gucci hadn't designed them for an overland expedition.

The lobby downstairs was quiet now, empty except for a black man standing near the door.

"Excuse me," Mark said to the woman behind the reception desk.

"May I help you?"

"Yes, I had intended to check out this afternoon, but my plans have changed. I need to keep the room for a few more days."

"Your name?" she asked as she stepped over to her computer.

"Mark Albright."

"Room two twenty-nine?"

"That's right."

"No problem, Mr. Albright. Just let us know when you'll be checking out."

"Thanks. Is the dining room still open?"

"No, but you can get sandwiches in the bar."

As he started toward the bar, the black man fell in beside him.

"Mr. Harjo?"

Mark felt a jolt of apprehension at hearing this stranger say his name, a name that still seemed alien to him, despite the revelations of the past few days.

"I need to talk to you."

"About what?"

"My father."

"Who are you?"

"Amax Dawson. Joe Dawson was my daddy."

"I wish I could tell you more," Mark said. "But that's really all I know."

Amax nodded, swallowed hard, then pushed back

from the table. "Excuse me for a minute," he said as he headed for the men's room in the motel lobby.

Mark watched him walk away, noticing that he had a slight limp. He was a handsome man, with smooth mahogany-colored skin, eyes a light shade of green and long, thick lashes of the kind women bought at cosmetic counters. Though he had probably thickened some around the middle, he still had narrow hips, broad shoulders and arms rippled with muscle.

"Hey, you guys ready for another round?" the bartender asked Mark.

"Yeah, I suppose so."

Amax came back to the table as the barmaid arrived with two bottles of beer, causing him to go for his pocket.

"You got the first ones." Mark handed the woman some bills. As soon as she retreated to the bar, he asked Amax, "Are you okay?"

Amax hesitated, then cleared his throat. "The day the gravediggers were shoveling out a hole for Dad's casket, O Boy Daniels had a crew on our land digging for a dead baby." Shifting his gaze to the mirror behind the bar, Amax stared at his own reflection, as if trying to put a name to the face looking back at him.

"I knew my daddy didn't kill anybody, knew he couldn't do a thing like that. But now and then . . ." Amax pulled at his lip. "Some kid at school would make a remark. Or I'd have a dream about my dad, see him on his hands and knees scooping out a hole down by the pond or behind the barn. Or maybe I'd just catch a stranger looking at me, his eyes telling me I was too young, too simple, to see the truth.

"And I'd wonder, you know? I'd think, What if . . ."

Amax ran a thumb around the rim of his beer bottle. "But I couldn't talk about that. Couldn't admit that sometimes I had doubts. I had to keep that to myself, keep all that guilt inside."

He wiped the back of his hand across his eyes. "Sorry. I haven't talked about this in a long time."

"You don't owe me an apology."

An outburst of laughter at the bar provided a brief distraction.

"Mind if I ask you a question?" Mark said.

"What's that?"

"How did your father know her?"

"Your mama?"

Mark nodded, acknowledging a word as strange as one from an undiscovered language.

"Daddy knew everybody in the county, I guess. He was a farmer who preached . . . or a preacher who farmed. Depended on what time of year it was.

"In the winter he was always out knocking on doors, promoting a revival or a new Bible study class. Praying with folks who were going through a bad time.

"Summers he'd show up at those same doors with a mess of okra or onions when we had extra. Tomatoes, corn. Whatever the drought didn't kill." Amax grinned. "Farming in Oklahoma might be a bigger test of faith than preaching.

"So he'd go by her trailer now and then. One of us would usually go with him. My mom, sometimes my sisters."

"Did you ever go?"

"Couple of times. Mostly I stayed busy trying to become the next Jim Brown."

"I was going to top Nolan Ryan in the record books."

Mark smiled. "Just didn't have a curveball. Or much of a fastball, either."

They were quiet then, Mark sipping his beer, Amax peeling the label from his bottle.

"Hey, Streak." The voice belonged to a tall, heavyset man passing the table.

"How you doing, Darrell," Amax said.

When the man joined a woman at the bar, Mark said, "Streak?"

"A name I picked up in another lifetime. I played ball at OU, then spent a couple of years with the Chargers. Punt returner. But I tore up a knee, so I came home, got a job coaching at the high school."

"I'm surprised."

"That they'd hire the son of a killer, or that I'd want to come back here?"

"Well, I—"

"This is Oklahoma. Sooner country. They don't care who you are as long as you can give them what they want. And that's a winner."

"Did you?"

"Yeah. I was part of it. But that's not why I came back." He took a swallow of beer, then stared at the lights of a jukebox. "I had some crazy idea that I could uncover the truth. Clear my dad's name.

"So I spent the next five, six years chasing dead ends. My wife finally made me stop. She thought I was going over the edge. But I think she'll see things in a different light now."

"How's that?"

"Because of you."

"You think my showing up is going to make much of a difference?"

"It might. See, I've always believed that whoever killed your mama lives here."

"What makes you think so?"

"Whoever did it knew my dad, knew how to get hold of his knife. And if the killer's still here, still alive, he's not going to be real happy when he hears Nicky Jack Harjo has turned up."

Chapter Twelve

The domino boys could have been the first to spread the news that a man claiming to be Nick Harjo had been plucked from the pool hall and carted off to jail. After all, they'd been witness to the scene, heard most of what was said, and watched O Boy take the man away.

The only problem was that two of the boys didn't quite get the story straight. And the two who did, didn't tell it.

Lonnie, his hearing aid low on battery power, had been able to follow most of the conversation about the dog bites on the fella's arm. But when Teeve whispered Nick's true identity to the sheriff, Lonnie had mistaken the name *Harjo* for *Cujo*, causing him—a longtime Stephen King fan—to conclude that the stranger had been attacked by a rabid dog.

Ron John O'Reily, still in the early stages of dementia, told quite a different tale. Though he knew what he'd heard when he heard it, by the time he reached the Quik Trip to buy a tin of snuff, his excitement was surpassed only by his confusion. Nevertheless, he was the center of attention when he announced to one clerk and five customers that he had seen Nick Nolte in the pool hall not more than an hour ago.

The Standingdeer brothers, Jackson and Johnny, were afflicted with neither hearing problems nor memory loss but were quiet, solitary bachelors who shared both an isolated cabin and their belief that talk led to trouble. Johnny, the least talkative of the two, occasionally went through entire days without speaking except to bid in the domino games. So after they left Teeve's Place, they went home, ate a supper of fry bread and beans, then watched the Cardinals game on TV, unaware that a lot of folks in town were penning up their dogs while even more were scouring the streets hoping to spot Nick Nolte.

But the fear of rabies and the search for a movie star would soon give way to the real story: Nicky Jack Harjo had returned from the grave.

That news was passed by a phone call from Olene Turner, a dispatcher in the sheriff's office, to Amax Dawson. Olene had been in love with Amax since she was sixteen, when he'd taken her to their junior prom. And though she'd been married and divorced three times in the past twenty-two years, her feelings for her high school sweetheart had never changed.

Amax, after spending time with Mark in the motel bar, had taken the story home to his wife, then called his sister, Zoe, who arrived at his house within minutes. They talked until midnight, but before Zoe left, they agreed to keep the news inside the family, at least for a while.

At home, Zoe waited for her husband, Foster, to

come in from his Saturday night poker game. Foster, himself not a Dawson, did not feel bound by the family agreement, so he felt no sense of betrayal when, the next morning, he whispered the news to his best friend, Jolly Strange, just after services ended at the AME Church.

Jolly and Foster, best friends since childhood, worked together at the plastic factory, but Jolly was also self-employed. He owned and operated a one-man business called Strange Lawncare, and on this particular Sunday he was doing Martha Duchamp's place.

Martha, bleary-eyed and shaky, poured herself an eye-opener of Jack Daniel's when she heard Jolly fire up his mower in her front yard. By the time he finished, she'd knocked back three more.

While Jolly waited at the kitchen door for Martha to retrieve her cash from the sock hidden in her freezer, he told her the story he'd heard from Foster Arnett, who'd heard it from his wife, who'd heard it from her brother, who'd been told by Olene Turner.

As soon as Jolly drove away, Martha poured herself a tumbler of bourbon, being it was past noon, and got on the phone.

The story, on the loose now, raced through the community like an unbridled child. Rumors climbed over backyard fences, skipped from street to street, romped down the aisles of Wal-Mart, tumbled through the Laundromat and cartwheeled through the park.

And like carriers of a virus, those who heard passed it on to others, causing an epidemic of gossip to spread from neighbor to neighbor, child to parent, doctor to patient, friend to friend.

Later, no one would give much thought to the path the news had traveled, but more than a few would be amazed at the speed with which the story sprinted past the city limits, jumped the river, galloped over eight counties and dashed across the state line.

Chapter Thirteen

Mark answered on the first ring, a call that jerked him from sleep.

"Good morning." The man's voice on the other end of the line, vaguely familiar, had a homogenized quality, stripped of accent, polished. "This is Arthur McFadden. I saw you yesterday at the radio station, but we weren't introduced."

Mark, never at his best before his first cup of coffee, mumbled a less-than-enthusiastic response.

"If you have time, I'd like to talk to you."

"When?"

"I'm downstairs now."

"Here? In the motel?"

"I go to early mass. St. Andrew's is just a block away, so . . ."

"I'll need a few minutes," Mark said.

"Fine. I'll be on the patio."

Mark pulled on the same clothes he'd worn the day before, reminding himself that he still had to make his way to Wal-Mart.

Arthur McFadden stood, offering his hand when Mark, squinting against the sunlight reflected off a small swimming pool, joined him at a table shaded by a faded umbrella.

"Sorry for barging into your day at this hour," he said as soon as Mark took a chair. "Coffee?" He offered a carafe.

"Thanks."

As Arthur filled a cup, he said, "I'm afraid I might have seemed brusque yesterday when you came to Kyle's office."

Mark sipped his coffee but made no response.

"I suppose my behavior was prompted, in part, by surprise. You're not the sort Kyle usually gives audience to."

"And what sort is that?"

"Aging hippies. Bizarre musicians with green hair and dirty fingernails. Drug dealers. Anyone looking to make a score." Arthur curled his lips in what was intended to be a smile. "Prevailing parlance, I believe." He inhaled deeply, held the breath for a moment, then said, "So. What did you think of my stepson?"

"Well . . ."

"I don't suppose I have to tell you that he's a troubled man."

"I wasn't with him long enough to make that kind of judgment."

"But you must admit that he's hardly in control of his emotions."

"I'm not quite sure what you're getting at."

"Let me come right to the point, then," he said as he stubbed out a cigar in the ashtray. "What is your business with Kyle?"

Mark guessed that Arthur's tone—demanding, superior

and authoritative—found in his stepson a soft and vulnerable target.

"It's really a private matter."

"I rather thought you'd say that. Under other circumstances, I might agree. But in Kyle's case, his business is my business."

"Oh? How's that?"

"Kyle is unstable. Manic-depressive. Alcoholic, addict since he was sixteen, seventeen. In and out of rehab, jail. Tens of thousands of dollars wasted, but . . ."

Mark could almost see dollar signs flashing in Arthur's eyes.

"In 1980, I was appointed by the court as his legal guardian, an arrangement of his mother's choosing, not mine. Because of her decision, I am responsible for Kyle. I trust that explains my interest in your dealings with him."

Mark helped himself to more coffee, less for the caffeine than to buy time as he decided how to play this.

"I'm an attorney, trying to settle an estate that leaves a piece of property to—"

"No, sir. You are not. You're here either because you're an impostor or because you actually believe yourself to be Nick Harjo."

"You mind telling me where you heard that?"

"The news is all over town. Nothing remains secret in DeClare for long."

"Apparently not."

"But my purpose in seeing you this morning is not to attempt to determine your identity."

"No?"

"No."

"Then why are you here?"

"Kyle said you were questioning him about Gaylene. I want to know why."

"I thought he might have some idea about who fathered her child."

"He denied knowing who that was, didn't he?"

"He expressed strong feelings for her, but he said their relationship was platonic."

"Well, Kyle doesn't have much of a grasp on the past."

"Meaning what?"

"Drugs have provided him the unique ability to rewrite history, and in doing so, he's made Gaylene a saint. He's probably convinced himself her conception was immaculate."

"So you're saying they were lovers?"

"I would have no way of knowing that, but she obviously had more in common with Mary Magdalene than with the Virgin Mary."

"You knew Gaylene well?"

"No, not especially. I gave her a job at the station when she was a senior in high school, but that proved to be a mistake on my part."

"Why?"

"Gaylene was lazy. Totally without ambition. And she wasn't particularly bright."

"That's odd. No one else I've talked to made those kinds of observations about her."

"Then maybe she didn't work for them. But I'll give her this: She was shrewd and beautiful. A combination that makes men like Kyle easy prey. Kyle had access to money. His mother is quite wealthy. So when I found out he and Gaylene had established a relationship, I had to let her go."

"But they continued to see each other."

"Unfortunately."

"If Kyle is the father . . ."

"He told you he wasn't."

"Nevertheless . . ."

"Kyle's quite upset. He was incoherent after you left the station yesterday and became unmanageable as the day wore on."

"I hate to hear that. Maybe if I talked to him again, I could—"

"I'm afraid that won't be possible."

"Why?"

"I had Kyle transported to a facility late last night. He won't be receiving visitors. Or phone calls." Arthur checked his watch, then pushed back from the table. "Well, I've taken enough of your time."

"I'm in no rush."

"But I am. Mass begins shortly."

"Before you go, let me ask you one question."

"I don't have any answers for you. And neither does Kyle."

Mark watched Arthur walk away, his shoulders hunched like he was moving against a strong wind, a burden balanced precariously on his back.

Following Hap's directions, Mark turned right at the first road past a one-lane bridge, then at a red mailbox took a left onto a graveled driveway bordered by blue spruce and magnolias. The drive climbed to the top of a hill, ending in front of a two-story log house with a broad wraparound porch.

As Mark was getting out of his car, Hap stepped

through the front door and came to the porch steps to meet him.

"Sorry to be late," Mark said.

"We don't keep to a schedule around here, especially on Sunday. Slept late myself."

"I had the same idea, but Arthur McFadden paid me an early morning visit."

"What was that about?"

"Kyle Leander. I had a conversation with him yesterday; McFadden sent him to rehab last night."

"Is there a connection?"

"McFadden seems to think so."

"You don't sound convinced."

"Kyle seemed agitated all right, but I got the impression that's not new. He's a pretty tense guy."

"He's been a mess since he was a boy, trundled from one institution to another."

"Yeah, so I was told. But I believe McFadden's trying to make sure to keep me away from Kyle."

"Wonder why?"

Just then a tall, angular man appeared in the doorway.

"Mark, this is my partner, Matthew Donaldson."

"Hi there." Matthew offered an open smile and handshake that could cause damage. "Hope you're hungry. I'm fixing brunch."

"Sure."

"Great. Just need a couple more minutes."

When Matthew went back inside, Mark said, "Does he know about me?"

"He knows you're a client from out of town. That's all."

Mark nodded, but it was an absent gesture, his eyes following a hawk circling high overhead.

"So, how are you doing, Mark?"

"Oh, better than yesterday, I guess."

"You're not sure?"

"The day's young. Still plenty of time for your sheriff to haul me back to jail . . . or break into my room again."

"Well, I have my doubts about O Boy being behind that little stunt."

Mark looked puzzled.

"If he wanted a copy of your birth certificate," Hap said, "he could get one from the Department of Records. No reason for him to take it from you. No, I don't think O Boy had a thing to do with it."

"Then who? Who else would want to see my damn birth certificate. Teeve? Ivy? Amax Dawson? No, I don't think—"

"Amax? How the hell did he find out?"

"A friend who works in the sheriff's office gave him a call."

Hap shook his head. "Amax tried for years to clear Joe's name, but he never got anywhere with it."

"He seems to think I'm proof that his father's innocent."

"You're proof that Joe wasn't a child killer, but proving he didn't kill Gaylene's another matter. After all these years, he'll—"

They looked up when Matthew rapped on the window and motioned them inside. As they started for the door, Hap said, "Listen, I should have mentioned this earlier . . ."

"What?"

"Uh, Matthew's cooking is . . . well, unusual."

"An adventure in eating, huh?"

"Yes, you could say that."

The first floor of the house, open and spacious, dominated by a massive fieldstone fireplace, was furnished with worn leather couches, heavy oak tables and large canvases of western art. Timbered beams crisscrossed the vaulted ceiling, Navajo rugs covered the floor.

"Nice place," Mark said.

"Thanks. We enjoy it."

The kitchen, permeated with the smell of pumpkin, was bright, the walls hung with knotty pine cabinets. In the center of the room a table was set for two.

"Are you sure you were planning on my joining you?" Mark asked.

"Absolutely," Matthew said. "I take lunch to the station every Sunday. I'll eat there."

"Matthew's a retired fireman," Hap explained, "but he hangs out there more than he did when he was getting paid for it."

"I've heard firemen are great cooks," Mark said, a comment that caused Hap to roll his eyes.

"We're not bad." Matthew ladled a watery orange liquid into soup bowls, where bits of something gray and slick floated to the surface. "Pumpkin squid bisque," he announced. "Enjoy."

Hoping to disguise his reluctance, Mark filled his soup spoon and brought it to his mouth, inhaling an unpleasant, vinegary odor. But with both Hap and Matthew watching him intently, he couldn't think of any way out.

His first and final taste of bisque, so bitter that his eyes teared, contained two chunks of squid that defied chewing as they swelled into rubbery globs, forcing him to swallow them whole.

"What do you think?" Matthew asked.

Managing a weak smile, Mark said, "I've never tasted anything quite like it."

"That's because it's one of my original recipes."

"Well, you're certainly inventive."

"Like I told you," Hap said, "Matthew's cooking is truly an adventure in eating."

Matthew beamed. "I've made spinach salad with yogurt dressing, cold fish mousse and a lima bean soufflé."

"Sounds wonderful, Matthew," Hap said, "but I know you need to get down to the station. Those guys will be getting hungry."

"Right." Matthew gathered up several grocery bags and headed for the back door. "Oh, I almost forgot. There's a mayonnaise cheesecake in the fridge."

"Go on. I'll take care of it."

"Okay. Bon appétit, gentlemen."

Hap went to the kitchen window and watched until Matthew's pickup pulled away. When he returned to the table, he picked up the soup bowls and emptied the bisque into the garbage disposal.

"Let's go back to my study, Mark, unless you've worked up a hunger for lima bean soufflé."

"I think I'll deny myself that pleasure."

Mark followed Hap to the far end of the house to a small room comfortably cluttered with law books, file folders, magazines and newspapers.

"Have a seat," Hap said as he removed a stack of legal journals from a worn wingback chair. Then he opened an unlocked wall safe, pulled out a brown paper sack and—beaming like a kid showing off his Halloween loot—dumped the contents on his desk. Candy bars, peanuts, Twinkies, pretzels, cookies, Pop-Tarts and chips.

"Breakfast is served."

"Thanks, but—"

"Wait!" Hap bent to a minifridge behind his desk,

produced two bottles, popped the tops and handed one to Mark.

"What's this?"

"Don't tell me you've never tasted a Chocolate Soldier."

"Afraid not."

"Oh, you are in for a treat."

Hap opened a package of Twinkies and handed one to Mark, who studied it with the look of a man about to bite into a frosting-filled grub worm.

"And this is . . . ?"

"A Twinkie! You mean to tell me you're twenty-seven, twenty-eight, and you never—"

"We didn't have junk food in our house."

"Junk food?" Hap frowned. "Now you've hurt my feelings."

Mark hesitated.

"Trust me. This will help you get past the taste of pumpkin squid bisque."

"Okay." Mark bit into the Twinkie, then took a swig of the chocolate milk.

"So?"

"Delicious."

"See? Lawyers never lie," Hap said as he peeled the wrapper from a Hershey bar. "Okay, let's try to figure out where to start." He grabbed a legal pad and pen. "You discovered this birth certificate after the death of your father. Right?"

"Yes."

"And you had no idea until then that you were adopted."

"None. And the name on the birth certificate didn't mean anything to me, but the date of birth, the same as mine, had to be more than coincidence. Then, when I saw the decree of adoption, of course I knew."

"You have the decree?" Hap's excitement was obvious.

"No. It was clipped to the birth certificate. Whoever took that got them both."

"Did you make a copy? Before you left California?"

"No, but there was also a statement from the attorney, dated February 2, 1972. It was for the adoption of a baby boy named Nicodemus Jack Harjo. The attorney was J. W. Downing; the charge was twenty thousand dollars."

Hap whistled through his teeth. "That was a hunk of money back then. Did you try to contact this Downing?"

"He retired in '83, died in '85. And his office was in a building that was demolished in '92. It's a parking garage now."

"Well, you've done some homework."

"Didn't learn much, though."

"Would you like me to follow up on this? See what I can come up with?"

"Like what?"

"Well, Mark, we've got a lot of damn blanks here. Like who transported that baby from Oklahoma to California? A man? A woman? The killer? And the couple who adopted you through this lawyer, Downing? What did they know? Any chance they were—"

"Look, Hap, if you're suggesting that my mother and father had anything to do with Gaylene Harjo's murder or—"

"Whoa. I'm not suggesting anything. I'm just asking questions. Same questions, I suspect, you've been asking yourself."

"My parents weren't perfect, but they were decent, honest—"

"Just not honest enough to tell you who you are."

A heavy silence settled between the two men until the phone on Hap's desk rang.

"Sorry, Mark. That'll be Martha Bernard. And she'll let it ring until I answer."

"No problem."

"Hello, Mother," Hap said into the receiver. "No, Jolly Strange didn't steal your shovel. I used it yesterday when you asked me to transplant . . ."

Mark wandered out of Hap's office and down the hallway, then stopped before a painting he hadn't noticed earlier.

The artist had worked in oil—two faces of an Indian woman . . . one young, hair black as ebony, dark, defiant eyes, unsmiling lips set in fierce determination. The second, the same woman grown old, hair gone white, face a geography of wrinkles. But the set of her jaw, the tilt of her unbowed head, and eyes that had refused and resisted revealed a spirit of defiance unaltered by her years.

Mark was so moved by the painting that he hadn't realized Hap was standing just behind him.

"What do you think?" Hap asked.

"It's powerful." Mark looked for the artist's signature but found instead a tiny spider painted with the face of a woman. "Who's the artist?"

"Gaylene."

Mark felt the fine hairs rise on the back of his neck, then rubbed at the goose bumps on his arms. "When did she do this?" he asked, unable to pull his eyes away from the painting.

"In her senior year of high school, I think. Yeah, she gave it to me just before she graduated."

"You knew her well, then."

"I watched her grow up. Her mother, Enid, worked for me at the bank for years. The family lived so far out of town, miles from the school bus route, so Gaylene rode in with Enid every morning, then came to the bank after school to wait for her mother to get off.

"So I saw Gaylene five days a week, from the time she started kindergarten until the day she turned sixteen and got her driver's license."

"Tell me about her."

"Oh, she was quiet. Very shy kid. Used to sit on a bench in the lobby, just outside my office.

"One day, I guess she was in the third, maybe fourth grade, I grabbed a book off my desk, an art book I'd ordered, and I took it out to her, asked her if she'd like to look at it. She said yes, not much excited by it. Just being polite, I think.

"But the damnedest thing happened. That book took hold of her. She simply fell in love with it. Every day for weeks, she'd come to my office, stand in the door, waiting for me to offer her that book. And you know what she did for two hours every afternoon? She'd copy from the prints in the book. She had a sketchbook filled with copies of works by Picasso, Cézanne, de Kooning.

"So I started bringing more art books to the bank, let her take them home, bought them for her birthday. When she was in junior high, her art class took a field trip to the Gilcrease Museum in Tulsa, a show of North American Indian art. And that did it for her.

"She was hooked. Determined as hell to become an artist. She would have, too, if . . ."

Hap didn't finish what he'd started to say. But he didn't have to. Mark knew the rest of the sentence, knew how it ended.

"What's the significance of the spider there in the corner?" Mark asked.

" 'Spider Woman' was the signature mark on all her work."

"Do you know why?"

"Something to do with Cherokee lore."

"And the connection?"

"Oh, I thought you knew. Gaylene was Cherokee."

September 14, 1967

Dear Diary,

Guess what? I made the basketball team! Coach said if I work hard, I might see some court time. I sure hope so. If I have to sit on the bench all season and watch Danny watching Becky, it's going to be a long season.

I asked Daddy if I could go to the all-school dance Friday night. I knew he'd say no, but no harm in asking. He says I can't dance or date until I'm sixteen and he doesn't want me going out with white boys.

Speaking of that, there's a new Cherokee boy in my class this year. His name is Oscar Horsechief and he's already had to fight because of his name. I understand that his family didn't have a choice about Horsechief, but why would they stick him with a name like Oscar? He's shy, but he seems nice. He's not nearly as cute as Danny Pittman though.

I think my bust cream is working. I don't jiggle yet, but my bra feels tighter. A little bit. I forgot to put the jar away night before last, but I don't think Mom saw it. If she had, she would have said something. I hate it when we have one of our "talks" because she does all the talking.

Spider Woman

November 17, 1967

Dear Diary,

Becky Allan fouled out of the game with Spiro tonight and Coach Dougless put me in while we were down nine points in the fourth quarter. I was real nervous at first, especially when I saw Danny watching me, but I settled down and focused on my game. I made four baskets. Three lay-ups and a free throw.

We won 59 to 52, but it was ruined for me because right at the end of the game, right after my three-point shot, some guy in the bleachers yelled, "Way to go, Squaw."

I wouldn't let myself cry, not out there in front of everybody, but I cried in the locker room after the game. The girls on the team all hugged me, but it didn't make me feel any better.

When I got home tonight, Oscar Horsechief called. He didn't say anything about what had happened, but I know he called to try to make me feel better. He's a good friend.

Spider Woman

Chapter Fourteen

Mark was surprised when he found himself parking the Mitsubishi in front of the pool hall. He'd just driven back from Hap's place, almost twenty miles from town, but as he turned off the ignition, he realized he couldn't recall the drive at all.

His mind was on the painting he'd seen and the girl who painted it—the girl who wanted to be an artist.

He tried to imagine what she would have looked like when she worked. Did she stand at the easel or sit? Was she right-handed or left-? Did she have small hands? Delicate fingers? Had she talked to herself as her paintings came to life? Or did she like silence broken only by the sounds of her brush strokes on canvas?

And Hap had said her artist's mark was always Spider Woman. "Always" meant there'd been other paintings. How many? Mark wondered. A few? Dozens? Did any still exist? If so, where would they be?

Questions. So many questions. But most of all, he

wanted to know who she was, this girl who had been his mother.

When he finally got out of his car, Mark saw the domino players at their table, watching him through the window. But when he stepped inside, they went on with their game, acting as if they hadn't noticed him.

A lone teenager was muttering to an image on one of the videoscreens and the pool tables were empty, but the lunchroom wasn't. Mark guessed from the way they were dressed that the diners, mostly elderly women, had just come from church.

Ivy, carrying a pitcher of tea, waved when she saw him. "Don't run off," she called. "I need to talk to you."

While he was waiting, Mark pulled a chair up to the domino table in one corner.

"Mind if I watch?" he asked.

"Okay by me," said Ron John O'Reily.

"How you feeling today?" Lonnie Cruddup asked, surprised to see a man with rabies up and walking around.

"Fine," Mark said.

Lonnie began to shuffle the dominoes. "You ever played moon?"

"Hell, Lonnie. He's from California," Ron John said, still believing their visitor was Nick Nolte.

"Well, that explains it, then," Lonnie said. "So what is it you all play out there?"

"They play polo," Ron John said. Then, to Mark, "Ain't that right?"

"Some do."

"Now that's something I'd like to try," Ron John said. "Go to one of them casinos and play polo."

"Do you mean keno?" Mark asked.

"Aw, hell." Jackson Standingdeer shook his head. "He means bingo."

"I saw James Bond do it in a movie," Ron John said. "He was in a casino, real fancy place, wearing a tuxedo, and he was sure as hell playing polo."

"You don't know a damn thing, do you," Jackson said. "You play polo on a horse."

"We gonna get on with this game or not?" Ron John yelled.

"Fine. But I know what I know and that's the end of it." Lonnie gave the dominoes one last rough shuffle, then each player drew.

"Bid four," Jackson said.

"Four?" Lonnie sneered. "You think you're playing with a bunch of little kinnygardeners? Hell, a blind man could make five with my hand."

"So, you bidding five? Or just saying you could make five if you was blind?"

"Five's my bid."

Johnny, the next bidder, studied his dominoes silently. Unblinking, unmoving.

"Goddammit, Johnny. You playing or having a stroke?"

Johnny hesitated, then said, "I'm gonna shoot the moon."

Lonnie roared. "He's had a stroke all right."

"He's bluffing," Ron John said. "Trying to bait me into shooting it over him."

"Remember what happened last time you shot it?" Lonnie asked. "You was picking up pieces of your own ass for a month."

Mark edged closer to the table. "What does it mean, 'shoot the moon'?"

"It means he's gonna go for all the tricks."

"The whole kit and kaboodle," Jackson said.

"Kind of like getting married," Lonnie explained.

"How's that?" Mark asked.

"Well, say you find you a woman you just can't get enough of. You want her so bad you can't eat, can't sleep.

"Now you know this is a woman who's gonna keep your bed warm on cold nights, make you potato soup when you're sick. She's gonna believe you even when you're lying. Hell, she's the only person in the world who's gonna know what you wanted that you never got, and what you got that you never wanted.

"But you know for certain there's gonna be times when this woman's gonna make you miserable. She's gonna bitch if you forget your anniversary. She's gonna want you to watch some crying movie on TV when there's a ball game you wanna see. She'll expect you to skip your poker game and keep her company when she's feeling blue. In other words, she's gonna be a pain in the ass some of the time.

"So, you gotta make a decision. What are you gonna do? Walk away from her? Or go for it all. Give her up? Or shoot the moon."

"Well . . ." Mark looked into one face after another while all four of the domino boys waited. They were sizing him up. And he knew that his answer would, for them at least, determine what kind of man he was.

Finally he said, "Well, I guess I'd shoot the moon."

Lonnie grinned, Jackson and Johnny nodded their approval and Ron John slapped Mark on the back.

"Okay, what are you boys up to in here?" Ivy asked as she came in from the lunchroom.

"Just talking about the game, Ivy," Lonnie said. "Believe this boy understands how it's played now."

"Mark, you start taking advice from that bunch, you're in for some hard times."

"You gonna bid, Ron John?" Jackson asked. "'Cause if you're not—"

"I'm thinking, Jackson. I'm thinking."

"Now there's a first."

Ivy went behind the counter and waved Mark over.

"Where've you been?" she asked.

"Hap's."

"Did he have any news?"

"I saw one of her paintings."

"Aunt Gaylene's?"

"Ivy, why didn't you tell me she was Indian?"

"I just assumed you knew."

Beginning to sound exasperated now, Mark said, "How the hell would I know?"

"You said you saw some pictures of her when you went to the newspaper office."

"She didn't look Indian in those," he said.

"Mark, what does an Indian look like? Huh?"

"Like those two brothers at the domino table," he said, almost whispering.

"Jackson and Johnny are full-blood Cherokees. Of course they look Indian. What about me? Don't I look Indian?"

"No."

"Well, I'm part Cherokee, part Creek. Almost everyone in this town has some Indian blood." Ivy folded her arms, leaned across the counter. "What's this about anyway? Does it bother you that you're Cherokee? Do I detect a bit of racism in all this?"

"No! But it's quite a shock. I knew even when I was a kid that I didn't have the look of a golden California boy, but I thought my great-grandparents were Mediterranean. That's what my mother told me, so—"

"Mark, you're going to have to rethink most of what you've been told."

"Yeah. I suppose so."

"Uh-oh. Here comes trouble," Ivy said when O Boy Daniels walked in.

"Thought I might find you here," O Boy said to Mark. "Went by the motel, then took a run out to Hap's place. Guess I just missed you."

"How did you know I went to Hap's?"

"Why? Was it a secret?" O Boy grinned with the satisfaction of having delivered the punch line to a good joke.

But Mark wasn't smiling. "Do you have some business with me, or is this a social call?"

"Came by to tell you I made an arrest in those break-ins."

"Will wonders never cease," Ivy said.

"You've got a smart mouth on you, girl. Just like your mama."

"Why, thank you, O Boy."

"Anyway, you're free to leave town, Albright. Or Harjo. Whatever you're calling yourself now. So you can take off whenever you're ready, but if I was you, I wouldn't waste any time."

"Why's that?"

"Had a call this morning. Some reporter in Tulsa asking questions about you. I didn't give him a damn thing, but that won't stop him. He's not going to let a story like this go. And if one of those sons of bitches knows about you, you can bet there's more on to it by now. Place'll be crawling with them."

As O Boy turned and started for the door, he said, "You have a good trip. And don't be such a stranger."

When the door slammed, Ivy said, "Isn't he charming?"

Mark walked to the front window, where he watched O Boy get into his patrol car and pull away. "Well," he said, "I guess Hap was right."

"What'd Hap say?" Lonnie asked, calling Mark's attention to the foursome in the corner, where the domino game had stopped, the players caught up in the goings-on around them.

Customarily, Mark would have been peeved at a near stranger butting into his personal business, but given the incongruity of this situation, he couldn't keep from grinning.

"He said the sheriff would be real enthusiastic about me leaving town."

"Hap was right," Jackson Standingdeer offered, his comment considered a downright outburst from a man who cared little for the spoken word.

"You know, Mark, as much as it hurts me to say this, O Boy's close to the truth about one thing," Ivy said. "Story like yours will cause a big stir around here, and I don't think you'll like being in the middle of it. Before this is over, you may wish you'd taken that flight back to L.A."

"You could be right, Ivy, but there's so much more I want to know. If I leave now, chances are I'd always wonder."

For a brief time, all movement, all conversation, in the pool hall ceased. The domino players in the corner, Ivy behind the counter, Teeve in the café doorway . . . they all waited.

Finally, Ron John O'Reily, in one of his more lucid moments, said, "I think you might ought to shoot the moon."

Chapter Fifteen

"You've got to remember, Mark, I was just a little kid when all that happened, so I only know what Mom's told me." Ivy slowed the van as she neared a one-lane bridge that crossed a dry creek bed.

"Then tell me what you know."

"Well, she was a hell of a basketball player, I guess. I've seen an old newspaper clipping with her picture; the caption says, 'Gaylene Harjo Named Player of the Year.' Several colleges were after her when she finished high school, but she decided on Northeastern, a state college in Tahlequah, because they offered her the best scholarship. Full tuition, books, room and board. All she had to do was sign a letter of intent and pass a physical.

"So, a week before she was scheduled to leave, she went to a local doctor for her exam. I don't know . . . an X-ray of an old knee injury, some other tests, I guess." Ivy glanced at Mark. "Evidently, she had no idea she was pregnant. If she had, things wouldn't have turned out the way they did."

"What things?"

"Grandma Enid planned a surprise party. See, having a Harjo go to college was really a big deal. A first. So she arranged for Grandpa to drive Gaylene into town to pick up the results of her physical, and while they were gone, everyone would come to the house—the basketball team, her friends, teachers, coaches. And the family, of course. The whole damn clan.

"They tied balloons to the fence, set up tables in the yard, put out a ton of food. Some of the kids had Roman candles and firecrackers. It was going to be a real celebration. Mom said nearly a hundred people showed up.

"So, they were all there waiting for Grandpa to pull in with Aunt Gaylene when they'd yell 'Surprise!' and set off their fireworks.

"But when Grandpa drove in, Aunt Gaylene wasn't with him. He parked his truck, walked straight into the house without a word to anyone, and that was that."

"What do you mean, 'that was that'? Where was she?"

"I don't know, but Mom said the next day she was living in one of Arthur McFadden's rental trailers. A little more than seven months later you were born. And she never did go to college."

"But what happened on that trip to town?"

"I assume her medical exam showed that she was pregnant. Grandpa probably found out at the same time she did."

"So he wouldn't let her come home?"

"I don't think she ever stepped foot inside his house again."

"How did her mother feel about that?"

"Oh, Grandma tried to talk to him, tried everything

she could to change his mind, but he was so damn hard-headed. He wouldn't listen.

"So she did what she could to help Aunt Gaylene. Kept her in produce from the garden, bought everything she'd need for the baby. Took her to the hospital when she went into labor. Stayed with her for a week when she came home with you."

"I don't suppose your grandfather was too happy about that."

"Probably not, but he couldn't do anything about it. Grandma's a strong woman. Independent as hell. Yeah, he obviously knew about it, but I doubt he ever mentioned it. That wasn't his way."

"He must've been fun to live with."

"Well, I know how it sounds, but he was really a decent man. Good husband, hard worker. But to his way of thinking, there was only one way to live. The right way. Which just happened to be his way."

"And having a pregnant unmarried daughter wasn't the right way, was it."

"No," Ivy said as she turned off the blacktop onto a recently graded dirt road.

"He must have had a lot of regrets when she was killed."

"I'm sure he did."

"Did he ever talk to you about it?"

"No. He didn't talk to anyone about it. Grandpa stopped speaking the day Aunt Gaylene was buried."

"We're here," Ivy said as she eased the van across a rusted cattle guard and onto a graveled drive leading to a freshly painted clapboard house.

The home was the first dwelling Mark had seen for

the last half hour or so, unless someone was living in the abandoned school bus or the burnt-out church they'd passed several miles back.

Even before Ivy parked, two hounds raced from a barn at the back of the property, barking while they circled the van.

"Why don't you give me some time alone with her. This is going to be a shock no matter how we do it, but maybe it'll be a little easier for her if you wait out here while I tell her."

"Okay."

"And here's another thing. She's going to call you Nicky Jack. Not Mark. And you're not going to correct her. She's an old lady and you're her grandson. Understood?"

"Understood."

As Ivy was climbing the steps, the door opened and a thin, dark woman with white hair and an open smile stepped onto the porch.

"Hi, Grandma."

"Well, hello, sweet thing." Enid embraced Ivy, then patted her belly. "How's our little one today?"

"Feels like he's playing kickball."

"Who's that with you?" Enid asked, shading her eyes against the sunlight. "That your mama out there?"

"No."

"Well, whoever it is, tell them to get out and come in."

"I will, but let's go inside first. I have something to tell you."

A look of alarm crossed the old woman's face. "Is it bad news, Ivy?"

"No, no," Ivy said as she drew her grandmother inside. "I'll tell you all about it."

When Ivy closed the door, Mark got out of the van to draw a breath of fresh air. A muscle just beneath his right shoulder blade had tightened up as it usually did when he was feeling tense.

He stretched, grimaced at the pain that radiated up to his shoulder, then began to walk. The hounds followed but kept a safe distance behind this stranger.

The doors of a one-car garage were standing open, so he took a look inside, where a workbench, clean and smooth, was topped by a Peg-Board containing straight rows of tools. On a shelf overhead, cans of oil, gasoline, anti-freeze, kerosene and paint were lined up neatly, their labels facing front. The walls were hung with coils of garden hose, rope, fan belts, extension cords and baling wire. Everything neat, everything orderly. All put in place by a man who lived the "right" way. His way.

At the back of the house, enclosed in a chicken-wire fence, Mark found a garden—straight, weedless rows of squash, corn and melons.

Behind the garden was a shed housing a tractor, lawn mower, sacks of livestock feed and bales of hay.

As he completed circling the house, he passed a tire swing, the spot beneath it bare where children's feet had rid the space of grass.

When he took a seat on the front porch steps, the dogs approached him timidly.

"So you want to be friends now, huh?"

At the sound of his voice, both dogs wagged their tails, then cozied up so he could rub behind their ears.

When the front door opened behind him, he stood and turned to see Enid coming toward him, her face wet with tears.

"I never gave up hope, Nicky Jack," she said as she

wrapped him in her arms. Then, holding him close, she whispered, "Thank you, Lord. Thank you for bringing my grandbaby home."

While Enid turned the chicken, sizzling on the stove, Mark watched every move she made. He'd been stealing glances at her since he'd walked into the house, but now, as she busied herself with cooking, he felt free to stare.

He was fascinated by their similarities—the color of their skin, the shape of their eyes, the contours of their lips. For the first time in his life, he was in the company of someone whose face resembled his own.

As she took a spoon from a counter drawer, she saw him watching her and smiled, causing him to flush with embarrassment.

After she slid a pan of biscuits into the oven, she rejoined him and Ivy at the kitchen table, covered with photographs, scrapbooks, newspaper clippings and school yearbooks. Mark was turning pages of an album, looking at pictures of Gaylene as a toddler, her face smeared with chocolate; then, at seven, she and two older boys wading in a creek; Gaylene, a teenager, climbing the town's water tower; and at her graduation, in cap and gown, giving a thumbs-up to the camera.

"Look at these." Ivy held out a handful of blue ribbons she'd picked out of a shoebox of memorabilia.

"Oh, she won all kinds of awards for her artwork," Enid said. "Won blue ribbons at the state fair in Tulsa three times."

"What happened to her paintings?" Mark asked. "Did she sell them?"

"No." Enid smiled. "Said they weren't good enough to make people pay for them. She just gave them away."

"Do you know who has them?"

"Well, let's see. My brother in Arizona; her old basketball coach. Rowena Whitekiller—she was Gaylene's best friend. They started kindergarten together and graduated together." Enid swallowed hard, trying to hold back tears.

"I think her art teacher at the high school, Irene Dobbins, had several, but she moved to Florida after she retired and I've lost track of her.

"Now and then, Gaylene would donate her paintings for fund-raisers. An auction or raffle, something like that. She gave one to the tribal office so they could sell chances on it to pay for some equipment at the dialysis center. She gave a couple to our church to raise money for new pews. And the United Way sold one at auction for over six hundred dollars, I think."

"She didn't keep any of them?"

"Just one. It was her favorite, but I don't know why. She said it was a self-portrait, but it didn't look anything like her. Matter of fact, it didn't even look like a human at all."

"May I see it?"

"I wish you could, but I don't know where it is. Gaylene took it with her when she moved into that trailer. And I don't know what happened to it. I saw it on her wall the last time I visited her, just two or three days before she was . . . a few days before she died."

"So you don't have any of her work."

"Not her paintings, no. But I have her sketchbooks, drawings she did in high school. Would you like to see those?"

"Yes, I would."

"Come on, then," Enid said. "Ivy, honey, keep an eye on that chicken, will you?"

"Sure, Grandma."

Mark followed Enid through the dining room, then down a hall past a bedroom and a bath to a closed door, which she opened almost reverently. And when she led him inside, she stepped softly as if she were entering a shrine. He knew, without being told, that nothing here had changed in the past quarter century.

"I used to come to this room every morning, long after she was gone. Pretend I was waking her for school. Sometimes I'd bring flowers from the garden, put them in a vase on her night table. She always liked—"

When her voice broke, Enid bent to snatch a dead leaf from the floor. Then, forcing control, she said, "Her sketchbooks are on a shelf in that closet. And her diary's in the top drawer of the desk. You can read it if you want to."

"You don't mind?"

"Why, honey, why would I mind? She was your mother, Nicky Jack." Enid touched his cheek with the back of her hand, then left the room, closing the door behind her.

Suddenly feeling weak in the knees, Mark sat on the bed where Gaylene Harjo had slept, surveying the room that had been hers for over seventeen years, and tried to see her there. A girl learning to put on lipstick, trying out her first pair of high heels, daydreaming about a future she would never have, this girl who became his mother.

On the top shelf of a bookcase in the corner, he found several high school textbooks and three library books thirty years overdue: *The Autobiography of Alice B. Toklas*, *A Vision of Paris* and *The Fabulous Life of Diego Rivera*. On the bottom shelf he discovered a stack of art books, three poetry collections, a French phrase book and several paperbacks, including *And Still the Waters Run*, *Black Elk Speaks* and *Custer Died for Your Sins*.

Standing in front of her dresser, he picked up a bottle of cologne, evaporated now but still holding the scent of honeysuckle. He opened her jewelry box, which contained a charm bracelet, two pairs of earrings and a peace pendant attached to a leather strap.

In her closet, he found clothes dating back to the sixties: tie-dyed shirts, bell-bottom jeans, peasant blouses, granny skirts. And a dress of soft cotton—pale yellow with small orange flowers, a dress he pressed to his face, inhaling the faint sweet aroma of honeysuckle.

On the shelf above the clothes, he found her sketchbooks. He carried them to a chair by the window, where he leafed through her drawings: several pages of hands—hands of children, praying hands, fisted hands, gnarled hands; women dancing; children laughing; a man and a woman embracing; horses; ears of corn; an old man fishing; nude men; nude women. Pages and pages of sketches that might have become finished paintings had there been time.

At her desk, he removed the diary Enid had told him he would find there. On its cover, printed in block letters, the words WARNING! THIS IS PRIVATE. IF YOU OPEN IT, YOU WILL BE CURSED.

Mark didn't know if it was the threat of a curse that made him feel uneasy or what he might learn about the girl who wrote it, but when he opened the diary, he felt a chill in the room.

Her first entry was dated January 1, 1966.

Dear Diary,

Mom said I could stay all night with Row tonight, so Daddy took me to town after supper. Mr. and Mrs. Whitekiller went to bed at ten o'clock, but we stayed up till after midnight. We watched the New Year's celebration on TV, then Row stole two cigarettes out of her mother's purse and we went outside and smoked them behind the garage. When we came back in, we called Danny Pittman's house, but his mother answered, so we hung up.

Row made twelve resolutions for the new year, but I'll bet she doesn't keep any of them. I just made three. I'm not going to smoke anymore; I am going to shoot one hundred free-throws every day; and I am going to study French because one day I will move to France.

Spider Woman

After Ivy served herself a second helping of green beans, she offered the bowl to Mark.

"No, thanks," he said.

"I guess this isn't the kind of food you're used to," Enid said, gesturing toward Mark's plate, where a cold biscuit and chicken leg remained untouched and the gravy on his potatoes had jelled.

He had barely gotten started on Gaylene's diary when Enid had called him to dinner, and now, with his mind still on those pages, he had no interest in food.

"This Rowena Whitekiller you mentioned earlier . . ."

"Her last name's Findley. Married a local boy a long time back."

"Where does she live?"

"Somewhere in Illinois, but I heard she was in DeClare a couple of weeks ago. Came back to be with her daddy, I imagine. Milton's got lung cancer, not got long to live."

"Do you think she's still in town?"

"Well, she might be. I haven't heard of Milton's passing."

"Why are you interested in her?" Ivy asked.

"I didn't get very far into the diary, but Rowena's there, on almost every page I read."

"Oh, she and Gaylene were close," Enid said. "Closer than most sisters, I think. And when Rowena got her driver's license, she was out here almost every night. They went everyplace together. Even double-dated until Rowena took up with one of the Warner boys."

"That caused a problem?"

"Gaylene didn't like him much. Said he was a trouble-maker. But that didn't break up her friendship with Rowena. No, they were crazy about each other right up till . . ." Enid pushed back from the table. "How about a piece of chocolate cake and a cup of coffee, Nicky Jack?"

"Sounds good."

"I'll help you, Grandma," Ivy said. But as she was stacking dirty dishes and gathering up silverware, the phone rang.

"Ivy, can you get that?" Enid called from the kitchen.

"Yeah."

The old rotary dial phone in the living room sat on an end table just inside the door.

"Hello? . . . Hi, Mom . . . Yeah, we were . . . What?" As Ivy listened, she turned to lock eyes with Mark. "Okay. We'll be there soon. Bye."

"Is something wrong?" Enid asked.

"Mom just got a call from Hap. He said DeClare is crawling with reporters."

Enid looked alarmed. "Why, Ivy? What's happened?"

"It's about Nicky Jack turning up." Then, to Mark, she said, "They know who you are."

February 9, 1968

Dear Diary,

Between first and second period I went to see if my pink sweater was in the lost and found closet. It wasn't, but when I was coming out, Danny Pittman walked by and he SMILED at me! I almost wet my pants.

Oscar and his Mom have started going to our church. They moved here from Cherokee, North Carolina, to live with her sister after Oscar's Dad went to prison for stealing a car while he was drunk. Oscar says they'll probably move back when his Dad gets out.

Our Sunday School class is having a hayride and a weeny roast this Saturday night. Oscar asked me to go, but I told him I had to babysit for one of our neighbors. I thought telling him a fib was better than saying I didn't want to go with him. I like him just fine, but I don't want him to be my boyfriend. I just don't feel about him the way I do about Danny.

Spider Woman

Chapter Sixteen

As they said good-bye, Enid, locking eyes with Mark, had taken his hand, then passed him Gaylene's diary, leaving him stunned. Here, in his hand, were the words of a mother he had never known, given to him by his grandmother, a woman who had not existed for him until today.

As Ivy drove him back to town, he was silent, staring into the night, its darkness relieved only by the van's narrow lights.

When she slowed on Main, a block from Teeve's Place where he'd left his car, he finally spoke.

"Ivy, I appreciate you taking me out there today. I'm not sure how I would have handled that by myself."

When she sped up and drove past the pool hall, Mark said, "Whoa. You just passed my car."

"Did you see that Ford parked on the corner?"

"No."

"The guy behind the wheel is Early Thompson, one of O Boy's deputies."

"And you think . . . what? That he's looking for me?"

"Could be. He's in an unmarked car, it's Sunday night, everything downtown is locked up and yours is the only other vehicle on the street. Maybe O Boy's keeping tabs on you."

"I'd be surprised. You heard what he said this morning. He's through with me, wants me to get out of town."

"That might be the problem. You didn't go."

"Well, what the hell. Just drop me at the motel. I'll pick up my car in the morning."

"Okay, but you could come home with me. Mom would love to have you. She . . ." As Ivy rounded the corner to the Riverfront, she said, "Uh-oh. Looks like you're a celebrity." TV and radio news vans were parked bumper to bumper in the motel drive. Cars and pickups lined both sides of the street. Ivy stopped as two young women crossed in front of the van to join another three or four dozen people milling around the motel entrance.

"You're going to have a devil of a time getting past all that," she said.

"You think so?"

"Sure. They've heard about you. Now they want to see you."

"But they don't know what I look like. If I work my way through the crowd, take my time to get inside, they'll think I'm there for the same reason they are: to get a look at this guy who's supposed to be dead."

"Is that right?"

"I'll blend right in."

"No, you *won't* blend in."

"How can you be so sure?"

"Because you don't look like you belong here. You're an outsider, Mark. It shows. Those clothes you've got on didn't come from Wal-Mart, and they don't sell shoes like yours at Payless. That watch isn't a Timex, the gold in your ring is probably twenty-four karat and you didn't get that haircut from Ernie at the Corner Barbershop.

"Face it, Mark. You're a California boy; you're not an Okie. You start for that motel, you'll never make it to the door."

"Bet you ten dollars."

"You're on. I'll wait for you right here. When you get back, pay me my ten bucks, then I'll take you to Mom's. You can spend the night with us."

No one seemed to notice Mark as he started across the lawn. And only a couple of people looked at him when he reached the edge of the crowd. But as he began to thread his way through, he heard a woman say, "That's him. That's got to be him."

"Hey!" a man shouted. "You're Nick Harjo, ain't you?"

Within seconds, the crowd closed around him. Flashbulbs blinded him as hand held minicams and microphones were stuck in his face.

"Mr. Harjo, where have you been since 1972?"

"Can you identify your kidnappers?"

"Have you been held captive all these years?"

Faces were blurred for Mark as bodies pressed close, so close that he could feel their heat.

"Was your arm injured during . . ."

"Mr. Harjo, my magazine has authorized me . . ."

"Nicky Jack, I lived next door to your aunt when . . ."

"Can I have your autograph for my . . ."

As Mark struggled, tried to push his way free, someone kicked his ankle, a hand snatched at his hair, an elbow jabbed into his ribs.

When he finally broke clear, he bolted, running for Ivy's van, but before he reached it, a man chasing him grabbed the back of his shirt, ripping the fabric from the collar to the sleeve.

Ivy had the motor running, and he was barely inside when she floorboarded it and shot around the corner.

"My God," Mark said, gasping for air.

"Well, you were right. You just blended right in, didn't you?" Ivy held out her hand, a signal for him to pay up.

"I don't suppose you'd take a check," he said.

"Not a chance in hell."

"Then how about I clean your van? I can guarantee you the job is worth more than ten dollars."

"What's wrong with my van?"

"It's a damn mess. More junk in here than—"

"Hey, this isn't junk. It's my stuff. Keeps me free."

"What does that mean?"

"Everything I need is in here. If I decide one morning to move on, I just grab my toothbrush, my keys, and I'm gone."

"Gone where?"

"The next place."

"Of course I don't mind, Mark," Teeve said. "We'll make up the Hide-A-Bed in the den. I just hope things settle down around here so we can all get some rest."

"What things?" Ivy asked.

"Oh, I've had more people at the door than you could fit in my hot tub."

"Mom, you don't have a hot tub."

"Yeah, but if I had one, they wouldn't all fit."

"How much of that cough medicine did you take?"

"I can't remember. It made me a little woozy."

"No kidding."

Teeve pulled a wad of tissues from the pocket of her bathrobe, sneezed, then blew her nose. "Nothing more miserable than a cold."

"Right. Now, who were these people that wouldn't fit in the hot tub you don't have?" Ivy asked.

"Well, let's see. Amax Dawson was the first to stop by, then a couple of women came in a TV car, which brought out the neighbors. O Boy was here, left one of his deputies parked out front for over an hour. And Opal Headen, she's the new president of the Ladies' Auxiliary, she wants to have a parade for you, Mark."

"Great." Mark propped an elbow on the kitchen table, then cupped his chin in his hand. "A parade. That's just great."

"And the preacher from First Baptist came to discuss a special service he's planning to welcome you back to the fold."

When the phone rang, Ivy made a move toward it, but Teeve waved her off. "Let the machine get it."

After three rings, they heard the voice of a man through the answering machine speaker.

"It's Brandon Miller again with the *Daily Oklahoman*. I still haven't connected with Nick Harjo. Want to make sure he has my number—555-782-6500. Thanks."

When the machine cut off, Teeve said, "I talked to him a couple of hours ago, and that's the third message he's left. He's persistent, but more polite than some of the others."

"What others?"

"A man who claimed to be Geraldo Rivera, but I don't think it was him; some woman from the *National*

Enquirer; a guy said he was with *Good Morning America*; a filmmaker in Florida, says he wants to make a movie of your life."

"Oh, God," Mark said. "Please let this be just a bad dream."

"Don't be so discouraged, Mark. I think we could turn a profit out of this." Teeve grinned. "The *National Enquirer* woman offered me five hundred dollars for a story and some pictures."

"Hold out for a thousand, Teeve."

"Oh, here's something odd. A woman named Lantana Mitchell called, says she wants to write a book about you."

"There'll be a lot of people trying to cash in on this," Ivy said.

"Yeah, but here's the thing about this Mitchell woman. She was here in '72, writing stories for the *Tulsa World*. I heard she was carrying on with O Boy then, but we had so many rumors making the rounds, no way to know if it was true."

"I'm really sorry," Mark said.

"What for?"

"For disrupting your lives like this."

"Why, Mark, you haven't done anything wrong. Besides, you're the most exciting thing that's happened around here since Ivy came home pregnant."

"Well, I'm glad to know our little community was enlivened because I got knocked up."

"Oh, honey, I'm just joking." A thump came from the back of the house. "What was that?"

"I'll see." When Ivy stepped into the den, a flash popped outside the sliding glass doors that opened to the patio. "Get the hell out of here!" she yelled at the retreating figure in the backyard.

"You okay?" Teeve called out.

"Yeah." After closing the drapes, Ivy returned to the kitchen. "Some creep just took my picture."

"Suppose it was that woman with the *National Enquirer*?"

"Right. She's been hiding out there behind your begonias all day, hoping for a shot of Mark."

"Then why would she photograph you?"

"Oh, they'll find a way to make me part of the story. Headline'll read 'Pregnant Woman Shielding Long-Missing Cousin Sees Face of Spider Man Emerge in Her Stretch Marks.'"

"Ivy, how do you think up these things?" Teeve said, laughing.

"I'm going to make sure we're locked down before someone tries to sneak in with a camera." Ivy started with the kitchen windows and doors, then disappeared down the hallway to the bedrooms as Teeve was seized with a fit of sneezing.

"Can I get you something?" Mark asked.

"Maybe a glass of water."

When Teeve regained her breath, she said, "Now, tell me, what did you think of Enid?"

"Well, we were both a little uncomfortable. I didn't really know what to say. And she was pretty quiet, too."

"She was probably too shocked to say much. But she's naturally quiet. Kind of shy. Don't let that fool you, though. She's a strong woman, been through a lot. Had more than her share of grief.

"Her youngest boy, David, drowned when he was

seven. Then she lost Gaylene, her only daughter. . . . And you, her first grandson.

"That left her with James and Navy, two brothers as different as sugar and salt. James is kind, thoughtful, dependable. Everything Navy isn't. And wouldn't you know, Navy was her favorite."

"Why?"

"Don't know, but I've seen it before. Mothers will favor the bad seed every time. Maybe they think that's the one needs love most. But make no mistake. I hold nothing against Enid. Nothing at all. She treats me more like a daughter than my own mother did. And I love her to death."

"You talking about me again?" Ivy said as she came down the hall.

"Sure am."

"Bolted all the doors, barred the windows, put fresh alligators in the moat and loosed the dogs. I think we're secure for the night."

Teeve coughed until her eyes teared.

"Mom, you sound terrible and you look as bad as you sound. If you're not better in the morning, you're going to see Doc Bruton."

"Oh, honey, it's just a cold. Gotta let it run its course. But I think I will go to bed. Mark, make Ivy help you with that Hide-A-Bed. It's tricky."

"I will."

"Good night, you two."

"Hope you rest well, Teeve."

"I'll check on you later, Mom, see if you're still kicking."

"No, you stay away from me," Teeve yelled from down the hall. "Don't want you to catch what I've got."

When he heard Teeve's door close, Mark said, "Your mom's great, Ivy."

"Yeah." Ivy smiled. "She'll do. You hungry?"

"I could eat a little something. But don't go to any trouble."

"Trouble?" Ivy forced a look of confusion, held it a moment, then snapped her fingers. "Oh, you didn't think I was going to cook, did you? See, when I cook, it means putting a bagel in the toaster or dribbling butter on my popcorn."

"So, you don't cook."

"Right. But I do eat." Ivy ran her hands across her midsection where she'd once had a waist.

"I suppose you're saying you've gained some weight."

"No, of course not. I've always looked like a Volkswagen."

Mark looked her up and down, then made a face, his look skeptical.

"Yes! I've gained forty pounds in—"

"That doesn't sound so bad."

"You didn't let me finish. I've gained forty pounds in my butt, another twenty in my belly, ten in my boobs. Throw in fingers and toes, and what've you got?"

"A Volkswagen?"

Ivy growled and flipped him with a dish towel.

Then, with no hint of teasing in his voice, he said, "I think you're lovely, Ivy."

They locked eyes as silence settled around them, time enough for Mark to feel a warm flush reddening his face and neck. What was it about this woman, he wondered, that caused him to act such a fool? Just yesterday, he'd been so furious with her that he'd yelled and stomped around like an angry child. And just now he'd told her she looked lovely.

He knew he looked ridiculous, standing in the kitchen in his torn shirt, his stained slacks and stocking feet, having delivered a line lifted from some sappy movie. But he wasn't Richard Gere and she wasn't Julia Roberts. He was a man trying to understand a life he'd never lived, and she was his pregnant cousin, a woman he shared nothing with except a lost history.

"Thank you, Mark," Ivy said. "No one's called me lovely for a long time."

He couldn't think of a response, had no clue, so to cover his discomfort, he wheeled, opened the fridge and peered inside. "How about I cook for you?"

"Yeah?" Ivy sounded skeptical. "Like what?"

"You like omelets?"

"Sure."

"Okay!" Feeling more sure of himself now, he started pulling out cartons and bottles and plastic bags. "Eggs, black olives, cheese. Onions. Salsa and ham . . ."

"I don't eat ham."

"How do you feel about turkey?"

"I don't eat anything with a face."

"So I can fix an omelet as long as I don't put a face in it."

"Right," Ivy said. "You know, I'm amazed that you know how to cook."

"Why?"

"'Cause you were a rich boy. Didn't you have servants? Butlers, gardeners, cooks?"

"We had a Mexican woman named Luz who did all the cooking. I learned by watching her."

Mark poured the eggs into the skillet, then sprinkled them with salt and pepper.

"You must have spent a lot of time in the kitchen," Ivy said.

"I did. Luz was my best friend. Besides, she cooked mainly just for me. My parents were hardly ever at home for meals."

"Why?"

"My father ate at his club; my mother almost always had dinner with her clients. So it was usually just Luz and me."

Ivy looked puzzled.

"What?" Mark asked.

"When we were at the trailer you went on about what great parents you had. Said they spent so much time with you. Made me think you were the center of their lives. But if they were never home . . ."

"You want to grate this cheese for me?"

"No. I want to know why you told me that stuff."

"I was being defensive, I guess."

"Being defensive? Or lying?"

"A little of both. My father never seemed to notice that I was around. And my mother was disappointed because I didn't become a movie star. I think I just never lived up to their expectations, but I can't blame them for the way I turned out."

"What way is that?"

"I've always felt like a misfit, but I never knew why until I came here."

"Mark—"

"I think this is ready. Let's eat."

Mark closed the book and switched off the lamp beside the Hide-A-Bed a few minutes past three. But he didn't feel sleepy. Not now. Not after the hours he'd spent listening to the voice of his mother speak to him from the pages of her diary.

She'd told him so much about her life, a life very different from his own.

While she was in high school, she'd worked as a waitress, baby-sitter, secretary and motel maid. She'd driven her father's ten-year-old Ford pickup, when she could get it, and for her senior trip, her class had gone to Six Flags over Texas.

He'd graduated from a private academy, and though he'd never worked a day while he was in school, he'd had his own Platinum Mastercard, the monthly charges paid by his mother. He received a new BMW convertible the day he got his driver's license, and his class had gone on a Caribbean cruise to celebrate the end of their senior year.

For her graduation, her parents gave her a portable record player; he'd gotten a five-thousand-dollar Bang & Olufsen sound system. She'd lived in a four-room house with her parents and two brothers. He, an only child, had lived in a seven-thousand-square-foot house in Beverly Hills with a swimming pool and tennis court. She had fished with her daddy in an old johnboat; he'd fished for marlin on his father's yacht, but only with a hired crew, never with his father.

A few days after his nineteenth birthday, he went to Paris on his spring break from college. She never went to Paris, never went to college. And she never turned nineteen.

Mark tried to clear his mind, tried to concentrate on

sleep, but he had too much going on in his head. He tried some of the relaxation techniques suggested by his therapist—deep breathing, visualization and recollection—but nothing worked.

It didn't help either that each time he moved, the bed groaned under his weight and a metal bar beneath the thin mattress pressed into his back just below his shoulder blades.

When he finally found a position he thought he could tolerate, he developed a restless leg—a prickling sensation that was only temporarily relieved by movement, which caused the bed to complain.

He'd never been a great sleeper, but for the past few weeks, his bouts of insomnia had ratcheted up a few notches. And tonight, after spending time visiting his mother's past, he wished desperately for the bottle of sleeping pills back in his room at the motel.

He didn't know if he was being kept awake by what he'd read in the diary or what he hadn't read.

She'd described in great detail basketball games in which she played, the plot of her favorite movie, a boy she had a crush on, a night spent at Rowena's house, a painting just finished.

He knew, when he closed the diary, that her favorite color was green, she didn't drink milk, she was allergic to pecans and she loved the names Shannon and Nicky, names she planned to give her children *if* she decided to have children.

He was struck from time to time to read an entry in which he discovered some similarity he shared with her. For instance, they were both crazy about the music of Dusty Springfield and Sam Cooke, popular in the sixties, "oldies but goodies" in the nineties; they both hated the smells of vinegar and mustard, the taste of sweet potatoes, liver and Brussels sprouts.

Both had played the flute in their high school bands; loved the poetry of Richard Wilbur and James Dickey; liked rainy nights and lightning storms.

But even though Mark now had a clearer picture of what his mother's short life had been, he was no closer to knowing what he most wanted to know: the identity of his father and the killer of his mother.

She'd stopped writing in the diary on June 28, 1970, just about the time she would have gotten pregnant with him. Yet there was no mention of a secret rendezvous with a classmate or an affair with a married man or a night of drinking that had led to a reckless encounter.

No new name appeared that would arouse suspicion, nothing that made him think she was hiding a guilty secret. No inkling of a backseat tumble at a drive-in, no clandestine meeting in an out-of-town spot. Nothing. Not even an innocent date for a hamburger and a movie.

And in one entry written in March of that year, she had confessed to still being a virgin. And that was the last conscious thought Mark had before sleep.

He didn't know when he had cried out, didn't know when he began to sob. And he didn't know when Ivy had slipped in beside him or when he first felt her warmth at his back as she held him and whispered, "It's okay, Nicky Jack, it's okay. Just a bad dream."

Chapter Seventeen

Mark awoke to the smell of coffee and the sound of Ivy humming along with a radio in the kitchen.

He hadn't slept well but didn't know why until he moved. As he sat up, a muscle spasm gripped his back where the metal bar beneath the mattress had punished him throughout the night.

He made several false starts before he managed to stand, and when he crept across the floor, he moved like a spider missing a few legs.

After a torturous journey to the recliner, where he'd tossed his clothes the night before, he found they'd been replaced by a pink terry-cloth bathrobe at least three sizes too small for him.

"Morning," he said as he shuffled into the kitchen.

"Hey, I was right. Pink's your color."

"Thanks." His body tilted at an unnatural angle as he hobbled in the direction of the nearest chair.

"Are you all right?"

"Now why would you ask a silly question like that?" he said, wincing with each painful step.

"Because you're walking like a wounded goose."

"Well, I just got up. I'm a little stiff."

"It's that damn Hide-A-Bed, isn't it. That bar that digs into your back."

"That's the one."

"Sorry. Guess I should have warned you."

"About what? That I'd be crippled for life?"

Ivy laughed. "Here, let me work on you."

As she moved in behind him, Mark said, "Hey, what are you going to do?"

"Make it better."

"Maybe this isn't such a good idea. Why don't I—"

"Tell me where it hurts. Here?"

"Couple of inches higher."

Ivy slid her arm around his chest. "Give me your right hand."

When he did, she pulled his hand under his left arm.

"What are you doing?" he asked, sounding more fearful than inquisitive.

"Moving your shoulder blade so I can get to that muscle. Now relax." She began massaging the knot of muscle, first with her fingers, then with her elbow, burrowing into the deep tissue. "Does that hurt?"

"Yes, but don't stop."

As Ivy pulled Mark's arm tighter, her belly pressed against his back, a dream from the night before tried to surface. He seemed to remember a woman trying to comfort him, cradling him in her arms as he wept.

The image was fuzzy, a dream with no beginning, no end, the edges ragged and incomplete.

"Better?" Ivy asked.

"I think so." He rolled his head slowly, testing for pain. "Thanks."

"Sit down, I'll get you some coffee. We have bacon and eggs if you want breakfast."

"Doesn't bacon have a face?"

"It does."

"So if I want some . . ."

"You have to cook it."

"I think I'll just settle for coffee."

"You got it."

"How's Teeve feeling this morning?"

"Good enough to go to the pool hall."

"You're kidding. She went to work with that cold?"

"She's not going to open the café, but she said if she didn't crank up the pool hall, the domino boys would cause her more grief than a bad cold." Ivy brought two cups of coffee to the table, then sat across from Mark. "I'm going down pretty soon, make her come home."

"You didn't stay here because of me, did you?"

Ivy shook her head. "Mom thinks she's the only one who can open up the place. I can't see much more to it than unlocking the door and turning on the lights, but she has her own way of doing things."

"I guess we all do."

"So, what've you got planned for the day?"

"I'm hoping to talk to Rowena Whitekiller. Her name came up again and again in the diary. With any luck, she's still in town."

"You want me to see if I can find out?"

"Would you?"

"Sure. I'll make some phone calls."

"Thanks. And while you do that, I'd like to take a shower. You have any idea where my clothes are?"

"Oh, Mom took them to the cleaners on her way to the pool hall."

"Then I guess I'm going to have to ask you to go to my room at the motel and grab me a shirt and pair of slacks. Unless you think I can get by wearing this?"

"I think we ought to steer clear of the motel for a couple of days. Someone there is sure to recognize me, and by now, they'll assume I know where you are."

"Then I suppose I'll have to borrow an outfit from you. You wouldn't happen to have something in linen, would you? Maybe a two-piece suit with a—"

"I went to Wal-Mart this morning, smart-ass. Bought you a few things."

"That's awfully nice of you."

"Didn't know if you were a brief or boxer man, but I see I guessed right."

When he glanced down, Mark discovered that his little pink robe was untied. "You're a naughty girl, Ivy," he said as he pulled his robe closed.

"Mark, the stuff I bought you, it's not exactly your style. I mean, I didn't have much choice in shirts and—"

"Don't worry. I'm sure whatever you got will be fine."

"That's great," Ivy said into the receiver. "Yes, I'll tell him. Thanks. Thanks a lot."

After she cradled the phone, Ivy looked up to see Mark standing in the doorway. He was wearing the clothes she'd bought him at Wal-Mart: stiff Levi's, a western-cut plaid shirt, cowboy boots, a belt with a brass buckle in the shape of a horse's head.

"I look like Howdy Doody," he said, his voice registering resignation.

"No, you don't." Ivy tried to sound reassuring but

couldn't quite manage it without grinning. "You look . . . well, like you belong here."

"Okay. I look like Howdy Doody in Oklahoma."

She gave it up then and fell back on the couch, hooting with laughter.

"You did this on purpose, didn't you," he said.

"I didn't. I swear."

"Listen, if you think I'm going out of this house in this getup, you're—"

"Not even to meet Rowena Whitekiller?"

"She's still here? You talked to her?"

"Just hung up."

"Did you tell her about me?"

"She'd already heard that you'd come back from the dead, but she didn't sound too anxious to meet you."

"What did she say?"

"Tried her best to get out of it. Her first excuse was a migraine, so I tried to set up something for later in the day. Then she said she had to go to the hospital, but when I suggested that you meet her there, she backed off real fast."

"What do you suppose is going on?"

"I don't have a clue, but she's sure as hell jumpy about something."

"So, am I going to see her?"

"Yeah, at her dad's place, but you'd better hurry before she changes her mind."

"Can I borrow your van?"

"I'm afraid it's not going to be that simple. Look."

Ivy parted the curtains to give Mark a view of the street. A TV van was parked in front of the house, a police cruiser just behind it. Two boys on bikes were riding circles in the driveway and half a dozen people had gathered three doors away on the corner.

"Mom called when she got to town. Said a TV crew followed her from here, then parked across the street from the pool hall."

"Then how in the hell am I going to get out of here? Try to outrun them?"

"I have a plan."

"Now I know why I'm disguised as Howdy Doody."

"Trust me, Mark. Just trust me."

Twenty minutes later, Mark was behind the wheel of a white paneled truck with multicolored logos on the sides advertising Noah's Ark Plumbing Service.

True to her word, Ivy had devised a plan. And so far it seemed to be working.

First, she'd backed her van out of Teeve's garage with Mark in the floorboard covered with a quilt. Then, closely followed, she'd driven five miles outside town to a prefab metal building, home of Noah's Ark Plumbing.

After she parked inside the shop garage, Noah Harjo, her cousin, closed the overhead door, exchanged shirts with Mark and gave him a Noah's Ark cap. A few minutes after Ivy and Noah took off in her van, leading a procession of vehicles back to town, Mark drove Noah's plumbing truck to a farmhouse where Rowena Whitekiller was waiting.

The woman who answered the door was nearly three times older and more than three times as large as the girl in the photo Mark had seen.

"Oh, my Lord. You look just like her." Then, glancing at the drive, she said, "Why are you driving that truck?"

"I'm hoping to avoid a crowd."

"What?"

"Too many people want to talk to me right now."

"Look, I don't want to get mixed up in this again."

"Don't worry. I wasn't followed."

Rowena hesitated as she checked out the road in both directions. Finally she opened the door, then led Mark down a narrow hallway into a living room furnished with large antique pieces. Because of her size, she moved slowly, with the gait of one suffering from bad hips and ruined knees.

"Your cousin told me you wanted to ask me some questions about Gaylene."

"If you don't mind."

"I don't want anything I say to you to end up in the newspaper."

"I can promise you that won't happen."

Rowena was quiet then, taking her time to study Mark. "You're like her, you know. In so many ways." She removed her glasses, then with the back of her hand wiped away the tears spilling down her cheeks. "Sorry. I thought I was ready for this. I mean, after the shock of hearing you were alive, I kind of adjusted to the idea. But now, well, it's a little spooky."

"I understand. This whole thing's pretty spooky for me, too."

"We started in kindergarten on the same day. Two scared little Indian girls and eighteen other kids, all white. They singled me out early, first recess. Girls singing 'Whitekiller, Whitekiller, cut your throat and drink your blood.'

"I cried, wanted to run off home, but Gaylene wouldn't go. She said if we ran once, we'd run forever.

And when the biggest bully in the class pulled my hair, said he was gonna scalp me, Gaylene whipped him.

"From then on, she looked out for me. And it was like that all the way through school. She played forward on the basketball team; I played guard. We wore each other's clothes, skipped school together, double-dated, told each other all our secrets."

"I'm hoping you'll share one of those secrets with me."

The change in Rowena's demeanor was immediate and obvious. Her skin paled, and a tic began to pulse beneath one eye; her fingers, trembling now, worried at a ragged nail.

"I don't know who your father is," she said, her voice taking on a defiant tone. "She never told me."

"But you were best friends. Why wouldn't she?"

"It wasn't my business. Not then, not now."

"What is it you're afraid of?"

"I'm not afraid."

"I think you are."

"Listen. I'm going to tell you what I told the sheriff almost thirty years ago. I don't know who got Gaylene pregnant. And I don't know who killed her."

"But you must have some suspicions."

"Suspicion gets people in trouble. And I don't need more trouble than what I've already got. I thought the world of Gay, she was the most important person in my life growing up. And I can't believe I'm sitting here talking to her son. In some ways, it's a bit like talking to her."

March 2, 1968

Dear Diary,

    I didn't write last night because we didn't get back from Oklahoma City until three this morning. It was a terrible night.

    First, we lost our last game in the regional tournament. Okemah beat us 63 to 61. Then, on the way home, our school bus had a flat and we had to stand outside while Mr. Peters, our bus driver fixed it. We almost froze.

    But the worst thing that happened was that one of the Okemah girls got mad at Keann Robinson who plays guard on our team and called her a nigger.

    Sometimes I hate white girls.

Spider Woman

Chapter Eighteen

When Mark backed out of the driveway, he got a glimpse of Rowena Whitekiller watching him from a front window of the house. She'd clearly been relieved when she said a hurried good-bye and wasted no time in locking the door behind him. He supposed she'd wanted to see him drive away to be certain he didn't hang around, waiting for her to step outside so he could hammer her with more questions.

He was sure she knew more than she'd told him, but he couldn't figure out why, after all these years, she was holding back. The only explanation he could come up with was fear. She was afraid of someone. The trick would be to figure out who it was.

As he neared Main Street, Mark realized he'd been driving aimlessly, no thought given to where he was headed. But finding himself close to town, he decided to delay meeting Ivy as they'd planned and instead make a quick stop at the Riverfront.

Since he was outfitted in the Noah's Ark shirt and cap, and driving the plumber's truck, he felt he had a decent chance of getting in and out of the motel without being recognized.

He might not have taken the risk except for the antibiotics in his room. He'd been taking them since he was bitten by the keeshond, and though he was probably in the clear as far as infection was concerned, he knew the smart way to go was to finish the prescription.

The crowd in front of the motel was larger than it had been the day before, but no one showed any interest in him or the truck turning in at the delivery entrance.

After parking in back, he grabbed a toolbox from the bed of the truck, then went inside.

On the way to his room, he passed the kitchen, where he saw a cook turning meat on a grill; outside the utility room he nodded to a woman pushing a laundry cart; in the hallway he dodged two small boys in bathing suits racing toward the pool; and he shared the elevator with an elderly man in a wheelchair. But not one of them paid any attention to the plumber passing through.

He half expected to find his room turned inside out again, but at first glance everything seemed to be in order. His unopened suitcase was still on the luggage rack, his clothes still on hangers, his shaving kit on the dresser where he'd left it.

When he sat on the bed to retrieve his prescription from the bedside table, he saw that the message light on his phone was blinking.

Most of the calls he listened to were from reporters hoping for an interview; others came from townspeople who were either friendly or bizarre. One was a man named Cozy who phoned to invite him to a poker game at the VFW. Another came from an unidentified woman who described her unusual tattoos and the body parts they adorned.

But the call that caused his mouth to go dry came from someone he knew quite well.

"Dr. Albright, this is Charlene," came the voice on the recording. "I am so worried about you," she said as she began to cry. "Please, please call me as—"

Mark disconnected without listening to the rest of the message.

Somehow the news from DeClare, Oklahoma, had made its way to Beverly Hills, and he had a pretty good idea of how that had happened. All the same, he dreaded hearing it confirmed, even as he dialed the number.

"Albright-Cushman Animal Hospital," she said.

"Hello, Charlene."

"Oh, Dr. Albright."

When he heard Charlene weeping at the other end of the line, he said, "Let me guess. The story's in the *Times*. Right?"

"Dr. Cushman said it's in *USA Today*, too, but without the photograph."

"Are you telling me the *Times* printed my picture?"

"I believe it's the same one that ran on the society page last winter when you chaired the Humane Society."

"Jesus Christ."

"But you look good." Charlene snuffled, crying at the same time she was trying to sound upbeat. "You're wearing your tuxedo."

"Wonderful. You can't imagine how relieved I am to hear that."

Either ignoring his sarcasm or oblivious to it, Charlene said, "Is it true, Dr. Albright? What they printed in the paper?"

"I'd just as soon not go into that right now, Charlene."

"Oh, I understand. Really, I do. But if there's anything I can do for you, anything at all . . ."

"Why don't you bring me up-to-date on what's happening there?"

"Well, of course, we've experienced a bit of a disruption since you've been gone, but nothing we can't handle."

In the background Mark could hear a man's voice—angry and insistent—the voice of his partner, David Cushman, demanding the phone.

"Charlene," Mark said, then louder, "Charlene," finally yelling into the mouthpiece, "Charlene!"

"I'm sorry, Dr. Albright. What did you say?"

"Put David on the phone."

"Certainly, but before—" She was stopped in midsentence as the receiver abruptly changed hands.

"Mark, how the hell did this happen?" David asked. "And more important, what are you going to do about it?"

"And hello to you, too, David."

"Do you have any idea of the mess you've created here? Can you—"

"I believe this conversation might be more pleasant for both of us if you could lower your voice a decibel or two."

At the same volume, David said, "You apparently had some information about this situation weeks ago, information you should have shared with me."

"But I didn't know the circumstances then. All I knew was that—"

"You might've given me a heads-up on this. If I'd had some warning—"

"David, I don't understand what your problem is."

"You don't understand? Well, let me see if I can help you out, Dr. Albright. A reporter and a cameraman showed up here this morning. They barged into the office while Reese Witherspoon was picking up her Yorkies, minicam in her face as the reporter fired off questions about a murder.

"I ran them out of here, but about the time they hit the sidewalk, Ms. Zellweger's limo stopped out front and they started in on her. Of course, she had her driver pull away. Didn't even take time to drop off her Abyssinians."

"And you think—"

"Within the hour, we heard from Eisner, Aniston, Cage and Spelling. All canceled."

"Because my mother was murdered? What does that have to do with them? Huh?"

"Mark, you know—"

"I'm a vet, David, not some Hollywood agent or director or producer."

"It's not about what you do or don't do."

"Then what's it about?"

"A questionable background."

"Let me see if I understand this. Hollywood found out I'm Indian, a Native American, a Cherokee. So now I have a questionable background?"

"Mark, you're not operating a clinic in Podunk fucking Oklahoma, gelding horses and worming cattle. This is Beverly Hills, where appearance is everything. The people we deal with can't afford to be associated with scandal."

"Right. No one out there's been arrested for shoplifting or possession or child porn."

"Now you listen to me. I've got thirty years of my life

tied up in this business. My reputation and my money are on the line here."

"I was wondering when you'd get around to talking money."

"Oh, now you've got a problem with money. Do you also have a problem with the Jaguar you drive or your house in Malibu?"

"Look, David, this business in Oklahoma will be wrapped up before long."

"Are you being held there?"

"Held?"

"By the authorities."

"No. I haven't done anything wrong."

"Then what's to keep you from walking away from it now? Just pack up and leave?"

"Goddammit, I'm not here on a vacation. I'm trying to find out—"

The sound of running water from behind the closed door of Mark's bathroom caused him to stop in midsentence. He cradled the phone soundlessly, then tiptoed across the room.

Just as he came within reach of the door, it opened and an attractive, middle-aged woman stepped out.

"Hello, Mr. Harjo," she said.

"Who the hell are you?"

"Or should I call you Dr. Albright?"

"I said, who are you? And what are you doing in my room?"

"Lantana Mitchell," she said, "and I'm here to help you find out who killed your mother."

Chapter Nineteen

"She started writing a book about it years ago, but she got sidetracked." Mark finished the Coke Ivy had brought him when she slipped out of the pool hall to meet him behind the café. "Then, when she heard about me showing up, she dug out her old notes and got interested in the story again. At least that's what she says."

"You sound like you don't believe her."

"Oh, she seems serious about getting a book out of it, but I think she's got another reason for being here."

"What's that?"

"She's got some unfinished business with O Boy Daniels."

"Good business or bad?"

"She detests him. I don't know what it's about, but she's obviously here to settle an old score."

"Great. Rowena Whitekiller is too afraid to tell you what she knows, and Lantana Mitchell's come back to carry out some kind of vendetta. Can't imagine either one's gonna be much help to you."

"Maybe not, but the Mitchell woman's determined.

She's checked into the motel, and the way she talked, she's in no hurry to leave. And I have a feeling that she just might dig something up."

"You really think so?"

"Well, I'm no detective, and it's pretty clear that the sheriff's not going to help, so I say let her go at it. Let's see what she can do."

Mark pulled off his Noah's Ark cap and wiped his forehead with his shirtsleeve.

"By the way, how's the plumbing business?" Ivy asked.

"Not bad. I've unstopped a couple of toilets, put in a new kitchen sink and dug up a busted sewer line. Dirty work, but it pays well."

Ivy took hold of one of Mark's hands, pretending to check for blisters, but when she rubbed her fingers over his palm, they exchanged a look, both knowing that something had just changed between them. After a moment, he pulled his hand away. To cover palpable awkwardness, she said, "Yeah, you're developing the tough skin of a real workingman."

"Hey, I wear gloves," he said, following her lead.

"I'm sure you do. Italian leather lined with cashmere."

"Shouldn't I be getting Noah's truck back?"

"Oh, I almost forgot. Hap called. He wants you to come by his office."

"Did he say why?"

"Nope. But he said you should use the back entrance because of the reporters hanging around out front."

"Okay. Where do I go?"

"Take the alley just south of Main Street. His office is a two-story brick between the old movie theater and the bank."

"What am I supposed to do about the truck?"

"Noah said he won't need it until tomorrow morning. He said if you bring it back this afternoon, he'll drive you to Mom's."

"Then I'll see you later."

Mark started for the truck; Ivy headed back to the pool hall, then stopped and turned.

"Hey. Would you take a look at Mom's hall toilet? After we flush, the water keeps running."

"Just jiggle the handle."

"And you call yourself a plumber."

Hap's secretary looked as old as the antique desk where she sat, but then everything in the office looked ancient.

"May I help you?" she asked, her voice like that of an older Katharine Hepburn.

"I, uh . . . I'm here about the leak in Mr. Duchamp's office."

"Why, there's no plumbing in his office. You're obviously confused. The restroom is down the hall next to the elevator."

"Well, I'll need to talk to Mr. Duchamp, since he's the one who called me."

"I haven't seen you before," she said, her tone suspicious. "Are you new at Noah Harjo's?"

"Yes, ma'am."

"How long have you been working there?"

"Not long. Now, if I could speak to Mr. Duchamp . . ."

"No, I'm afraid that's quite impossible. You don't have an appointment. And Mr. Duchamp is not available without an appointment."

Just then, the door behind the secretary's desk opened

and Hap said, "It's all right, Frances. I was expecting this gentleman." Then to Mark, "Come in."

As Mark passed her desk, Frances made no attempt to hide her disapproval.

"Have a seat, Mark."

"She's tough."

"Frances? Yeah, she started here with my father fifty-two years ago. I inherited her. Good thing, too. She knows more law than I do."

Hap's office, in contrast with the one dominated by Frances, was a hodgepodge of framed movie posters, comic book art, life-size plastic statues of Superman and Wonder Woman and a large rug adorned with Disney characters. And at the center of it all, Hap, wearing faded jeans, a plaid shirt with frayed cuffs and a haircut that made his head look lopsided.

"I see you've gone into a new line of work," Hap said. "Any chance you could take a look at the—"

"I've heard all the plumber jokes I need from Ivy."

"Anyone see you come in?"

"Not that I know of."

"Lots of people poking around town hoping to corner you," Hap said.

"Yeah, but they're not looking for a plumber."

"But they're desperate to find Nick Harjo. And they won't stop until they do."

"Sounds like you have something in mind."

"How would you feel about a press conference?"

"Would that end it? Make them back off?" Mark asked.

"Oh, hell, no."

"Then what's the use?"

"Sometimes stirring up the media, putting yourself

out there, can lead to some answers. Someone who has information might step forward."

"Why?"

"They want their fifteen minutes of fame, want to be in the spotlight for once in their lives."

"So you think—"

"There's a slim chance the killer is still around. And if he is, this story making national news is bound to make him nervous. And besides, there's almost always someone who was close to the killer, or someone who saw or heard something who didn't come forward twenty-seven years ago, but who might talk now."

"What about offering a reward?"

"Can't hurt," Hap said.

"I'll put up twenty-five thousand."

"I can kick in another ten. And I know a few others who'll pony up. We can probably come up with fifty thousand. So when do you want me to set this up?" Hap asked.

"The sooner the better."

"How about tomorrow morning, say, ten o'clock."

"Fine."

"We'll do it here, outside, in front of the office," Hap said. "I'll write up a statement; you come early, look it over. If you feel it's okay, you read it, but take no questions. After you're finished, we'll come in, lock the door. No reporters get in."

"Do you know Lantana Mitchell?"

"Name sounds familiar."

"She was working for the *Tulsa World* in '72. Spent a couple of weeks here writing for the paper."

"Oh, the gal who was sleeping with O Boy. Sure, I remember her. A real go-getter."

"She showed up this morning. Checked into the motel. Says she's going to write a book about it."

"As I recall, she had a book published. True crime. I think it sold reasonably well, at least in this part of the country. So, what does she want from you?"

"Information."

"Yeah, don't they all. By the way, I've requested a copy of your birth certificate. But seems I wasn't the only one. A woman I know in the Department of Vital Statistics said she had another request. And guess who it came from."

Mark shook his head.

"Oliver Boyd Daniels."

"So he didn't take the original from my room."

"Apparently not."

"Then who did?"

"If we knew that, we'd be way ahead of the game."

Mark was on his way to return Noah Harjo's truck when he saw the Hook 'Em Bait Shop just ahead, and since O Boy's pickup was gone, he decided to pull in.

Carrie Daniels was alone in the shop, where she was restocking canisters of insect repellent. If she recognized Mark from his previous visit, she gave no sign of it.

"Help you?" she asked.

"Just stopped in for something cold to drink."

She went on with her work without conversation, and Mark had the feeling she was the sort of woman who was familiar with silence.

He took a bottle of Chocolate Soldier from the cold case, opened it and took a long swallow. "You have Twinkies?"

"Over there on that rack." She pointed across the room.

At the counter, he handed her a hundred-dollar bill.

"Don't you have anything smaller?" she asked.

"Sorry."

"Well, I can't change this."

"I can give you a credit card."

"We don't take credit cards."

"Then how about I put this back in the cooler. I didn't drink much." He was hoping to make her smile, but her expression didn't change.

"Don't worry about it," she said. "The price of a drink and a Twinkie isn't going to bankrupt this place."

"No, I can't do that. You gave me a freebie when I was here a few days ago."

"Yeah, I know."

"I tell you what. Next time I'm in, I'll pay you. In cash."

"Let's just call it even. For the favor you did Kippy when you were here."

"How is your boy?"

"The same. Kippy's always the same," Carrie said.

"Seems like a nice kid."

"I didn't know who you were before. But I know now."

"Guess almost everyone around here does."

"Can I ask you a question?"

"Sure."

"Why did you come back to DeClare?" she asked.

"I wanted to meet my mother. My birth mother."

"You didn't know she was dead until you got here?"

"No."

"Then why did you lie, say you were a lawyer named Alford or Alcorn?"

"I didn't lie to you."

"No, but you lied to my husband. And not many people lie to Oliver and get by with it."

"I'm sorry if I caused you trouble."

"You know, you seem like a decent guy, but you being here stirs folks up. Especially Oliver, him being sheriff and all. He's not real happy when he's stirred up."

"Well, I don't plan to stay around long," Mark said.

"That's probably a good idea. And I think it'd be better for me and Kippy if you didn't come out here no more."

"Am I bothering you?"

"No, but Oliver wouldn't like me talking to you again."

"I can't understand why it would bother him for me to stop in to buy a soda."

"Please, mister," she said, "just don't come back."

Not far from the bait shop, Mark passed Kippy walking beside the highway carrying a fishing pole and coffee can. Mark turned the car around, driving slowly some distance behind Kippy until he climbed through a fence, waded through high weeds and disappeared into a grove of trees.

Mark parked on the shoulder, then followed in Kippy's path, which led to a pond where two cows stood knee-high in the muddy water near an earthen dam.

Kippy was threading a worm onto a fishing hook when he heard steps behind him. Turning, he saw Mark and smiled.

"You gonna fish, too?"

"No. But you don't mind if I keep you company, do you?"

"If I catch Old Tom, you can take him off the hook for me, but you'll have to be careful, 'cause catfish have real sharp teeth."

"Yes, they do."

"But don't tell my daddy you helped me, 'cause he don't want me to talk to you no more."

"Why?" Mark asked.

"He said your mama died and you were real mad. Are you mad?"

"No. I'm sad, though."

"I know why. It's 'cause when someone dies, they never come back. Not people or dogs or babies or horses or squirrels or dogs.

"I had a dog named Skippy. He was a receiver 'cause he was supposed to go pick up birds my daddy shot. But Skippy didn't like dead birds, so my daddy kicked him and he died because Skippy was a piss-poor receiver.

"Mama buried Skippy down by the creek, but I dug him up so he could chase his ball, but he didn't. He didn't eat the bone I brought him, either. And he didn't even try to get away when I picked ticks off his ears. He was dead, I guess."

"Yes, it sounds like he was."

"I almost died when I was little. I had to have an operation on my heart 'cause my heart didn't work right. And the doctor charged a whole lot of money." Kippy laughed. "Mama says I have a heart that's richer than she is."

"But your heart works right now, doesn't it?"

"Yeah, but if that doctor made a mistake, I would be

dead. Just like Skippy. And when you're dead, you never come back. Never, ever, never."

Later that afternoon, Teeve was on the front porch watering her hanging baskets when O Boy pulled up and parked in the driveway, causing a commotion among the reporters and cameramen who'd been at the curb all day waiting for some action.

As O Boy sauntered toward the house, a woman with a microphone trailed him.

"Hey," Teeve yelled at her. "You're on private property. *My* property. Back your ass up to the street or I'll call the law."

"Evening, Teeve," O Boy said.

"I mean the *real* law."

Ignoring her sarcasm, O Boy smiled. "How're you feeling? Heard you've been nursing a pretty bad cold."

"Is this a social call? You come to inquire about my health?"

"Well, I'm a sociable guy. You know that. And I'm here to socialize with your houseguest."

"Who?"

"Come on, Teeve. Everybody in the county knows he's been staying with you."

"I've heard those rumors, too."

"I aim to talk to him, Teeve." O Boy's smile had disappeared, and his voice had turned ugly. "Now."

"Then I'd better let you in before you shoot me."

O Boy followed Teeve inside and back to the den, where Ivy was reading and Mark was asleep in the recliner. When Teeve touched his shoulder, he jumped, then blinked several times as his eyes adjusted to the light.

"Your friend the sheriff is here," Teeve said.

"After our last conversation, I didn't think I'd be seeing you again, Harjo."

"Why is that?"

"Figured you'd hightail it back to Hollywood, seeing as how our town seems to cramp your style."

"I'm adjusting."

"That's nice. But if I was you, I wouldn't get too comfortable here."

"I have the feeling you're about to tell me why."

"Be my guess that someone thinks you've overstayed your welcome in DeClare."

"Now why would you say that?"

"Hear you and Ivy went out to Arthur's trailer couple of days ago. You want to tell me about that?"

Ivy said, "He wanted to see where—"

"I'm not talking to you, Ivy."

"Ivy drove me out, we looked around," Mark said. "I walked through the trailer, then we left."

"Did you find anything of interest?"

"No."

"Have you been back out there?"

Mark shook his head. "Once was enough."

"Well, won't be much reason for you to go back now. Someone set fire to it a couple of hours ago."

"Set fire to it? Why in the hell would anyone want to . . ."

"I think whoever torched that trailer was sending you a message."

"Which is?"

"Someone wants you gone."

April 5, 1968

Dear Diary,

Martin Luther King was killed yesterday evening. It was on television all night long. Today in study hall we were talking about it and I started crying. Richard Graham who is a senior asked me what was wrong. When I told him, he laughed and said, "So another nigger bit the dust."

I got so mad I hardly remember slugging him in the stomach, but Row said I hit him so hard he threw up. I got sent to the principal's office, but Mr. Gordon didn't do anything to me. He said if he'd been there, he might've hit Richard, too.

Spider Woman

Chapter Twenty

Mark had seen plenty of press conferences on TV; still, he wasn't prepared for the pandemonium awaiting him as he and Hap stepped through the door and onto the sidewalk in front of Hap's office.

More microphones than Mark could count had been mounted onto a lectern, and there was constant movement from the crowd that spilled into the street as people with cameras and minicams jostled for position.

Reporters began shouting questions as soon as Mark and Hap appeared, and when the crowd surged forward, two policemen stepped in to escort Mark to the lectern.

When Hap raised his hand and said, "Good morning," the gathering quieted. "My name is Hap Duchamp, attorney of record for Dr. Mark Albright, who has asked me to announce that a reward of fifty thousand dollars is being offered for information that leads to the arrest and conviction of the killer or killers of his mother, Gaylene Harjo, in 1972."

A murmur ran through the crowd, someone whistled and a few actually applauded.

"Now, Dr. Albright will read a brief statement he has prepared, but he will decline to answer questions at this time."

Hap moved aside, allowing space for Mark at the lectern, but his feet wouldn't budge. His mouth had gone dry, and an unsettling sensation low in his stomach was threatening some kind of rebellion.

"Mark?" Hap whispered. "You ready?"

Mark nodded, stepped reluctantly to the lectern, then looked over the crowd, where he saw Arthur McFadden and O Boy Daniels shoulder to shoulder.

Hap tried again. "Go on."

Mark studied a typed statement he held in a trembling hand, the statement he'd read several times in Hap's office, but the words were now indecipherable, the characters seeming to belong to another language.

Mark cleared his throat, then said, "I'm glad," but his voice failed him, so that the words came out sounding like "Ham gad."

When someone laughed, he glanced up once again, but this time he spotted Ivy standing near the back of the throng. She winked and gave him a thumbs-up.

Finally, he placed the sheet of paper flat on the lectern, then focused on the typed lines until the words emerged as English again.

"I'm glad to have the opportunity to speak to you this morning," he said, his voice growing stronger.

"A short time ago, I discovered that I was adopted when I was ten months old. Curious about my birth mother, Gaylene Harjo, I came here to DeClare, intending to meet her. But soon after my arrival, I discovered she had been murdered and I was presumed to be dead. As you can see, that is not the case."

Two teenage girls on the sidewalk giggled but were quickly silenced by a stern-looking woman beside them.

"I plan to remain here, welcoming the chance to talk to someone, anyone, who might have information important to me and the family I've recently met.

"Please, if you think you can help at all, in any way, come forward. You can reach me through Mr. Duchamp's office.

"Thank you."

As they planned, Mark and Hap retreated immediately into Hap's office, where Frances locked the door as soon as they were inside while a barrage of questions echoed from the street.

"I've never seen so much traffic on this road," Ivy said. "Nothing much out here but the Green Country Plant Farm, a small nursery."

"Maybe there's a sale on roses," Mark said.

"I have a sneaking suspicion we're not the only ones driving fifteen miles from town just to see a trailer."

"A burned trailer at that."

"Well, the story was in today's paper, along with that dorky picture of you in a tuxedo. And with your press conference, there's bound to be a lot of curiosity."

"I thought I looked quite debonair."

"I thought you looked dorky."

After Ivy negotiated a turn, she put her hand low on her abdomen and said, "Okay, kid. Settle down."

"The baby?" Mark asked.

"Feel right here." Ivy took Mark's hand and placed it flat against her belly.

"That's quite a kick. Girl or boy?"

"I don't know."

"You've had an ultrasound, right?"

"Sure, but I asked my doctor not to tell me the sex."

"Any particular reason?"

Ivy's expression changed, but Mark couldn't read it. "Yeah," she said. "A very particular reason."

When the van topped a hill, they saw two dozen slow-moving vehicles stretched out ahead of them.

"This is incredible," Mark said.

"Lets you know what an exciting place DeClare is. A trailer burns and half the town comes out to gawk."

Movement was slow but steady. And the nearer they got to the trailer, the stronger the smell of smoke. Several blackened tree stumps still smoldered, and wooden fence posts, burned away at the bottom, hung from strands of barbed wire.

Crime scene tape had been stretched across a wide area, and the fire chief's bright red SUV was blocking the turnoff to the trailer; standing just off the shoulder of the highway, a man in a baseball cap was waving cars on by.

Ivy said, "That's Matthew."

When she pulled up and parked behind the SUV, Matthew yelled, "Sorry, ma'am. You'll have to keep moving. No one's allowed . . ."

As she rolled down her window, he grinned, said, "Hey, Ivy," and tipped his cap.

"Thought you retired, Matthew."

"Yeah, I have. Just rode out here with the chief, see if I could lend a hand."

"I think you two have met," Ivy said, gesturing to Mark.

"Hello again," Matthew said. "I didn't know until this

morning who you were. Hap's real closemouthed about this business."

"I didn't get a chance to thank you for brunch."

"Why don't you come back next Sunday? You, too, Ivy. I'm doing something with tofu and curried figs."

"I appreciate the invitation," Mark said, "but—"

"Looks like there was a hell of a grass fire out here," Ivy said.

"I'd say it burned off four, five acres, but it started in the trailer. Of course, everything's so dry, it all went up. Chief's back there now with the fire marshal and a couple of state boys, but it's arson, that's for sure."

"Any idea who started it?"

"Kids, maybe. Doesn't look professional. Found the empty gas can, box of kitchen matches. We'll have to wait to see if they can get any prints."

"O Boy came by last night," Ivy said. "Seemed to think somebody might be sending a message to Mark."

"Must be easier ways than this."

"You think someone was trying to get rid of some evidence out here?" Mark asked.

"Can't imagine there'd be anything left to find. The law went over this place with a fine-tooth comb. More than once, too. Been a number of transients in and out of the trailer for years. I understand a homeless family lived here for months. And kids discover it all the time. A good place to have sex, do some drugs. What in the world would have been left to find?"

"Yeah, you're probably right."

When a car pulled up behind Ivy's van, Matthew waved them off. "You can't park here," he yelled. Moments later, the car drove away.

"We'd better get out of your way," Ivy said.

"Sorry I can't let you all back there."

"That's okay," she said. "We're just like everyone else. Curious."

"Oh, I don't know. I think you've got more than curiosity invested in this."

"Matthew, you take care." Ivy started the van.

"Will do. By the way, construction isn't finished at Tinker Junction," Matthew said.

"They've been working on that junction for over a year."

"Yeah, but it's a real bottleneck out there now with all this traffic. If you're headed back to town, I'd take Sowell Road."

"Thanks, Matthew."

As Ivy pulled away, Mark said, "You've no idea how close we came to danger."

"What kind of danger?"

"Tofu and curried figs."

"Gosh, I haven't been on this road in years," Ivy said. "I think the last time I was out here was for Kippy's welcome home party."

"Welcome home from where?"

"He had heart surgery when he was eight or nine. Spent weeks in the hospital. When he got out, Carrie had a party for him. Most of the kids in our church came."

"So, the Daniels lived out here."

"Yeah. That was their house." Ivy pointed to a clapboard house with peeling paint, a sagging roof and a broken window covered with masking tape. A rusted-out hull of a pickup shared the yard with a few chickens and some hounds.

"How long did they live here?" Mark asked.

"Years. I think they were living here when Kippy was born. And they didn't move until after his surgery."

"And this road's less than a mile from the trailer?"

"Aunt Gaylene's trailer?"

Mark nodded.

"Well, it's a lot less than that if you go by foot," Ivy said. "Cross the creek and it's probably no more than a quarter mile."

"So they were neighbors when she was killed."

"Where are you going with this?"

"I don't know." Mark stared at the house until they were well past it. "But it's interesting."

Chapter Twenty-one

Teeve waited for Lonnie Cruddup to shuffle out so she could put the CLOSED sign in the window and lock the door. As he walked past her, he was still grumbling about being "evicted" before closing time.

He was always the last of the domino boys to leave and always the one who complained about the pool hall shutting down at six o'clock, which he called "the shank of the evening." He often whispered to his gang that Teeve, twenty years his junior, was "an old manless woman" who went to bed with the chickens for want of something better to do, whereas, he pointed out, his libido was just waking up when the sun went down.

Lonnie wanted his acquaintances to think he was a man for whom the night was long and full of lusty adventure. Unfortunately, all he had to look forward to at home was drinking a glass of Metamucil, injecting insulin in his thigh, scooping poop from the cat litter box and watching an hour of *Matlock* before bed.

But he was especially upset at being turned out today, not because it was ten till six, but because Ivy had, only a few minutes earlier, arrived with Nick Harjo, causing Lonnie to turn up his hearing aid. He recognized this as an opportunity to redeem himself with the community after having spread the erroneous news of a stranger in town with rabies.

He'd been able to catch a bit of the whispered conversation between Mark and Teeve taking place at the counter, something about O Boy Daniels' old house on Sowell Road. But before Lonnie could discover the point of the discussion, Teeve had sent him packing.

She watched him push his way through some reporters outside the pool hall, then she joined Ivy and Mark in the café, where Ivy was washing out the coffeepot and Mark was attempting to sweep, though it was obvious he was a stranger to the broom.

"I've been thinking about your question, Mark," Teeve said, "and I don't remember Gaylene ever mentioning O Boy coming to her trailer. Now, Kippy came by from time to time when he managed to slip away from Carrie. She tried her best to keep him home, but he escaped every once in a while and crossed the creek."

Mark nodded, thoughtful as he made jabbing swipes with the broom.

"Be honest with me, Mark," Teeve said. "Do you think O Boy had something to do with Gaylene's murder?"

"He might. When Ivy told me he'd lived near the trailer back then . . ."

"No more than a stone's throw," Teeve said. "I've thought from the beginning that he was involved."

"Whoa! Hold on, you two," Ivy interrupted. "He's scum all right, but I can't see what reason he'd have to kill Aunt Gaylene unless he was the one who got her pregnant and she threatened him with blackmail."

"Ivy, trust me. If the man who made her pregnant is the same man who killed her, Oliver Boyd Daniels is the last guy I'd want it to be. I just can't quite imagine calling O Boy 'Dad.'"

Teeve began to cough as she fanned at the cloud of dust rising in the room.

"You're not much with a broom, are you, Mark."

"Am I doing something wrong?"

"Have you ever swept before?"

"Sure," he said defensively. "I've vacuumed. Once or twice."

Teeve coughed again.

"Here," Ivy said to Mark. "I'll sweep; you take out the trash. Mom, go home! We'll finish up in here."

"I think I will," Teeve said. "This cold just keeps hanging on." She retrieved her purse from beneath the counter, then started for the door. "Don't forget to—"

"Empty the cash register, turn off the air conditioner, unplug the microwave and make sure both doors are locked," Ivy said in a singsong voice, a monologue long memorized.

"See you all at home."

"Bye."

"Where do I take these?" Mark held up two plastic garbage bags.

"That Dumpster." Ivy pointed through the kitchen window, then watched as Mark went out the back door and crossed the narrow strip of grass behind the café to the alley.

He didn't want to touch the closed Dumpster, which was filthy and reeked with the smell of decay, but he didn't have much choice. Making a face that projected his distaste, he tossed in the bags, then returned to the café bathroom and scrubbed up like a surgeon preparing to perform a transplant.

When he came out, Ivy said, "Think you need a tetanus shot?"

"Hey, that thing is a receptacle for germs that don't even have a name yet."

She grinned, then bent to put a can of Comet into the low cabinet, but when she stood up, she lost her balance.

"Ivy?"

She grabbed the counter for support but was unsteady on her feet.

In two strides, Mark was across the room. He wrapped her in his arms and led her to a chair at one of the dining tables.

"What happened?" he asked.

"I got dizzy," she said, her face beaded with sweat, her skin the color of eggshells.

He placed his fingers on her wrist to check her pulse. "Has this happened before?"

"No."

"What about your blood pressure?"

"It's been normal. One twenty over eighty." When Mark let go of her wrist, she said, "What do you think, doc? Will I live?"

"It wouldn't hurt for us to get you to the hospital, have you checked out."

"Nah. I just stood up too fast."

"Ivy . . ."

"Really. I'm feeling better."

"Truth?"

"Truth."

"Well, you look better." He wet several paper towels at the sink, then sat beside her and began to sponge her face and neck.

"Oh, that feels good," she said, letting her head roll toward him. And suddenly their faces were only inches apart.

Later, he would wonder how it happened, why he leaned forward those few inches separating them, why he kissed her . . . and why she kissed him back.

But at that time, he didn't have any questions. He didn't stop to think it through. The kiss was, pure and simple, the thing he wanted most to do.

Then, several moments later, the reality of what was happening hit him: he was kissing his cousin. Not a "hi, cuz, how you doing" kind of kiss; not a "haven't seen you in ages" kind of kiss; not a family reunion kind of kiss. This was a passionate kiss between a woman and a man.

When he pulled back, he seemed on the edge of panic. "Oh, my God," he said.

"What's the matter?"

He jumped up then and backed away from the table. "Ivy, I don't know what to say."

"About?"

"I'm so sorry." He began to pace, avoided looking her in the eyes. "So sorry."

"Hey, Mark, it was just a kiss."

"No, it wasn't just a kiss and you know it."

"Then what was it?"

He put his palms together, raised his hands beneath his chin, a prayerful gesture, like a sinner asking for forgiveness. "We can make ourselves forget this ever happened."

"Why? I enjoyed it! And I don't know why you're so upset."

"I think you do."

"No, dammit, I don't!"

Mark started to speak but changed his mind. When Ivy stood, he offered her a hand for support, but she shook it off.

He followed her from the café, through the pool hall and out the front door, which she locked, the only one of her mother's instructions she followed.

"You sure you're all right?"

"I'm just fine."

When she started toward her van, Mark said, "Good night," causing her to turn back to look at him.

"Aren't you coming?"

"No, I'm going back to the motel."

"Until . . . ?"

He shrugged.

Ivy studied him for several moments, then said, "Why? Because we kissed?"

"Can you think of a better reason?"

"No," she said, sounding less angry than sad. "I guess not."

Mark knocked on Lantana Mitchell's door shortly after ten that night. He'd been in his room since leaving the pool hall, debating whether or not it was time for him to go back to California, back to his practice, back to his life.

This trip had turned into a nightmare. He was no closer to learning who his father was than when he'd arrived; his mother's death remained a mystery; and he was beginning to have weird feelings for his cousin. His *pregnant* cousin.

When he'd returned to the motel earlier in the evening and read the note Lantana had slipped beneath his door, his first thought had been to ignore it. He figured his life was complicated enough already.

But later, his curiosity kicked in, so he decided to take her up on her invitation.

"Thanks for coming," she said as she led him inside. "I wasn't sure you would."

"Why? Because you ambushed me yesterday?"

"Well, just so you know, I don't make a habit of hiding in motel bathrooms."

"I doubt you've even been in many motel bathrooms."

"More than you can imagine, dear." She smiled, revealing a set of porcelain veneers that had cost her— or somebody—a hefty price. "Drink?" She held up her own glass, which was almost empty.

"Sure."

She was wearing a blue silk *peignoir*, but she hadn't removed her makeup, which had been artfully applied and recently touched up, an indication that she'd been pretty confident Mark would show up. When he'd seen her the previous day, her hair—the color of champagne— had been swept back and held in a tight chignon. But now it was loose, falling gently around her face.

She was just one side or the other of fifty, but either way, he thought, she made fifty look good.

"What would you like?" She gestured to the top of the TV console, where she'd set up a small bar—vodka, Scotch, bourbon, a bucket of ice.

"Scotch, please."

Mark took a seat on the far side of the coffee table,

which held a basket of fruit and a vase of long-stemmed yellow roses. A desk at the side of the room held a laptop, several leather-bound notebooks and a couple of Mont Blanc pens.

When she handed him his drink, she said, "So, how are you dealing with this Oklahoma culture?"

"Not particularly well."

"You're pretty much a fish out of water here, aren't you."

"There've been a few surprises."

"Like discovering that 'public transportation' here means pickup trucks?"

"Well, in Beverly Hills it means Jaguar convertibles."

"I know. I lived in L.A. for several years."

"Where are you from?"

"Eldorado."

"Just east of Sacramento. Right?"

"No. Just east of Elmer."

Mark looked puzzled.

"Eldorado, Oklahoma," she said. "Born and raised."

"I wouldn't have guessed you were from this part of the country."

"'Cause I don't speak Okie?" she asked, switching to a dialect marked by drawn-out vowels and a nasal twang. She went back to the bar, where she poured herself another drink. "Now that voice didn't cost a penny," she said, reverting to the delivery she had cultivated years earlier after working with a voice coach. "But this one cost my ex-husband some money." She laughed then, a deep, throaty laugh fueled—in part—by vodka.

"Do you have two personalities as well?"

"Of course. I'm a Gemini. And I happen to know you're an Aries."

"You seem to know a lot about me."

"I've done some research."

"Then I'm at a disadvantage. All I know about you is that you're a writer and you have an ex-husband."

"Actually, I have two ex-husbands, but one of them didn't have any money, so he doesn't count."

"Tell me about yourself," Mark said.

"How far back do you want me to go?"

"Why not start with Eldorado."

"Hardscrabble town. Population five hundred, give or take a few dozen. More churches than bars, but more drunks than preachers. My dad was both. I couldn't wait to get out.

"After graduation, went to Tulsa, got a job as a secretary at a television station, worked my way up to the evening news. Stayed with that until I found a man with money and power.

"He moved me to L.A., remade me for big-time TV, put me on the air, and I was a hit. When he dumped me for a twenty-year-old, I came back to Oklahoma and started to write. End of story."

"And now you've had three books published."

She faked a look of chagrin and held up one finger.

"You told me yesterday that you'd—"

"I lied. I was just trying to impress you."

"Why did you feel the need to impress me?"

"Because I want you to agree to let me write your story."

"Well, I don't suppose I could prevent that. Not legally. Besides, you seem pretty damn intent."

"You can't . . . and I am. But I'd prefer your cooperation. It's easier to write true crime when someone involved is willing to help."

"I'm curious."

"About what?"

"Why are you so determined to write this story?"

She took a deep breath, then leaned forward and put her hand on Mark's, a gesture intended to convey comfort. "Mark, what happened to you, your mother . . . that's a tragedy. I'm sympathetic to that." She withdrew her hand, drained the last of her drink, then returned to the bar. "But from a writer's point of view, this is a hell of a story. Sure to be a best-seller."

"So it's the money?"

"It doesn't have a damn thing to do with money."

"Then what?"

"O Boy Daniels." She filled her glass, took a long, slow swallow. "I've despised the man longer than most marriages last."

"Do you want to tell me why?"

"Have you ever hated anyone, Mark? Hated with pure, sweet passion?"

"No."

"Well, you should. It's fun. You can entertain yourself for hours thinking up the most punishing schemes."

Mark smiled, shook his head, then put his unfinished drink on the table. "Look, Ms. Mitchell, I don't know what kind of game you've got going on in your head, but I'm not going to play it. Whatever your reason is for wanting to get even with O Boy Daniels—"

"Oh, I don't want to get even. I want to get ahead."

"Then you'd better count me out." He stood, started for the door.

"But you want to know who your father is, don't you?"

She spoke softly so that Mark, unsure of what he'd just heard, stopped and turned to face her.

"Gaylene Harjo was arrested nine months to the day before you were born." She looked, for the moment, like a woman accustomed to conquest. "She spent some time in jail, Mark. O Boy Daniels' jail."

June 23, 1968

Dear Diary,

I've been out of school for four weeks and I'm already bored. Nothing to do out here but work. Mom leaves me a list of chores every day and Daddy expects me to work in the garden all the time.

Row can get her drivers license in August if she passes the test, so maybe the end of summer vacation won't be so bad. If she fails her test, I'll kill her.

The only good thing about being out of school is that I can work on my art, at least when Daddy's not around. He thinks it's a waste of time, so I don't draw or paint unless I'm sure he'll be in the fields all afternoon. Mr. Duchamp bought me a set of charcoal pencils for my birthday, so I've been working in my sketch book. Last week I started on a self portrait, an abstract I'm going to call "The Girl in the Looking Glass."

Oscar called today. He starts baling hay next week and he says he can't wait to get out of his aunt's house. They had another argument last night because he was playing his radio past ten o'clock. She says it keeps her awake, but he says she gripes about everything he does. He wants to make enough money this summer that he and his mom can move out and get their own place, but he said she's drinking again, so she might lose her job at the grocery store.

I guess I shouldn't complain about being so bored.

Spider Woman

Chapter Twenty-two

Mark had passed only one car since leaving the outskirts of DeClare some thirty miles back, but at three in the morning, he hadn't expected much traffic.

Even though his directions had been exact, he missed the final turn to the cabin. As he turned to double back, three empty Chocolate Soldier bottles rolled across the back floorboard and banged against the door. When he approached from the opposite direction, his headlights had picked out the PRIVATE DRIVE sign Kyle Leander had told him to watch for.

After leaving Lantana Mitchell's room and returning to his own, Mark had phoned Hap to tell him what he'd just heard. But because of the late hour, the answering machine took the call. He didn't leave a message. Then he drove to Teeve's, hoping to find Ivy's light on. It wasn't.

The phone was ringing when he got back to his room. He half expected it was Lantana calling; he figured her for a drunk who didn't like drinking alone. But the voice on the other end of the line belonged to Kyle.

Now, less than an hour later, Mark was parking in front of a rough-hewed cabin covered with a tin roof, an ancient air conditioner rattling in one of the windows. In the yard a NO TRESPASSING sign was partially hidden by the jimsonweed and Johnson grass. As he waded through, his Howdy Doody jeans picked up the spiny seeds of sandburs.

Just as he reached the narrow plank porch, Kyle burst through the front door and crushed him in a bear hug.

"Oh, Nicky Jack. Didn't I tell you that you were alive? Huh? You remember what I said? 'He's out there somewhere,' I said. You remember that, little man?"

Hoping that a positive answer would gain his release, Mark, his mouth buried in Kyle's beard, his breath restricted by the pressure on his ribs, managed to nod.

"And here you are. Gaylene's baby."

"Thanks," Mark said, though he had no idea what he was thankful for until Kyle let him go.

"Everyone at the hospital was talking about you, Nicky Jack. The nurses, the staff. Then someone left a newspaper in the day room and I saw your picture."

"Kyle, I'm sorry I didn't tell you who I was the day we met, but it just didn't seem to be the right time."

"If you want to understand time, read *Einstein's Dreams.*"

"Yes, I think you mentioned that before."

"Well, come in." Kyle nudged Mark toward the door. "Let me get you a beer."

"Sure."

The low-ceilinged room was furnished with bunk beds, a threadbare couch, an empty gun cabinet and two folding chairs at an unfinished pine table, its surface scarred and scorched by decades of burning cigarettes.

Part of the space included a kitchen with open shelves, an avocado-colored refrigerator and a yellowed, apartment-size gas range.

"Is this your place?" Mark asked.

"It's Arthur's, but he doesn't come out here anymore. Hasn't been here in years."

The walls held cobweb-covered trophies and dusty framed photographs: mounted heads of bear, leopard, antelope and pictures of a much younger Arthur, rifle in hand, posing with his kills—a gutted deer hanging from a tree; an elk, its sightless eyes open; a gazelle shot in the neck.

"Looks like your stepfather's quite a hunter."

"Pretty gross, huh?"

"I suppose some people would be impressed."

"Not Gaylene. She was an animal lover, you know. She hated this place."

"Did she come out here a lot?"

"Only once. We came out to go swimming on the day she graduated. The river runs through the back of the property. She saw these"—Kyle gestured toward the heads—"said she'd never come back. And she didn't."

Mark paid special attention to a photo of Arthur and O Boy standing on either side of a two-hundred-pound marlin dangling from a weighing hook, each toasting the other with a bottle of whiskey. Someone had scribbled a date at the bottom of the picture: "June 1974."

"How about you? Do you hunt?" Mark asked.

"Man, I don't even *eat* meat."

Kyle finished a beer he'd left on the kitchen counter, then got two more from the fridge, popped the tops and brought them to the table.

"Listen, Kyle, I want you to know I feel bad about what happened to you after we talked at the radio station."

"Oh, that's fine." Kyle screwed up his face in concentration, then stared at Mark, his expression absolutely blank. "What happened after we talked at the radio station?"

"Arthur told me you had to be hospitalized because our conversation upset you so much."

"Well, don't worry about it," he said, memory kicking in. "Arthur puts me away whenever he feels like it. I get on his nerves sometimes."

"I see." Mark nodded to show how reasonable he sounded. "So when were you released?"

"Wasn't. I'm just taking a break."

"You're taking a break?" Mark was dumbfounded.

"You look like her, you know. Like Gaylene."

When Kyle's eyes filled with tears, he reached into his shirt pocket and pulled out a carefully folded tissue. Inside were several capsules, which he popped in his mouth at the same time and then washed down with beer.

"Hey, are you supposed to do that?" Mark asked, obviously alarmed. "What did you take?"

"I don't know. Demerol, Zoloft. Some Valium, maybe a couple of Darvocet."

"That's a lot of drugs, Kyle."

"Hey, I don't do drugs anymore. Been clean and sober for . . . well, for a long time."

"Kyle, how did you get here?"

"Hitched."

"Maybe I should take you back." Mark sounded more than a little concerned.

"Nah. Arthur will come and get me."

"When?"

"Depends on when he finds out I'm gone."

Despite trying not to, Mark laughed.

"You sound like her, too." Kyle upended his beer, then asked, "You ready for another?"

"No, thanks."

"If you're hungry—"

"Kyle, was Gaylene ever in jail?"

"No! Lord, no! Why would she go to jail? She wasn't like me. She didn't drop acid, didn't do mushrooms or smoke pot. She didn't shoplift, never grabbed some old lady's purse. Hell, she never even stole a car."

"Well, she sounds just about perfect."

"The most perfect creature God ever made. She was an angel."

Mark noticed that Kyle was a bit unsteady as he went to the fridge for more beer. The drugs or alcohol or both had started to kick in.

"She was so sweet, Nicky Jack. So gentle," Kyle said, slurring the last two words. "She loved weeping willows and rainbows and rabbits and . . ." He wept then, openly, unashamed. Finally, he took three more capsules that he dug from his pants pocket.

Sensing that Kyle might soon be out of it, Mark said, "When you phoned me at the motel, you said you had something to show me."

"That's right. I do." He staggered as he returned to the kitchen and took a cigar box from one of the shelves. When he brought it to the table, he said, "Everything in here was part of her in one way or another."

He opened the lid, took out a silver key chain in the shape of a dove. "Gaylene gave me that for Christmas. And she found this in the river." He put a cobalt blue marble on the table. "This was hers; she left it in my car," he said, holding up a tube of lipstick. "We picked these

the day we drove to Tahlequah for the bluegrass festival."
He removed some dried stems of goldenrod from the
box. "And this here is her senior ring."

"These things mean a lot to you, don't they, Kyle."

"Yes. That's why I'm giving them to you."

"Kyle . . ."

"I want you to have everything."

"I can't do that."

"Nicky Jack, she'd want you to have them."

"But that's all you have left of her."

"Oh, no. I have so much more. I have her memory.
You got cheated out of that."

September 5, 1968

Dear Diary,

*I can't believe what just happened. Danny Pittman called me!
He really did! He told me he broke up with Becky last week because
she was getting too serious. Then he asked me to go to the drive-in
with him Saturday night. He said he'd wanted to ask me out for
a long time. I must be dreaming.*

Spider Woman

September 6, 1968

*Mom said I could spend the night with Row Saturday and we
could go to a movie if it was okay with Daddy. He grumbled about*

it, but finally said yes. Row has her license now and her folks said she could take their car tomorrow night. We'll go to the drive-in where I'll meet Danny, then after the movie I'll find Row and we'll go back to her house. I can't wait! A date with Danny Pittman! Daddy will ground me for life if he finds out. Especially since Danny is a white boy.

Spider Woman

September 7, 1968

Danny was waiting for me on the last row of the drive-in just like he said he would. When I got to his car, he said we should get in the back seat so we could see the screen better. I was real nervous until we started talking about school. He's a senior this year. Pretty soon, he put his arm around me and pulled me so close I bet he could feel my heart beating. Then he put his finger under my chin, turned my face to his and kissed me. It was just as wonderful and sweet as I dreamed it would be. When we stopped, I didn't know what to say and I guess he didn't either because he kissed me again. But this kiss was different. He stuck his tongue in my mouth and mashed his mouth so hard against mine that my teeth were cutting into my lips. He tasted like sour milk and he was sweating so much his forehead was slick. I tried to back away, but he pushed me down in the seat and ran one hand under my blouse, the other up my skirt, his fingers pulling at the elastic of my pants.

By then, his whole weight was on top of me and I could only take little quick breaths. I thought I might suffocate, so I bit down on his tongue. Real hard. When I did, he reared back, said shit and called me an Indian bitch, but I didn't care. I shoved him as hard as I could and pulled myself out from under him. He didn't try to stop me as I got out. I think his tongue was hurting too much.

I ran to Row's car where she was watching the movie, but we left right then and went back to her house. Her folks were in bed, so they didn't see me. Good thing because my top lip is swollen and bruised. Row got some ice to put on it, then she held my hand while I cried myself to sleep.

Spider Woman

September 9, 1968

Dear Diary,

Today was the first day of my junior year and on my way to my American history class, I passed Danny who was walking down the hall with his arm around Becky. He lied about breaking up with her so he could try to get into my pants. When he saw me, he smiled and said, "Hi, Gaylene," like nothing had happened.

I've thought about telling Becky how he cheated on her, but I won't. She's never done anything to hurt me, so I'm not going to hurt her. I figure she's going to be hurt enough by Danny Pittman.

Spider Woman

Chapter Twenty-three

"Did she tell you why Gaylene was in jail?" Hap asked.

"She said it was a DUI."

Hap took the last bite of a chocolate doughnut, licked his fingers, then brushed flakes of icing from his shirt while Mark opened his second Twinkie of the day.

"Do you trust her, Mark?"

"Lantana? I can't think of a good reason why I should. She was drinking—and she's obviously no stranger to vodka. In addition, she hates O Boy Daniels. I believe she'd say or do anything to cause him trouble, but I don't know the reason. She wouldn't talk about that."

"Any chance he's the one who told her Gaylene was arrested?"

"She claimed the information came from an anonymous source in 1978 when she was living in L.A. So, to answer your question: No, I don't trust her."

"Still, if it's true, then somebody who was at the jail that night might be able to provide some answers. Or, if she was stopped for DUI, she might've had a friend in the car with her. And that would most likely have been Kyle Leander or Rowena Whitekiller. Right?"

"Kyle didn't know anything about it."

"But maybe he lied to you. Suppose it would do any good for you to talk to Rowena again?"

"I don't know." Mark rubbed the stubble on his chin, unconcerned that he hadn't shaved in two days. "Maybe."

"I'll ask for a copy of the arrest report and the jail blotter. And if Gaylene was jailed, there'll be a prisoner property receipt."

"What's that?" Mark asked.

"A list of whatever she had on her person. Purse, keys, money, jewelry. Problem is, records weren't computerized here until the mid-eighties. And even if those documents are available, the sheriff's not required to hand them over. Now, if I could get a judge to back me up, I might be able to—"

"We don't have a damn thing tied down, do we, Hap."

"Not yet, but we're not finished. I have a lead on a woman who was a secretary to the attorney in California who handled the adoption. Maybe . . ."

"Yeah," Mark said. "Maybe." He got up and went to Hap's office window, where he looked down on Main Street.

"You need some rest," Hap said. "Why don't you go to your room, sack out for a few hours."

"I'm going back to Arthur's cabin, check on Kyle."

"You worried about him?"

"Hap, that much medication could've killed him. I was afraid he might die in his sleep, so I sat and watched him breathe for a couple of hours after I got him to bed."

"Well, do yourself a favor when you get back to town.

Take the afternoon off. Read a book, go fishing. Hell, get drunk. Do something to put this out of your mind for a while."

"Sure," Mark said, but he didn't sound convincing.

"If I have any luck at O Boy's office . . ."

"You know what we have, Hap? Ifs. Nothing but a hell of a lot of ifs. *If* Lantana's telling the truth, *if* Gaylene was in jail, *if* O Boy cooperates, *if* Rowena knows what happened, *if*—"

"Give it a little more time. You never know when or where the answers will surface."

"*If*, Hap. We don't know *if* the answers will ever surface."

Both doors to the cabin were locked, but by looking through the windows, Mark could see that Kyle was not inside. Nobody—living or dead. No overturned chairs or broken glass caused by a staggering drunk, a stumbling addict. Nothing out of place.

The beer bottles left on the cabinet and table just hours before had disappeared. Even the quilt he'd used to cover Kyle had been folded neatly on the foot of the bed.

Behind the cabin, Mark inspected a windowless shed. The chain and lock that held the door was rusted and covered with cobwebs.

As he started back to his car, he noticed a graveled path leading away from the cabin and into a cover of pecan trees. Thirty yards from where he'd started, the path circled an outcropping of bedrock. That's where he heard the rush of water.

Seconds later, he was standing on the bank of the river, water cascading over boulders upstream. From the sound, a long hidden memory surfaced.

He was five, maybe six, standing ankle deep at the edge of a clear stream, watching his father flyfishing near the far bank. His mother and his aunt Edna, both in bathing suits, sat behind him on boulders along the bank.

He knew they were talking about him because he heard his name. And though he didn't understand the conversation, he could tell from her voice that his mother was angry.

"You've never had children, Edna, so how is it you're so certain of what I should do?"

"Child psychologists say these children should be—"

"'These children'?! We're not talking about 'these children.' We're talking about Mark. My son."

"It's easy to hide it from him now, Helen. He's hardly more than a baby. But sooner or later, he's going to find out."

"You don't know that."

"Take my advice. Tell him now."

"He wouldn't understand."

"No, he won't. But keep telling him so that later on, when he does understand, he'll be comfortable with it. It'll be old news."

"What makes you so sure, Edna? You read a magazine article at the beauty shop and now you're an expert?"

"You're setting yourself up for disaster, Helen. When he discovers the truth, he'll feel like you betrayed him. And he might not be able to forgive you for it."

The rain started as a light shower just minutes after Mark drove away from the cabin, but by the time he reached town, the sky had opened up.

He drove by the farmhouse where he'd met Rowena

Whitekiller, intending to stop, but the driveway was crowded with cars and pickups. A funeral wreath hung on the front door.

He drove on to town but detoured past the pool hall when he saw Ivy's van. He'd been mentally rehearsing what he would say to her the next time they were together, but the pool hall was not the place to deliver that speech.

As he drove by a liquor store, he decided to take Hap's advice. He found a parking place just across the street, but by the time he got inside, he was soaked.

He asked the clerk for a bottle of Dimple Pinch, his favorite Scotch.

"Never heard of it," she said.

He settled for a bottle of Dewar's, took it to the counter and handed the woman his credit card.

Eyeing him suspiciously, she asked, "Aren't you that Nick Harjo?"

"Mark Albright," he said. "Just like the name on the card."

"Well, you sure look like that guy in the paper."

"Yeah, that's what someone else told me."

The rain was beginning to let up when Mark pulled into his motel, but apparently the deluge had sent the reporters running for cover. Even so, he wasn't taking any chances. He parked in the back and slipped in the service entrance.

When he reached his room, he was pleased that no note was waiting beneath the door and no one was hiding in his bathroom.

He stripped down to his briefs, hung his dripping clothes on the shower rod and had just poured himself a drink when he saw that the message light on his phone was flashing. He sat on his bed and ran through the recordings—calls from Lantana, Teeve and Frances Boyd, Hap's secretary. He was disappointed that Ivy hadn't called.

Even with all the lights on, the room seemed dark, so Mark pulled back the drapes to discover that the sun was out. He opened the sliding glass doors and stepped onto the balcony.

The river, swollen now, frothed and foamed as it crashed against the boulders along the bank. And the needles of the pine trees, freshly washed to a deep, rich green, shimmered with droplets that blinked like clear crystals.

Later, he would remember hearing the first shot in the instant before the door behind him shattered, showering him with tiny fragments of glass. And he would remember the second shot, the bullet ricocheting off the brick wall only inches above his head.

But he would never remember the sound of the third shot or recall how he felt as his body lifted, then fell backward into the silence of the motel room.

Chapter Twenty-four

Even with an IV in his arm, an oxygen apron in his nose and EKG monitors attached to his chest, it took Mark a few minutes to figure out where he was when he regained consciousness. But he had no idea why he was there.

A woman in blue scrubs was standing beside his bed, writing on a clipboard. "Hello," she said when she saw him watching her. "I'm Dr. Alkoff."

Mark's lips formed a response, but his brain didn't follow through.

"How are you feeling?" she asked.

It took him a couple of tries, but he finally managed to mumble, "Like hell."

"Headache?"

"Worst ever."

"I'm not surprised. You have a knot the size of a golf ball right here." She gingerly touched a spot just behind his ear. "Any dizziness? Nausea? Blurred vision?"

"No. What's going on? Did I fall?"

"You don't remember anything about what happened to you?"

"No."

"Can you tell me what day it is?"

"Wednesday, I think."

"Your name?"

"Mark Albright. Or Nick Harjo. Take your pick."

She smiled. "Ordinarily that answer would get you a free ride to the psychiatric ward. But in your case, it works. I read about you in the paper." She finished writing, then placed the clipboard on a table by the bed. "Any pain in your leg?"

Mark tried to raise his head, grimaced with the effort, gave up.

"Probably be best if you didn't move around too much."

"What's wrong with my leg?"

"You have a bullet wound in your thigh."

Still foggy headed, Mark was sure he'd misunderstood the doctor's statement. "What did you say?"

"A bullet wound."

He tried to reconcile what she'd said with an image of himself aiming a gun, but he couldn't see it, couldn't see himself buying a gun or even holding one.

"That's impossible," he said. "I don't think I have a gun."

"You didn't do the shooting."

"Who did?"

"Sheriff Daniels is waiting to talk to you about that," she said.

"A bullet wound," he said, reality beginning to kick in.

"Fortunately, it's a through-and-through, didn't involve bone, artery or nerve. Even missed muscle."

"You know, I've treated dogs that've been shot, cats, even an iguana, but—"

"Then you know the drill. I gave you a local anesthetic so I could clean the wound and put in a few stitches. We're loading you up on antibiotics to prevent infection. You're not allergic to any medications, are you?"

"No."

"We'll give you Demerol for the pain, but first—"

"Except for this headache, I'm not in any pain."

"Trust me, when the local wears off, you'll know you've been shot. Now, let's get you to X-ray for an MRI, see about that head injury."

"Did someone hit me in the head, too?"

"Apparently you did that when you fell into your room. At least that's what the paramedics surmised."

"How long was I out?"

"An hour or so. Long enough that we need to see if you have a concussion."

Mark took a deep breath, held it several seconds, then exhaled audibly.

"You okay?" she asked.

"As okay as I can be knowing that someone tried to kill me."

Mark was sleeping when a nurse drew the curtain separating his bed from the one nearest the door.

"Sorry if I woke you," she said, "but you've got a roommate now. He's just back from surgery. Can I get you anything?"

"No, thanks."

After she left the room, Mark felt himself drifting off

again until he heard Ivy's voice. "Hi," she said. "How're you doing?"

"Not so bad."

"You seemed to be resting well."

"How long have you been here?"

"About an hour."

"I don't remember sleeping. Can't remember much, actually."

"That's okay. Don't try."

Taking his hand, she bent over him and kissed his cheek. "I'm glad you're doing so well."

"Yeah. I just . . ." He closed his eyes for a few seconds, then, with sudden awareness, said, "I was shot, wasn't I."

"Yes, but you're going to be fine."

"Who did it?"

"No one knows yet, but Hap said O Boy's got every one of his deputies searching the woods behind the motel."

"Was Hap here?"

"He didn't want to wake you. He came back up with me after we'd eaten, but you were still asleep."

"What? You left me all alone? Helpless and in pain?"

"Helpless and in pain, maybe . . . but not alone. There's a security guard right outside the door."

"You're kidding."

"Huh-uh."

"Whose decision was that?"

"Hap's." Ivy looked a little sheepish when she said, "Mine."

"You think whoever shot me didn't get the job done? You actually believe someone's going to come to the hospital, sneak into this room and try again?"

"It's possible."

"And it's also possible that the shooting was accidental. Someone might have been hunting."

"Hunting what?"

"I don't know. What's in season now in Oklahoma?"

"Smart-aleck veterinarians from California."

"Seriously. Maybe some kid was squirrel hunting or target shooting."

"Yeah. And you were the target."

"I have to go to the john."

He pressed the button that connected him to the nurses' station.

"I could help you, you know."

"Not a chance in hell."

"Well, if that's the way you feel, guess I'll take off."

"Yeah, you should. I'm about ready for another shot that will send me back to la-la land."

"Okay." Ivy dug in her bag, pulled out a paperback book. "Maybe when you feel better . . ."

"Thanks."

"Then . . ." She made a move toward the bed, then backed away. "You feel better soon."

"I think . . ."

"Mark, if you—"

"Ivy, we need to talk about yesterday."

"What happened yesterday?"

"Come on. Stop playing games."

"Okay, let's talk."

"I'm sorry about what happened."

"You told me that already."

"Help me out, Ivy. We're in a very awkward situation here."

"All right. Let's lay it out," she said. "We've spent a

lot of time together over the past week. We get along, we like each other. Right?"

"Right."

"You're extremely vulnerable right now, and I seem to be your strongest ally. Then, in an irresolute moment, you kissed me. And I kissed you back.

"But when that happened, you came to the horrible realization that you were kissing a woman whose belly looks like a giant water balloon. You remembered that I'm going to have a baby and you are not the father. Sudden humiliation caused you to recoil, fearing our friendship was damaged. How am I doing so far?"

"You're way off the mark."

"Let me finish. You're humiliated and guilty; I'm humiliated and angry. I run out of the pool hall, you run back to the motel. And then you're shot. I didn't do it, by the way. I was mad enough to shoot you, but I didn't. I'm a better shot than that. If I'd wanted to kill you, we wouldn't be having this conversation. End of story."

"No. Maybe the end of *your* story, but not mine. I kissed you because you're a desirable woman—energetic, bright, compassionate, beautiful. My guilt had nothing to do with you being pregnant. None. When I said it wasn't right that we kissed, I wasn't even thinking about that."

"Mark, you don't have to be kind about this. I know how I look, and I understand my situation. I don't expect you or any man to find me desirable."

"You're wrong, Ivy. And if we weren't cousins, I would be—"

"Cousins?"

"I just don't feel comfortable with that."

"You think we're cousins?"

"Ivy, Navy Harjo was a brother to Gaylene Harjo. Right?"

"Right."

"And if my understanding of family structure's correct, that makes us cousins."

"Yes, if Navy *Harjo* were my father, we would be."

"Hold on."

"Navy adopted me when he married my mom."

"Are you telling me—"

"We're not cousins, Mark. We're not even blood related."

Chapter Twenty-five

When Teeve walked into Mark's hospital room just before seven the next morning, she found him in a chair eating breakfast.

"Let me guess," she said. "French omelet, pork terrine, baked grapefruit and walnut molasses bars with peach butter."

"Close. Very close. Try artificial eggs, synthetic bacon, make-believe coffee and fake toast with counterfeit butter."

"And how is it?"

"Truly disgusting," Mark said.

"Complaining about hospital food is a sure sign of recovery."

"Well, I'm not ready to leg wrestle yet."

"You have a good night?"

"Great night. An extremely attentive nurse woke me up every fifteen minutes to ask me if I needed a sleeping pill."

"You look pretty good considering someone tried to kill you less than twenty-four hours ago."

"Doctor says I'll probably be discharged later today."

"Lord, Lord. They send you home nowadays before the bleeding's even stopped."

"I think if you can survive a night in the hospital, they figure you're able to hit the road."

"Well, you call the pool hall when you're ready to go."

"Thanks, Teeve, but I'll just grab a taxi and go to the motel."

"Don't be ridiculous. You're coming back to my house."

"No, really. I think it would be best if I didn't."

"Is this about that nonsense between you and Ivy?"

"She told you what happened?"

"Yeah, I had to laugh. I figured she'd told you she wasn't Navy's child, and she assumed I'd told you. Anyway, I'm glad you two have hit it off. You're good for her right now."

"Ivy's great, Teeve, but—"

"I know, I know. She's got a quick temper. And she's not a very trusting person. I blame Navy for that. When he left us, she was brokenhearted. And once he was gone, he just forgot her. Never phoned, never wrote. Not a word, even on her birthday."

"What about her real father?"

"Oh, honey, that was so long ago, he doesn't seem any more real to me than some soap opera character.

"I was seventeen, thought I was in love, got pregnant. He left here before Ivy was born, got killed in Vietnam. Bless his heart, he never even knew he fathered a child."

"Does Ivy know all this?"

"I never tried to hide it from her. But truth is, she lost two dads and I think that's the reason she's never married. She just can't seem to let herself trust men. Don't know if she told you she was engaged once. When she was living in Vermont."

"No, she didn't."

"She sent out invitations, bought a dress, had everything planned. Then, a week before the wedding, she called it off."

"Did she tell you why?" Mark asked.

"Never did. But that's her way. She keeps too much inside."

When an aide came in to pick up Mark's tray, Teeve said, "Well, I'd better get to the pool hall before the domino boys break down the door. Now, you promise to call when you're ready to get out of here?"

"Teeve, I'm not completely comfortable staying at your place."

"Why?"

"If it's true that someone was trying to kill me, he's still out there. And once he finds out he didn't get the job done, he might try again. Better the motel than your place."

"Honey, Navy left an arsenal in my closet. And I know how to use every gun there. You leave the protection to me and I'll leave the caregiving to Ivy. I don't know how she is with people, but I've seen her doctor hamsters, cats, birds, mice. She saved all of them, but they ended up neurotic, so be careful. She'll baby you, mother you, pamper you and drive you crazy, but she'll get you through it."

"Sounds like the treatment is going to require more patience than the injury."

Teeve waited until the aide left the room, then she closed the door. "Mark, I want to ask you to do me a favor."

"Sure."

"Talk to Ivy about this baby, will you? I'm a little worried."

"About what?"

"Well, I don't know if this'll make any sense to you. It'll probably sound like I'm off on a tangent, just borrowing trouble."

"Tell me, Teeve."

"Ivy doesn't seem to have any plans for this baby. She hasn't picked out a name, isn't curious about whether it's a boy or a girl. She hasn't shopped for the stuff she's going to need. No diapers, no gowns, no blankets. Doesn't show any interest in baby furniture. I told her to turn my sewing room into a nursery, but she hasn't done a thing about it, hasn't even bought a bassinet."

"Maybe she's just procrastinating, putting everything off until the last few weeks."

"Mark, she's down to the last few weeks." Teeve shook her head. "The truth is, Ivy isn't excited about becoming a mother. And I want to know why."

Mark was hobbling from the bathroom on crutches when he found O Boy waiting in his room. "Didn't know I had company," he said.

"You look to be in better shape today."

"I'm doing okay."

Mark propped his crutches in the corner, then slid onto the bed, his feet dangling over the side.

"How about your head? You were pretty messed up yesterday, didn't make a whole lot of sense. Doubt you remember much of our conversation."

"I can recall some of it, but there are a few gaps."

"That's why I'm here. I want to talk about one of those gaps," O Boy said.

"Go ahead."

"You didn't tell me you were with Kyle Leander yesterday morning."

"Not much to tell. He called, asked me to meet him at his stepfather's cabin. I did. We talked for a couple of hours, then he went to bed, I went back to the motel. That's it."

"Did you know he'd escaped from the nuthouse?"

"I knew he'd been in a psychiatric hospital for a few days, but there was no talk of an escape. He said he was taking a break, so I assumed he'd checked himself out."

"You don't check yourself out of the nuthouse. That's why they have bars on the windows and locks on the doors."

"Where is Kyle now?" Mark asked.

"That's what I'm trying to find out. Thought you might have some idea."

"I don't have a clue. I left him at the cabin, didn't see him again."

"No, you probably didn't. But I believe he saw you."

"Where?"

"Through the scope of a rifle when you were standing on that motel balcony."

Two hours later, Mark was back at Teeve's house with Ivy hovering. When she came from the kitchen with a fresh ice pack, he said, "The one that's on here now is still cold."

"The doctor said change them every hour. And that's what I'm going to do." She shot him a look that said the routine was non-negotiable; she was in charge.

And in his present condition, he knew he had little choice. She had leaned his crutches against the fireplace mantel across the room, then stretched him out in a recliner, two pillows on top of the raised footrest so that his bandaged leg—exposed by the baggy shorts she'd made him wear—was elevated. *Really* elevated. For the moment, he looked about as helpless as a turtle on its back.

But she'd made sure that anything he might need was within his reach. On an end table beside his chair, she'd assembled his pills, a bottle of water, thermometer, cordless phone, paperback books and the TV remote.

"Can I get you some fruit? Bananas? Apples? Grapes?"

"No, thanks."

"How about some ice cream? We have strawberry, vanilla and black walnut."

"I'm fine, Ivy."

"Want me to read to you?"

"I don't think so."

"Maybe you'd like for me to rent some movies. You like comedies? Or do you—"

Mark was relieved to hear the doorbell, which sent Ivy to the front of the house.

Moments later, when she returned, she was followed by Hap. "Hey, Mark," he said, "tap-dancing yet?"

"Great. Another stand-up comic."

"Hap, can I get you something to drink?" Ivy asked.

"I'm not going to stay long, Ivy. Don't want to tire out your patient."

"No chance of that," Mark said. "Nurse Ratched will tell you when your time is up."

"Ingrate." As she left the room, she said, "I'll be in the

kitchen, Hap, if you need anything. But your client can fend for himself."

"So, Mark, other than being abused by your caregiver, how're you doing?"

"Not bad."

"I don't know if you've heard that Kyle's in jail."

"Oh, damn."

"One of O Boy's deputies picked him up out on I-244. He was trying to hitch a ride. I suppose he'll be arraigned in the morning."

"Charged with?"

"Attempted murder."

"That's just nuts. Kyle didn't shoot me."

"Probably not."

"I don't believe it's in him to try to hurt anyone. Besides, he had no reason to harm me. No reason at all."

"Well, this isn't the best time for you to get upset, Mark. You can't do anything about Kyle right now, and neither can I. But I have another piece of information, one that might prove to be valuable."

"What's that?"

"I made contact with Sybil Sokolowski in Long Beach."

"Who the hell is Sybil Sokolowski?"

"Former secretary to J. W. Downing, the lawyer who handled your adoption. She was also his lover from 1968 until he died in '85."

"She told you that?"

"She did. Said she had no reason to keep it secret now because Downing's widow died a couple of years ago. But here's the bombshell."

"Drop it."

"The house he bought her in Long Beach has a basement, and that's where he stored his records after he retired. And not only does she still have them, she found your file. Copies of your birth certificate, the decree of adoption, receipt for payment. Even found his notes."

"So . . ."

"It was a woman who showed up in Downing's office with a ten-month-old boy in her arms. A woman who said she was Gaylene Harjo."

It was almost midnight when someone tapped at the front door. Teeve had been in bed for a couple of hours, and Ivy had fallen asleep on the couch watching *The African Queen* on TV. But Mark was still awake, propped up in the recliner, reading.

"Ivy," he said, waking her, "someone's at the door."

"What time is it?"

"Ten till twelve."

"Who comes to visit at midnight?"

"I don't know, but I'll be surprised if it's a social call."

The gaggle of reporters had thinned a bit until news got out that Mark had been shot, an event that caused them to swoop back in. Even so, the Harjo routine had taught them that no one came to or went from Teeve's house much after nine, so Ivy was more than a little curious about this late night caller.

When she looked through the small window in the front door, she saw a short, fat woman looking back.

"I'm Rowena Whitekiller," the woman said when Ivy opened the door as far as the safety chain would allow. "We talked on the phone the other day."

"Yes." Ivy removed the chain, then said, "Come on in."

"I was wondering if I could see Nick Harjo for just a

few minutes. I know he was shot, I read about it in the paper, so if he doesn't feel like seeing me—"

"Hello," Mark said as he crutched into the foyer.

"I really won't stay long, I promise. I know it's awfully late, but I'm leaving town early in the morning."

"You all go in the kitchen," Ivy said. "I'm going to turn in. Oh, Mark, you're sleeping in my room tonight."

"Why?"

"You'll rest better in my bed."

"But—"

"Good night."

"Night, Ivy."

When Rowena and Mark were settled at the kitchen table, she said, "Your cousin called you Mark."

"Well, I'm not quite ready to be Nick Harjo just yet."

"Oh. Yeah, I guess that must seem strange."

"It does."

"How's your leg?"

"Other than being sore, I'm fine. It's just a flesh wound."

"Do they know yet who shot you?"

Mark shook his head.

"Listen," she said, "I'm afraid I wasn't very nice when you came to my dad's house the other day."

"Oh, I understand. Your father."

"We had graveside services today."

"I'm sorry."

"Thanks. I listed his house with a Realtor, packed up a few things I'm going to have shipped to Chicago. That's how I came across these." She took an envelope from her purse and removed several photographs. "I thought you might want to have them."

The first photo Rowena handed to Mark was a picture

of Gaylene at twelve, straddling her bicycle in front of an old movie theater, the marquee announcing *The Sound of Music*. "See those Band-Aids on her face and neck?" Rowena asked. "Gay had been in a fight with a boy who was throwing rocks at her dog."

"You called her Gay?"

"And she called me Row. Here she is at Falls Creek, where we went to Baptist Assembly one summer. That's where she got her first kiss. A boy from Anadarko."

"How old was she then?" Mark asked.

"Fourteen, I think. Now this one was taken at the Western Days Parade. That's her riding on the back of the convertible. She won the Miss Cherokee Beauty Contest that year.

"And here we are, me and Gay, in our caps and gowns right after graduation. My daddy took that. I had it enlarged and framed." Rowena swallowed hard, trying not to cry.

"Look at this. Her first day of work at the Hungry Hawk Café. See, her paper hat and apron are both red, white and blue. It was the Fourth of July."

Finished now, Rowena put the photos back in the envelope and handed it to Mark.

"I'm glad to have these," he said. "Thanks."

"You're welcome." She put her hands on the edge of the table as if she were going to push back. But she didn't. "I want you to know something. When you asked me if I knew who got her pregnant, I told you the truth. She never told me, I never asked.

"But there's something I didn't tell you or anyone else because I promised Gay I wouldn't. I even swore on my grandma's grave to keep it secret."

She sucked in her breath, then cast her eyes toward

the ceiling and whispered, "Gay, I'm hoping this is what you'd want me to do. But if it's not, please forgive me."

Then she turned to Mark and said, "We were celebrating her letter of acceptance to OSU. It came that afternoon.

"A boy we knew who worked at the liquor store sold us a pint of orange-flavored vodka. We went to the river, Gay and me, and drank it all.

"We were in my dad's car and I was driving when we started back to town, but on the way, I had to stop and throw up, so she took the wheel to drive us to my house. O Boy stopped us out on East Main, took her to jail for drunk driving."

"What about you?"

"He let me go."

"Rowena, did you ever make a connection between her arrest and—"

"When you were born? Yeah, I did. It was nine months. Exactly nine months."

November 7, 1968

Dear Diary,

Last week I finished that book And Still the Waters Run, *which I read for the paper I had to write for American history. Today I got my paper back from Mr. Houser. He gave me a D-. He had drawn a red X through everything I wrote about the Trail of Tears, and had written "Undocumented" across the top of each page. When I held up my hand to ask about it, he ignored me.*

Finally, I spoke up and asked him if he had read the book or if

he had even heard of Angie Debo. I told him I could prove everything I wrote because it was in her book. Mr. Houser got furious
and kicked me out of class. But I didn't care. I knew my paper was
good, I knew Angie Debo was telling the truth, and so was I.

Spider Woman

December 8, 1968

Dear Diary,
    I finished a drawing today of an old Cherokee man looking
across a flat and empty plain. Nothing but trees standing stark
against a gray sky. I call it "The Day the Buffalo Went Away."
I'm going to give it to Oscar Horsechief for Christmas.

Spider Woman

Chapter Twenty-six

Ivy was in the kitchen when she heard Mark clunking around in the next room. "You decent?" she yelled.

"No."

"Good." When she walked in, she found him standing on one crutch, trying to pull on the cutoffs that fit over his thickly bandaged leg. "Sleep well?" she asked.

"Dreamed I had a bullet hole in my leg."

"How weird is that?" As she helped him into the shorts, she said, "Amax Dawson just called. Said he needs to see you."

"Did you ask him to come over?"

"He drove by here a little while ago, but was scared off by the reporters and satellite trucks out front."

"Can you drive me to his place?" Mark asked.

"He's reluctant to have you come there. Afraid you'll be followed. And he told me this is too big to talk about over the phone. He says he and his source have to remain anonymous."

"His source? Sounds like he's found himself a 'Deep Throat.'"

"Let's hope so," Ivy said.

"Well, if he won't come here, and he doesn't want me to go there, what am I supposed to do?"

"I've already worked that out."

"Great. Am I going to be a plumber again?"

"Not this time."

"Meter reader? Tree trimmer?"

"Put on your shirt, smart-ass. We're going out."

At a few minutes after nine, Ivy helped Mark into her van, ignoring the reporters who yelled questions at them from the street. As she backed out of the drive, both she and Mark acted oblivious to the hubbub around them.

Two vehicles followed them to the DeClare Medical Clinic, where Ivy dropped Mark off at the front door before she put the van in the parking garage.

Unhurried, he took the elevator to the third floor, to room 305, the office of Dr. Alkoff.

The waiting room was crowded. Mark took a seat between a woman with a cast on her leg and a teenage boy with his arm in a sling. When two reporters walked in, one took the last empty chair, which was across the room from Mark; the other stood near the window.

Five minutes later, a nurse opened a door at the end of the waiting room and called, "Dr. Albright?" Mark pulled himself up with his crutches and followed her through the door and down the hall.

"Here you are," she said. "The doctor will be with you shortly."

Amax was smiling when Mark entered. "Any problems?" he asked as they shook hands.

"No, it went just the way Ivy set it up. She could probably have a career with the CIA."

"How do you know she doesn't? Here, I'll take those," he said as Mark settled in a chair and handed off his crutches. "I heard Kyle Leander's been arrested for the shooting."

"O Boy's arrested him, but I'm pretty sure he didn't have anything to do with it."

"You have any suspicions?"

"I have the feeling O Boy was involved some way, but it's just a gut feeling. Nothing I can prove."

"Maybe I've got something here we *can* prove, something he can't slither away from."

Leaning forward, Mark said, "Let's hear it."

"Do you remember how I found out about you, about who you really are?"

"Some friend of yours who works at the sheriff's office, wasn't it?"

"Olene Turner. We used to date back in high school, been friends ever since. Well, she showed up at my house before dawn this morning to bring me this."

Amax handed Mark a box the size of a book, its lid wrapped in gift paper, bright yellow bow taped to the top.

"A birthday present?" Mark asked.

"No, but she wanted it to look like one. She didn't believe anyone at O Boy's office would follow her, had no reason to think they'd even suspect she had access to this, but she didn't want to take any chances. Go ahead. Take the lid off."

Mark opened the box and lifted out several pieces of paper folded in half. "What is this?"

"Copies of an arrest report on Gaylene Harjo. A jail blotter. And a prisoner property receipt. All signed on the night of June 28, 1970."

"My God, Amax. How did your friend get hold of these?"

"Olene is tight with one of the deputies who got wind that the sheriff was out to destroy some records having to do with an old arrest. When she heard it involved Gaylene Harjo, she kept her eyes open. Saw O Boy empty a file cabinet drawer into a box and take it to his office. When he was called away to an armed robbery, she went through the box, found this file and copied it. Then she replaced it in the box where she'd found it and brought these to me.

"Now, I've made the connection between the night she was in jail and the date you were born. Isn't too hard to figure what happened, is it?"

"You're thinking she was raped while she was in jail."

"And there's a good chance that whoever raped her is the same man who killed her."

"Let's not jump too far ahead, Amax. We ought to take this one step at a time."

"I've been taking those steps for so many damn years now, and I still haven't been able to clear my daddy's name. But this," he said, tapping his finger on the arrest report, "proves that O Boy is guilty of something. And I won't stop until I find out what it is."

"Can you blame him?" Mark asked. "All this time trying to prove his father's innocence, and now believing he's so close."

"I know," Hap said, "but Amax can't go running into O Boy's office waving these papers, accusing him of rape. There's always the possibility that what he's guilty of is covering up for someone else."

"Sure, but who?"

"I don't know. But you've got to consider this: Not all pregnancies last exactly nine months. She could have gotten pregnant a few days earlier or a few days later, which means that June twenty-eighth is not necessarily the day you were conceived.

"Secondly, even if she did get pregnant at the jail, it doesn't mean she was raped. As far as we know, she never reported an attack. So, it could have been consensual sex. After all, Rowena said Gaylene was drunk."

"But if it wasn't rape, or even consensual sex," Mark said, "then why would O Boy work so hard to cover it up?"

"I don't know. Yet."

Hap shuffled the papers in his hand and began to read aloud from the property receipt. "Brown plastic purse, two keys, comb, lipstick, billfold with nine dollars, seventy-four cents, fabric belt, senior ring, charm bracelet, pair of imitation pearl earrings.

"Everything was accounted for when she was released; she signed the receipt at ten forty-three."

"So that means she got back everything taken from her before she was put in a cell."

"Right. And if she . . ." Hap looked puzzled. "This doesn't make any sense," he said. "According to the arrest report, she was stopped on East Main at nine oh-seven p.m. for 'going left of center, then swerving onto the shoulder.'

"But this property receipt shows she was released at ten forty-three p.m. Now if she was so drunk she couldn't control the vehicle, how did she sober up in an hour and thirty-six minutes?"

"What are you getting at, Hap?"

"Someone got her out while she was still drunk. And

I doubt it was family. Didn't you say she made Rowena swear she would never tell anyone? Obviously Gaylene was trying to make sure the Harjos didn't find out."

"And it wasn't Rowena because she was drunk, too."

"So, who's the first person comes to mind?"

"Kyle Leander."

Kyle looked like a walking coma when he was led into the courtroom. Glassy-eyed, he stared straight ahead but appeared to see nothing. His head bobbed as if it were attached to his shoulders by springs, and he was so slack mouthed that a thin line of drool ran from his lower lip to his chin.

He had, Mark guessed, been given a fishbowl full of drugs from which he could choose his favorite colors.

He was wearing an orange jumpsuit several sizes too small and three inches too short, handcuffs and shackles, which caused him to walk stiff legged and heavy footed.

Even though Kyle was probably the one who bailed Gaylene out of jail when she was drunk, and although he might have been the one who got her pregnant that night, Mark couldn't help feeling sorry for him as he was paraded in front of the packed courtroom.

The arraignment lasted less than five minutes, so pat that the performers might have been reading from a script. The upshot was that Kyle was judged incompetent to understand the charges brought against him so was ordered by the judge to undergo thirty days of psychiatric examination at the Haven, the institution from which Kyle had recently taken a "break." Hap said he wouldn't be surprised if Kyle was put back in the same room he'd just escaped from.

When court was adjourned, Hap led Mark through the

judges' lounge so the media couldn't follow, then out the back door to his car, a 1988 Chrysler that looked like a Dumpster inside.

"How in hell am I going to get a chance to talk to Kyle?" Mark asked.

"I don't think you will. At least not here. They'll take him back to his cell until the hospital sends transportation for him. Between now and then, I'm certain he won't be allowed any visitors."

"Well, if Kyle is the one who got her out of jail that night and took her to Arthur's cabin, then—"

"Mark, do you know your blood type?"

"Sure. It's AB positive. Why?"

"Let's find out what Kyle's is. We might be able to determine whether or not he's your father."

"And how will we do that?"

"What are friends for?"

Hap parked outside the office of Drs. Westfall and Kenders, then suggested Mark come inside to wait.

"This might take a while, depending on how busy they are in there. And it's too hot for you to sit in the car. My air conditioner's gone kaput."

Inside the office, Mark took a seat in the patients' waiting area while Hap went to the counter, where a black woman slid open the window between them and shook Hap's hand.

"Hi, Happy," she said, a smile lighting up her face. "Haven't seen you in a month of Sundays."

"Barb, you're looking good."

She stood up, turned around and struck a model's pose. "Lost twenty-two pounds."

"I can tell. How's Henry?"

"He found every pound I lost." She laughed.

"And how about Rebecca?"

"Becca's making good grades, staying out of trouble. Since you got her out of that jam last winter, she's headed in the right direction. I can never repay you for that."

"Oh, you might be surprised."

"What can I do?"

"I need to talk to you for a few minutes, Barb. Privately, if that's possible."

"Sure, come on back."

Mark watched Hap go through a door that said PERSONNEL ONLY, then saw Barb close her window and disappear into an office behind her desk.

On the table beside him, Mark found copies of *Parenting*, *Healthy Living* and *Newsweek*, a March issue that he'd read months ago.

He picked up the copy of *Parenting* and read the lead article about the first six weeks of a newborn's life. Then, just as he'd started a true-life story of a mother who gave birth to triplets, an elderly couple came in. The man held the woman's hand and guided her to a seat.

"What time does the movie start, John?"

"Honey, you're here to see Dr. Kenders."

"Oh."

"You want your sweater on? It's cool in here."

"Maybe when the movie starts," she said.

The old man noticed Mark sitting near the corner and nodded, then helped his wife into her sweater, not easily accomplished. "There," he said. "Would you like to look at a magazine?"

"No, silly. The lights will go down soon. What time does the movie start?"

"You're here to see the doctor, Mildred."

Mark could remember such ramblings from his mother in the months before she stopped speaking entirely, but by that time, she was already in Ambassador Manor, an Alzheimer's care facility in Burbank.

He had gone to see her every morning, to feed her breakfast when she would eat, to clean up the mess when she wouldn't. But his visits had gradually diminished until, finally, he'd stopped going at all. He'd felt guilty, but not guilty enough to make himself sit beside her, making inane conversation that she neither understood nor responded to unless one of her less than human sounds could be considered a response. But now, watching the couple across the room, he felt the stab of regret.

When Barb returned to her seat behind the counter and reopened her window, she said, "Good morning, Mildred. John. How're you all doing today?"

"What time does the movie start?" Mildred asked.

"Let's get you in to see Dr. Kenders first."

"I'll take you to the movie this afternoon, Milly," John said.

When Mark stepped up to the counter, Barb smiled and said, "You're with Happy, aren't you."

"Yes."

"He'll be out in just a second."

"I wonder if you could sell me this?" Mark showed her the copy of *Parenting* he'd been reading.

"No, but I'll give it to you."

"I'd be glad to pay."

"Absolutely not," she said.

"You ready?" Hap asked as he joined Mark at the counter.

"Sure."

"Thanks again, Barb," Hap said.

"You and Matthew come to the house for dinner when you get hungry for my chicken and dumplings."

"Soon. Bye now."

When they neared the car, Hap said, "Kyle's blood type is O."

"And that means?"

"He's not your father."

"I brought you something today," Mark said, handing Ivy the *Parenting* magazine. "While I was waiting in the doctor's office for Hap, I read an interesting article about the bond that's formed between baby and mother during the first six weeks. Thought you might like to see it."

"Thanks," Ivy said. She leafed through the magazine for about thirty seconds, then tossed it on the kitchen table.

"When is your baby due?" Mark asked as he poured himself a cup of coffee.

"You know what I'm hungry for?" Ivy said as she opened the refrigerator door.

"Pickles," Mark guessed.

"No! I think that's an old wives' tale." She made a face. "The thought of a pickle makes me about half-sick. No, I want stuffed olives dipped in peanut butter."

"That's certainly one of my favorites. But you still haven't told me."

"Told you what?" Ivy asked.

"Your due date."

"Oh, it's another six, seven weeks," she said. "Here they are." She took a jar of olives from the door of the fridge, then went to the cabinet for peanut butter.

"Smooth," she read on the label. "Damn. Extra crunchy's the best."

"Have you picked out a name yet?"

"A name?"

"Yeah, for the baby."

"No. I don't know if it's a boy or a girl."

"Well, say it's a boy. How about Roger?"

"That sounds good." She dipped an olive into the peanut butter, then popped it into her mouth. "Um." She dipped another, held it out to Mark.

"No, I only eat mine with crunchy," he said.

"Purist."

"Stella if it's a girl?" Mark asked.

"I'll consider it. You want a cookie?"

"Huh-uh."

Ivy opened a box of ginger snaps and dipped one into the peanut butter.

"You think you and the baby will live here with your mom?"

"She put you up to this, didn't she."

"Up to what?"

"Giving me the third degree about this baby."

"No! Well, not exactly. I mean, I'm interested, too. Interested in knowing when your baby's coming, what you're going to name it and—"

"Where I'm going to raise it, how I'm going to afford it. Just a few casual questions, huh?"

"Sorry, Ivy, if I've gotten too personal."

"Mark, I'm going to level with you, but I hope you won't tell my mom. This news needs to come from me and me alone. I just haven't told her yet."

"Told her what?"

"I've decided to put the baby up for adoption."

April 30, 1969

Dear Diary,

I went out with Oscar tonight. We ate at the Dairy Queen, then went to the Plaza to see The Heart Is a Lonely Hunter. *It was really good. Made me cry.*

Oscar held my hand when we left the theatre and when he took me home, he kissed me once after we parked in front of my house, and again when he walked me to the door.

He's a good kisser.

Spider Woman

May 28, 1969

Dear Diary,

I got a summer job today working for Arthur McFadden at the radio station. I'll have an office right at the front of the building and my own desk. My job will be to answer the telephone, do all the typing and filing. Mr. McFadden, my boss, said if I do a good job, he might let me work at the station part-time after school starts next fall.

I met his stepson, Kyle Leander, while I was there. He's a lot older than I am, but he doesn't act like it. I've heard he's strange and takes drugs, but I don't know if that's true. Guess I'll find out though because I start tomorrow.

Spider Woman

Chapter Twenty-seven

Mark was already awake when he heard Teeve in the kitchen, but he stayed in bed, feeling some unnamed dread about the new day.

Soon he heard coffee brewing, smelled the bread baking and the sweet, rich aroma of vanilla, which made him think of Luz and her world-class flan that seemed to cure any illness, heal any wound.

He dozed again but roused when he heard Ivy's bare feet padding into the kitchen. Suddenly his dread had a name.

"Ivy!" Teeve said. "Honey, what are you doing up at this hour? Are you okay?"

"Got any peanut butter left?" Ivy asked.

"So you're the one who's been at the peanut butter. First it was mayonnaise, now—"

"I can't find the olives," Ivy said.

"Olives?"

"Here they are."

"What are you doing?"

"Eating breakfast."

"Olives and peanut butter? I can't even imagine the kind of appetite that child of yours is going to have. You know, when I was pregnant with you, I craved ketchup. Put it on eggs, peas, apples. Made ketchup sandwiches. Funny how pregnancy—"

"Mom, I got up early because I need to talk to you before you go to the pool hall."

"Good. I've been hoping you would."

"Yeah, I figured that's why you sicced Mark on me last night, trying to get information."

Mark cringed. Not so much at the conversation taking place in the next room as the fact that he was overhearing it.

"Well, Ivy, you haven't told me what your plans are."

"First of all, some of this stuff is just going to happen, Mom. This baby is coming with or without a plan."

"But what about later?" Teeve asked. "Are you and the baby going to stay here with me? You know I'd love that, but if you decide you want to have your own home, I understand. Kate Morey down at the end of the block, she's putting her house on the market, moving into one of those assisted living places. Now, Kate's house is nice. And reasonable, too. I could help you with the down payment."

"Mom, I won't be staying in DeClare. I'll be moving on. Probably head somewhere in the Northwest."

"Oh, honey, I was so hoping you two would stay here with me."

"You're not listening, Mom. I said *I'll* be moving on."

Teeve looked stumped. "I don't get it. You. You'll be moving on. What about the baby?"

Mark covered his head with his pillow, trying to block

out the conversation that was going to tear the two women apart.

"Mom, I know this is going to be hard for you to understand, and it's going to hurt you. So much. But . . . well . . ."

"Say it, Ivy."

"I've decided not to keep the baby."

"What does that mean?" Teeve asked, her voice taking on a different tone.

"I'm going to put the baby up for adoption."

Following a silence that seemed to last a lifetime, Teeve said, "I don't believe you," her voice brittle, thin. "You wouldn't do that. You couldn't."

"I can. I have to. Not for me, but for her."

"A girl? You've had an ultrasound?"

"No. But I know. Somehow I just know."

"A granddaughter." Teeve choked back a sob. "And you're going to give her away. Like a book you're not interested in reading. Or a plant you don't want to take care of. You're just going to give her away."

Mark heard Teeve sit heavily in a kitchen chair, could imagine her with her elbows on the table, her head in her hands, unable to hold back the tears.

"Mom, a child needs two parents, and in my case, since I'm not gay, that would mean a mother *and* a father. I can't be both."

"Of course you can. I was."

"You did a hell of a job of it, too. But I'm not you. You were able to manage me, a home, a business. I can't do that."

"Then stay here with me. You know I'll help."

"No, you raised one child. You don't need to raise another. That wouldn't be fair to you or to her."

"Ivy, you would be a wonderful mother."

"Mom, I've worked with kids being raised by one parent. Women and men worn down by lack of money and time. Never enough sleep, never enough energy. Going without health care, trying to make the rice and beans and milk last until payday. Their kids in day care, preschool, after-school centers because Mommy or Daddy works two jobs, takes classes at night, prays their car's transmission and tires will last until they get their tax refunds.

"It's a scary world, especially if you're trying to raise a child alone, but if you have a partner, someone to help you make the big decisions, someone to take over when you're too tired to fix supper, someone to take turns staying up with a sick baby, then the bad times must seem bearable."

"Ivy, you've never been scared of anything."

"You're wrong. I was scared when Navy left us. Scared when I'd see you cry, scared whenever someone came to the door at night, scared when you'd have to leave me alone for the time it took you to go to the drugstore for my cough syrup or antibiotics or—"

"But Ivy, there's no guarantee that the people who take . . . take your baby—" Teeve's voice was broken by weeping.

"No, I get to have a say in who adopts her. I've been to the Chosen Child Agency in Tulsa. I can choose the adoptive parents. I can find a couple who can give my baby the kinds of advantages I can't. Education. Travel. She'll know music and art.

"She'll have the luxury of being a child who won't have to face the humiliation of signing up for free lunches, who won't be made fun of because she doesn't

wear the right kind of clothes, who will never have to
bring her friends home to the low-income housing where
she and her mother live."

"Ivy," Teeve said, "I've always believed there are very
few decisions we make that can ruin our lives. But giving
up your child is one of them. It will be a mistake you'll
regret for the rest of your life. And there's no going
back."

After Mark turned the burner off under the eggs, he
poured batter onto the waffle maker and switched on the
coffeepot. He set the kitchen table for two, adding bright
green place mats, matching napkins and a vase of zinnias
he'd picked from Teeve's garden.

Then he went as quietly as he could down the hallway
to Ivy's closed bedroom door, where he heard her crying.
He started back to the kitchen, trying not to make any
noise, but the rubber tip from his crutch made a
squealing sound against the hardwood floor.

"What are you doing out there, Mark?" Ivy asked.

"How do you know it's not your mom?"

"She left for the pool hall a half hour ago."

"Oh."

"Don't you have anything better to do than stand out
there listening to me blowing my nose?"

"Thought you might like to join me for breakfast."

"I've already had breakfast," she said.

"Yeah. Olives and peanut butter."

"What've you got?"

"Waffles and scrambled eggs."

"I'm not hungry."

"Okay." Mark returned to the kitchen, took up the
eggs and the waffles—golden brown now—arranged

them on two plates and placed them on the table along with two glasses of milk.

He'd just sat down and poured syrup on his waffle when Ivy came in and sat opposite him.

"Looks like you were pretty sure I'd take you up on your offer," she said.

"No, but I hoped you would."

At first, they ate in silence. Finally Ivy said, "I guess you heard everything earlier this morning."

"Afraid so."

"I really hurt my mother."

"Probably."

More silence.

"What about you?" Mark asked.

"Me?"

"You're hurting, too. More than your mom, I suspect."

Ivy stared at him as she began to cry again.

"I'm sorry, Ivy. I didn't mean to say anything that would make this worse for you."

"Then don't be nice to me. Don't feel sorry for me, don't fix me breakfast, don't try to make me feel better. I don't deserve it."

"Okay." Mark grabbed her plate, picked up his own and took them to the sink.

"Hey, I wasn't finished with that."

"Yes, you were. Your nose just dripped into your waffle."

Ivy reached into her blouse pocket, pulled out a tissue and wiped her nose.

"Now, you stay right there," Mark said. "I've got something to show you."

He left Ivy snuffling at the table, went to the den and returned with a small duffel bag. He sat down and began to remove items from the bag, lining them up on the table, one at a time. He took out a blue bootie, Gaylene's diary, some photographs, a tube of lipstick, a key chain, some dried goldenrod and a senior ring.

"Where did you get all this stuff?" Ivy asked.

"From Kyle. Rowena. Enid."

"Why are you showing me these?"

"Because they're all, in one way or another, connected to my mother. But they're just things." Mark stared at Ivy, unblinking. "Do you know what that means?"

Ivy shook her head.

"It's all I have of my mother. Pictures, some old flowers, a ring. But no memories. I have no memory of her. Not one memory of the woman who gave me life. I'm never going to remember her reading to me or kissing me good night; I'm never going to recall her teaching me to swim or giving me my first bike. I will never recollect a birthday cake she baked for me, or her warning about looking both ways before crossing the street, or telling me not to run with scissors."

"But you're not in my situation. You don't know—"

"Ivy, I don't know if your decision is right or wrong. That's not for me to say."

"Mark, you were adopted, and even though your folks weren't as warm and loving as they could have been, they gave you a safe life."

"Safe?" Mark was thoughtful for a few moments. "Ivy, I never felt like I fit in. Had no idea why, but I suppose it was my personality. I've always been insecure, but I covered it by being obnoxious. Tried to make everyone think I was superior.

"But something was not quite right. When I asked

where I got my dark skin or my black hair, the answer was my grandfather who died before I was born. Any pictures of him? Any pictures of me as a baby? No, they were conveniently destroyed in a house fire. Where did I get this scar on my head? Easy answer. I fell down some steps when I first started to walk.

"Was I damaged by any of that? Yes, I think so. In a very subtle way. I developed some vague disapproval of who I was because I didn't look or behave like my parents. At times, I just didn't feel like I belonged.

"Maybe that's why I failed at so much."

"Failed. You haven't failed. You have a successful career, your own clinic. You own—"

"Yes, but it's not what I thought it would be. I became a vet because I love animals, wanted to relieve their suffering, help them live more comfortably. Or die without pain. I suppose I saw myself as a rescuer.

"But what I've ended up doing is cosmetic surgery. Scrotum tucks on aging dogs, breast reductions on cats that were allowed to deliver too many litters. I've performed a nose job on a poodle because the owner thought her precious 'Pearl' felt self-conscious about her appearance. I've done penile implants on animals more interested in sleep than breeding and eye jobs on Pekingese so they wouldn't look so Asian."

"That seems so wrong."

"It was. It is."

"Then why do you do it?"

"Because of my father. It was his clinic; he called the shots. And I was still trying to please him. Guess I still am."

"But there's more to what you do than implants and nose jobs."

"Oh, now and then I get to save a pet that's been hit by a car or has a kinked bowel or tumor. And sometimes I put down an animal that's in misery. But mostly I'm a plastic surgeon to the pets of Beverly Hills, owned by people about as real as paper flowers.

"But Ivy, you're the most real person I've ever known. And I think your child would be so lucky to have you for a mom. For sure, she'd have more than this." Mark gestured to the objects he'd placed on the table.

"And she'd never have to say, 'I have no memory of my mother. Not one memory of the woman who gave me birth.'"

July 8, 1969

Dear Diary,

Oscar came over this evening to tell me good-bye because today he joined the Marines. He had to get his mother out of jail last night because she was arrested on a public drunk charge. He said he's had enough.

I wish he had finished school first, but he said he had to get away and the military was the only way he knew how. I just hope he doesn't get sent to Vietnam. Lots of American boys are getting killed over there.

Spider Woman

Chapter Twenty-eight

After Ivy left for a doctor's appointment, Mark put the dishes in the dishwasher, rinsed out the coffeepot and wiped off the stove and cabinet, all the while thinking about her, about what he'd said to her. He felt uncomfortable at some of the comments he'd made, felt like a pretender to wisdom he didn't have. After all, who could know better what she should do than Ivy herself?

When he started repacking the duffel bag, he looked at the photos again, then picked up the ring, Gaylene's senior ring. He studied the design, the stone, the facsimile of her high school and the year, 1970.

Then something occurred to him, something he should have picked up on earlier.

Kyle said he'd taken Gaylene to Arthur's cabin only once, the day of her high school graduation.

But if Kyle had told the truth, Gaylene had been at the cabin with someone else, because according to her diary, she and her classmates didn't receive their senior rings until *after* their graduation, sometime in May.

He grabbed Gaylene's diary and began to leaf through pages until he found the entry of May 15, 1970.

Dear Diary,

Today I graduated which, I think, makes me an adult. Funny though, I still feel like a kid. Mom and Daddy got me a record player in a case with a handle. It looks like a suitcase when it's closed. I'll take it with me when I leave for college. (I can hardly wait.) Row gave me "Ticket to Ride" by The Carpenters and Kyle got me a Mickey Mouse watch.

After school, Kyle took me out to Arthur's cabin by the river to go swimming. The cabin's real creepy, animal heads on the walls. Kyle got high and wanted us to go in the river naked, but I wouldn't. I put on my bathing suit and told him if he didn't wear his underwear, I wasn't going to go in, so he did.

I tried not to look at him, but I peeked twice. He has skinny legs and a lot of hair on his chest and his low belly, real low on his belly. When he got out of the water with his wet underwear, I could see the outline of his thing.

If Daddy found out I went out there with Kyle, he'd kill me. But I had fun.

Spider Woman

Mark read the rest of the entries, mostly mundane accounts of school and work at the radio station. And though he'd read them before, they took on new meaning now. In one, dated May 14, Gaylene wrote about Arthur giving her a raise and bragging about her work, which made Mark wonder why she was fired a short time later for being "lazy," "totally without ambition" and "not particularly bright," as Arthur had claimed.

Then, the May 23, 1970, account confirmed what Mark remembered about the ring.

Dear Diary,

Row and I went to the high school this morning to pick up our class rings which finally came in. A week after we graduated. If the company hadn't screwed them up last fall, we could have worn them almost our entire senior year.

Mine has a sapphire, my birth stone, and I love it. I'm never going to take it off.

Spider Woman

Curious now, Mark shuffled back through the photographs Rowena had given him until he found the picture of Gaylene in her Hungry Hawk uniform.

It was taken on the Fourth of July. And she was not wearing the ring she vowed never to take off.

Lantana Mitchell handled the Porsche like she'd driven the Grand Prix. She'd lost the satellite truck five blocks from Teeve's and outraced the TV van before she reached the city limits. And she hadn't slowed down since.

After Mark had phoned, explained to her what he needed, she'd taken over. An hour later, when they were on the road, he'd asked a couple of questions about how they would manage this charade. She'd smiled. Clearly charades was a game she enjoyed.

Finally she'd told him to relax, assured him she'd "checked things out" and there would be no problem.

Making the decision to call her had come about through a process of elimination. He couldn't ask Ivy to drive him after their go-round this morning, and Teeve was far too upset to be dealing with him. He thought about asking Hap, but he seemed to be a pretty much go-by-the-book guy, so Mark finally settled on Lantana. He figured she was just shrewd enough to pull this off.

She'd already programmed the global positioning system for their destination, the Haven, so rarely had to check the locator screen on the dash.

"Neat car," Mark said.

"What do you drive?"

"I'm in a rental."

"No, I mean in L.A."

"Jaguar," he said, remembering their earlier conversation. "Convertible." His embarrassment showed.

"Hey, Mark. You live in Beverly Hills. What else *would* you drive? A bondoed Chevy four-by-four?"

She had talked very little at first, but when she did, he could tell she was excited about being involved in this "caper," as she called it. He supposed the word, for her, conjured up risk, danger. Something outside law and order. And if he had to guess, she wasn't much of a law-and-order woman.

She lit a cigarette with a slender gold lighter, with "Love from D.L." engraved on its side. After a right turn at a junction where she ran a stop sign, she glanced at the GPS screen and said, "Ten more miles, give or take a tenth."

"I'm curious," Mark said. "Have you been in your room the past couple of days waiting for me to call?"

"Now, sugar, don't get me wrong here. You're important to this story, of course, but you're not the only one. For instance, I've spent a good deal of time with Lige Haney. You know who he is?"

"He's the blind journalist works for the local paper."

"Yeah, he's blind all right, but he sees more of what goes on in DeClare than most people who *can* see."

"Did he have anything interesting to tell you? Something you didn't already know?"

"He sure did."

"Care to share with me?"

"No," she said, her tone making clear that her response was one she didn't intend to elaborate on. "But we'll talk about it in a day or two. When I'm ready.

"For now, you need to do the talking. Tell me what you hope to learn from Kyle Leander."

By the time Mark filled her in on the senior ring saga and why he needed to connect with Kyle, they'd arrived at the Haven, a three-story brick building constructed in southern plantation style—broad porch, thick columns.

"All right," Lantana said when she parked in the back of the visitors' lot. She opened the trunk, got out an aluminum walker and a pair of hospital scrubs. "Put these on." She handed him the clothes, which caused him to glance around for a place to change. "Come on, Mark. Modesty is the second most overrated virtue in the world."

"What's first?"

"Honesty."

After he was dressed, she draped a lightweight shawl around his shoulders, put his crutch in the trunk and handed him the walker.

"Follow me," she ordered.

She led him away from the parking lot and into a heavily wooded area, where they dodged wasps and stepped lightly for fear of snakes. When they emerged, they were at the back of the hospital in a magnificent park, the grass so soft and green it looked like a carpet.

A white granite statue of a ten-foot-tall angel stood in the middle of a lake. Glorious flower beds were broken up here and there by wrought-iron benches, water installations and topiary in the shapes of penguins, giraffes, elephants and bear cubs.

Several patients, identifiable by their scrubs, which were identical to the ones Mark was wearing, wandered the garden or sat on the benches, some accompanied by staff—those dressed in white—and a few obviously in the company of family.

As Mark started down one of the sidewalks, Lantana was at his elbow, whispering instructions. "Shuffle, Mark. Let your shoulders droop a bit. Look vulnerable."

"Hell, I *am* vulnerable."

"Then quit hiding it. Stop and turn to me occasionally as if you're in need of reassurance."

Mark took another ten steps, then turned to Lantana. "Please reassure me that they're not going to strap me into a straitjacket and toss me in a padded room here."

"They won't! Well, they *probably* won't. Do you see him?"

"No."

"He should be out here. I called to see what time he would 'take the sun.' They said between one and two."

"There he is. Sitting on the other side of the lake, the bench left of the giraffe."

"Okay. Take your time. The worst thing you can do here is act like you have a purpose."

"You sure know a lot about this place."

Mark leaned heavily on the walker and kept his head down until they passed a woman having a rambling conversation with God.

"You know, Lord, that I shouldn't be here, but my daughter, the little bitch, had my water shut off and killed my cat, so I'm asking you to strike her dead, but make it look like an accident. Lord, at bingo tonight, call B-seven, my lucky number. I can win a trip to Hawaii, first class. They serve strawberry daiquiris in first class, the best damn daiquiris you've ever tasted, Lord. Oh, one more thing . . ."

Mark locked eyes with Lantana, who whispered, "See what can happen?"

Finally they reached the bench where Kyle was sitting, apparently asleep—eyes closed, chin on his chest, mouth open.

"Kyle. It's me, Nicky Jack," he said, expecting little, if any, response or recognition.

But Kyle opened his eyes, jerked upright and hugged him. "Dude. You're in here, too. Cool!"

"No, I'm here to see you."

"That is just too awesome." Kyle seemed overjoyed. "How's your leg?"

"Fine."

"Nicky Jack, you know I didn't do that. I've never

even held a gun. Well, only once, but that was for a robbery and it wasn't loaded."

"That's not why I'm here."

"Who's the pretty lady?" Kyle asked.

"Friend of mine. Lantana Mitchell."

"Hi," she said. "I was around here in 1972, but I believe you were away."

"Drying out?"

"Yes, I think that's what I heard."

"Well, take it from me. It's not all it's cracked up to be."

Mark said, "Kyle, I've got some questions I'd like to run by you if you feel up to it."

"Aw, man, I feel great. Go ahead."

"Okay. Why did Arthur fire Gaylene at the radio station?"

"Fire her? He didn't fire her. She quit."

"Do you know why?"

"She said there was no particular reason, she just wanted to do something else that summer before she went off to college. But I don't know. She didn't make as much at the Hungry Hawk as she got paid at the station. Finally, though, it didn't really matter, did it." Kyle's eyes filled with tears.

"Were you surprised when she left?"

"If I'd been there, maybe I could've talked her out of leaving. 'Course, that was just selfishness on my part, 'cause when she was there, I could see her every day." He smiled. "Every day." He turned serious then. "It happened while Arthur had me stashed away again."

"Kyle, you're doing fine. Feel like one more question?"

"Sure, Nicky Jack. For you, anything."

Mark explained that he'd learned from reading Gaylene's diary that the seniors did not receive their rings until *after* graduation owing to some screwup by the company. As a result, she couldn't have lost it at the cabin when Kyle took her there on May 15, because she didn't get her ring until May 23.

Kyle seemed unable to comprehend what he'd just heard. He cocked his head to one side, ran his hand over his beard and squinted as his eyes searched the sky.

"Kyle?" Mark said, hoping to bring him back to earth. "Do you understand the situation I just described?"

"Nicky Jack, I found her ring under a cushion of the couch in the cabin. Nearly two years after she was killed."

"Then maybe, I mean . . . well, there's a chance she went to the cabin another time. Sometime later. With someone else."

"No! She wouldn't do that, she didn't even like it there."

"Kyle, what if she didn't want to go, but someone didn't give her a choice?"

"You mean, like *forced* her to go?"

"Yeah, maybe."

"Who would do that?"

"That's what I was hoping you could tell me."

"No one ever went to the cabin unless Arthur invited them. He had the only key."

"Then where did you get yours?"

"I swiped it from his key ring the day I took Gaylene out there, but he never found out. I put it back soon's I got to town."

"So, do you think Arthur took her to the cabin?" Mark asked.

"Arthur? Why would he?"

"Kyle, there's a good chance Gaylene got pregnant that night."

"What? I don't understand why you'd say that."

"Because I was born nine months later."

"Arthur? No! No! Gaylene would never have had sex with him. Not with Arthur. She wouldn't have!"

"*Not* if she had a choice," Mark said.

"No, man! That's not right."

"Maybe it's not, Kyle. But Gaylene did go to jail on the twenty-eighth of June. DUI. And someone did pick her up just an hour or so later, while she was still drunk."

"Was it Arthur?"

"I can't be sure, but whoever it was probably took her to his cabin."

"Oh, God. He raped her, didn't he. And she couldn't do anything about it. No one was there to help her. Oh, God."

Kyle began to rock back and forth on the bench, his arms wrapped around him like he was trying to hold himself together.

"You know why I couldn't help her?" Kyle said. "Because Arthur, that bastard, had sent me away again. Had me locked up. But if I'd been here with her . . ."

Kyle started to wail, making loud, high-pitched sounds like an animal in pain.

Lantana scooted in beside him, put her arm around his shoulder and made soothing sounds, but he was beyond anything anyone could do for him as he struck out at her, one of his elbows jabbing her face just beneath her right eye. Totally out of control.

As two men in white rushed him, Kyle broke away, made a wobbly dash for the trees. But he never got there.

After a clumsy struggle, they subdued him and dragged him, still screaming, toward the building.

Lantana got them down the road in a hurry until she stopped at a service station, where she washed up and got some ice on an eye that was swelling and turning darker by the minute. She had a tear in her panty hose just beneath her knee, where an ugly bruise was spreading.

"You okay?" Mark asked as she slid back beneath the wheel.

"Probably a little worse than I look."

"Lantana, I'm sorry I got you into that."

"You couldn't have known how he was going to react."

They were quiet for a while on the way back to town. Lantana tried conversation a few times but was met with silence as Mark, his head turned toward the window, watched the scenery fly by without seeing any of it.

Finally, as they reached the edge of DeClare, Mark said, "Kyle's right. Arthur did it. He got Gaylene out of jail while she was still drunk, took her out to his cabin and raped her."

Chapter Twenty-nine

Arthur McFadden, pacing in his office with a cell phone at his ear, a cigar in his mouth, didn't realize Mark had entered the radio station and was watching him from the doorway.

"Yes, I understand that," Arthur said into the mouthpiece, then, with his free hand, rubbed at the bridge of his nose as he listened to the voice on the line.

Now, with the realization that this man could be his father, Mark saw him in a very different way from the two previous times they'd come face-to-face. Every feature, every gesture, every movement, took on new meaning.

Arthur was tall; at his prime he'd probably been six two or three, about Mark's height. And he was terribly thin, a characteristic Mark might have attributed to the old man's health or age—except for the framed photos he'd seen on the walls of the cabin. Arthur had always been slender. So had Mark.

The only facial feature Mark thought similar to his own was Arthur's chin, square with a bold jawline. Other than that, Mark believed himself to favor Gaylene Harjo more than Arthur McFadden, a comforting feeling.

Arthur walked with his left shoulder higher than his right, just as Mark did, and both men had a tendency to drag their feet a bit with their steps.

But Mark knew, without a doubt, that he could find many similarities between himself and most men if he looked hard enough. And the characteristics he'd identified in Arthur that were much like his own certainly didn't indicate that this was the man who had fathered him.

When Arthur finally noticed Mark standing in the doorway, he said, "I'll have to call you back. Someone's here."

As soon as he snapped the cell phone closed, and even before he acknowledged Mark's presence, he got his jacket from a coat-rack in the corner of the room and put it on as if he were preparing for a business meeting.

"That was the head of security at the Haven," Arthur said. "I've spoken to him twice and to the nursing supervisor once. You and your lady friend caused quite a stir out there this afternoon."

"Yes, I suppose we did."

"In our last conversation, our *only* conversation, I asked you to leave Kyle alone. I thought I had thoroughly explained his reaction to seeing you, which was a disaster. But apparently you didn't listen, or else you went there with the purpose of agitating him. In either case, the outcome is the same."

"Exactly what does that mean?"

"Kyle has been removed from the general population of the hospital."

"Meaning a padded cell," Mark said.

"You, and you alone, Mr. Harjo, or whatever you call yourself, are responsible for making his recovery so much more difficult than it needs to be. As a result, he's sedated and under constant watch."

"Kyle's always sedated, isn't he?"

"Today's circumstances were markedly different. He tried to end his life."

The statement hit Mark hard, but he worked at not losing his focus, remembering that he was talking to a man who was a liar, probably a rapist, perhaps a killer.

"I don't believe I'll accept the responsibility for that, Mr. McFadden. Why don't you add that to *your* list of credits."

"I think before you say anything more," Arthur said, "you should know that I've already spoken to my attorney, Paul Perkins. As Kyle's guardian, I am filing legal action against you on his behalf, for harassment and mental anguish."

"I'm curious. Did the nursing supervisor tell you why I went to see Kyle?"

"I doubt the 'why' of it has any merit."

"Then I don't suppose you know that I went to the hospital to ask Kyle about Gaylene Harjo's arrest for DUI on June 28, 1970."

Arthur's response was silent but palpable. His skin glistened with a sheen of perspiration, his breathing accelerated and his upper body slumped, just slightly, such a subtle gesture that it was barely discernible. When he made his way to the chair behind his desk, he took a monogrammed handkerchief from the inside pocket of his jacket and dabbed at his forehead.

"I don't see how that concerns Kyle or me."

"Oh, I believe you do. I know that Gaylene was jailed

for driving drunk, but she didn't stay behind bars very long because O Boy Daniels called you to pick her up and take her home."

"Why would *I* take her home? She worked for me, but that was it. I never took her to dinner, never took her on a business trip. Never bought her a birthday present. And I *never* took her home."

"But you took her to bed, didn't you."

"No, of course not!"

"I have proof that you picked her up at the jail."

After hesitating just a moment too long, Arthur shrugged. "Okay. Say I did. She didn't want her parents to see her drunk, made me swear I'd never let them know, then asked me to drive her to Rowena Whitekiller's."

"And you did. But not before you drove her to your cabin, where you raped her."

Arthur took a deep, steady breath, made a quick switch from defense to offense, then said, "Mr. Harjo, in addition to the charges I'm filing on behalf of Kyle, I will be charging you with defamation of character. Mine."

"Oh, I wouldn't want to damage your character."

"You know, I don't believe, have never believed, that you are Gaylene Harjo's son. I think he was murdered at the same time his mother was."

"Then why am I here?"

"Two reasons come to mind. The first: blackmail. I suspect you stumbled onto what happened here in 1972. You did some research, found out who the major players were and how they fit into the events that took place here and figured you could pull this off. Easy pickings, you thought, because you're a con man and because you're about the right age. You assumed your threat to expose me as the bad guy who got sweet little Gaylene Harjo pregnant would induce me to hand over a substantial amount of money.

"Well, wake up, genius. We're about to enter the twenty-first century. No one gives a damn anymore about a girl who screwed half the men in town and got knocked up by one of them."

Mark could feel his rage building, wanted more than anything to put his fist through Arthur's mouth, feel teeth splintering, a jaw cracking, a tongue gushing blood. But he held himself back, knowing the relief of hurting Arthur would come later. He just had no idea that he wouldn't be the one to inflict the pain.

"Who would care? My ex-wife? No. The hicks who listen to my station? Why, they'd love it. A hint of Jerry Springer right here in DeClare, Oklahoma. And a scandal would ultimately result in increased advertising revenue."

"All publicity is good publicity, huh?" Mark said.

"So I've heard."

"And the second reason?" Mark asked. "You said you could think of at least two reasons for my coming here. The first was blackmail. I'm waiting for you to tell me about reason number two."

"If," Arthur said, "and I repeat *if*, you could prove what you have alleged—"

"Which wouldn't be that much of a stretch since I was born nine months after you raped Gaylene."

"Then you could lay claim to being my son."

"And how would I profit from that?"

"You would be my next of kin, the only child of a single man without living parents, my only sibling a half-brother. Oliver. When I die, you would be in a position to inherit my entire estate."

"What estate? A two-bit radio station? Or maybe you own a collection of *Reader's Digest Condensed Books*? Would I also inherit your phony accent? Or perhaps I'd get Kyle."

"Oh, that would be a nice payback, wouldn't it? Yes, I rather like that notion."

"Do you like it enough to submit to a DNA test to determine paternity?"

Arthur found enough humor in the question that he actually smiled.

"You know," Mark said, "it's possible to have the test performed even without your consent."

"Well, let's say you do that. And let's say the test reveals that Gaylene and I fathered a child. You. Nick Harjo. Then here's a scenario you should perhaps consider.

"I picked her up at jail, took her to the cabin, we had a couple of drinks. We screwed, had a good time, and as a result, she had a baby. I don't think that's a crime. I believe that's called consensual sex.

"Now, let's consider another scenario. The one you came up with. I picked her up, took her to the cabin and raped her. Problem is, I could never be charged with that crime. The statute of limitations has expired."

"You bastard."

"That, I believe, would best describe you, Mr. Harjo." Arthur, with a smug grin, leaned back in his chair. "Of course, there could be one other reason you came here to confront me with these allegations."

"What would that be?"

"After all this time, you've suddenly decided you

want to know your daddy, your papa. Your loving father. Well, I hate to disappoint you, but all you've gotten for yourself so far is unsubstantiated evidence, some unreliable theories and just a little more truth than you were prepared to handle.

"Now, get your slimy ass out of my office. Son!"

Lantana, who'd driven Mark from the Haven to the radio station, was sitting in the front office, the space that served as a waiting room. She was using a four-year-old edition of *Radio Journal* as a prop to create the impression that she hadn't moved from her chair since she and Mark had arrived. In truth, she'd been on the prowl all over the building and even managed to eavesdrop just outside Arthur's door for a good part of the conversation between the two men.

When she heard Mark coming down the hall, she could tell from the sound of his crutch hammering the floor that he was furious.

"You okay?" she asked as he passed her without a word, going for the front door.

Outside, she had to hustle to keep up with him, a man on a crutch, followed by a woman wearing a ridiculously high pair of heels.

After they got in the car, she started the engine, turned on the air conditioner and said, "You want to talk about it?"

"No."

"Okay. What do you want to do?"

He stared straight ahead, curling his hands into fists.

"Huh-uh," she said. "Don't even think about punching my dash. That would make two lawsuits filed against you. One by Arthur, and one by me."

"You were listening?"

"Of course. Didn't you expect me to?"

"No. Yeah, I suppose. I don't know."

"So, is the DNA test on or not?"

Suddenly, his anger spent, he turned to look at her. "God, I forgot. The ashtray was right there on his desk and I forgot. I just wasn't thinking."

"I was." She pulled a plastic bag from her purse. Inside was a cigar stub.

"Where did you get that?"

"In the control room while you two were dancing around one another at the beginning of the bout, like two boxers, each eager to throw the first punch."

She took a second plastic bag from her purse and a rubber glove. After she put it on, she opened the bag and took out a swab.

"Open your mouth," she said.

He did; she ran the swab along his inner cheek, then dropped the swab in the bag and sealed it.

"Where did you get this stuff?"

"A DNA kit."

"What happens now?"

"I take this to Tulsa, to a lab where I have a special friend. He'll begin testing today." She glanced at her watch. "I'd better call him so he'll wait for me. Then, with the right kind of luck, we should have the results by tomorrow."

"Then let's go to Tulsa."

"You don't want me to drop you off somewhere?"

"Nope."

Neither spoke until they were on the Broken Arrow Expressway to Tulsa, but once they hit the four-lane, Lantana said, "Mark, you remember when we were at the Haven today and you said I seemed to know my way around?"

"Did I say that?"

"I spent some time in a psychiatric hospital much like the one Kyle was in. But now, after seeing where he was, I suppose they're all pretty much the same. People with invisible damage go in; people with invisible cures come out. Sometimes."

"Lantana, are you sure this is something you want to tell me?"

"It's okay. It has to do with what happened here a lifetime ago. My lifetime.

"I got mixed up with O Boy Daniels. I was a girl, twenty-one that winter. Now, don't get me wrong, I was no virgin, but I didn't really know much about men. Not much about sex, either, but I thought I did.

"Anyway, I slept with O Boy to get what I wanted— the story. Unfortunately, I also got what I didn't want— a pregnancy."

"Did he know?"

"Yeah. I needed money for an abortion, so I went to him, asked him to help me."

"Let me guess," Mark said.

"The son of a bitch laughed at me. Flipped me some coins, told me to buy a bottle of quinine. Said that would fix my problem.

"Long story short: I took two hundred dollars to a door marked 'Private' in the back room of a resale shop. Got my abortion, along with a perforated uterus, hemorrhage, peritonitis and septicemia. I think my 'specialist' used a rusted corkscrew."

"Lantana. I'm sorry."

"P.S. Eight months later I had to have a hysterectomy.

Twenty-one years old. No kids for this gal. None. Nada. Never."

With that, she pressed her foot down on the gas pedal, watching the needle on the Porsche's speedometer race toward a hundred.

That night, just after eleven, Mark crawled into the bed Ivy had vacated for him.

He and Lantana had gone to dinner in Tulsa after they left Future Diagnostics, the lab where Lantana's "friend," Harold Madrid, worked as a geneticist. He had explained that his lab work was not certified, which would have required a signed consent form by the alleged father.

But Mark didn't care if it was certified or not. He just wanted an answer. Just one definitive answer.

By the time he and Lantana had returned to DeClare and she dropped him off at Teeve's, Ivy was asleep on the Hide-A-Bed and Teeve was snoring behind her closed bedroom door.

Just as Mark was reaching to turn off the lamp beside the bed, he heard a phone ring once, answered, he supposed, by Ivy in the den. A minute later, she came to his open door wearing what she'd worn the night they'd met—a Sierra Club T-shirt and cotton underpants. The only difference was that the shirt was tighter across her belly now and the underpants didn't bag as much as they had ten days ago.

"Mark." Something in her voice told him bad news was on the way. "That was Hap on the phone. Kyle Leander just killed Arthur McFadden."

September 8, 1969

Dear Diary,

Mrs. Dobbins, my art teacher, is encouraging me to devote more time to my sketch book, so I've promised myself to draw every day no matter how busy I am. Sometimes, when there's nothing to do at the radio station, I work on my drawings.

Becky Allan quit the basketball team today. When she turned her suit in to Coach Dougless, she told her she's too busy to play this year because she's a senior, but the real reason is she's pregnant. Everyone in school knows, I guess, because Danny told it just before he dumped her.

Spider Woman

Chapter Thirty

If the folks of DeClare thought they'd had enough of the deployment of the media's forward units after word of Nick Harjo surfaced, then they were certainly ill prepared for the battalion that infiltrated town after Arthur McFadden's murder.

An hour after the shooting, both sides of the street leading to Arthur's condo were bumper to bumper with satellite trucks, vans and SUVs, all bearing logos of radio and TV stations as well as newspapers from cities and small towns.

The entrance to the grounds was closed, crime scene tape stretched between two granite towers topped with carriage lamps. Several of the TV stations had already set up with lights and cameras trained on the reporters being filmed, a guard pacing behind them.

The only other way to get into the Lakewood Garden Estates was to scale the six-foot rock fence surrounding the condos or know the Turtle Creek Road that ran half a mile away and would require a dark walk through rattlesnake-infested rock gullies and ridges.

Even so, the area was alive with the residents, a few fearless souls who'd walked from Turtle Creek Road and several young people who'd scaled the wall. They were all milling around Arthur's condo, which was also cordoned off by yellow police tape.

When O Boy drove up to the gate, the guard lifted the yellow crime tape so the cruiser could drive beneath it, and even though O Boy had already investigated the crime scene, viewed the body and set up the crime units, he roared from the gate to Arthur's place as if the killing had just been called in.

O Boy knew the technicians had finished dusting for fingerprints, the photographers had finished taking their shots and others in the units had collected fibers, hair and suspicious particles. Still, he drove like a fireman trying to save children from a blaze.

Mark wasn't quite sure why he was riding in the front seat beside O Boy. He was clearly not a suspect in the murder, as Kyle had called the sheriff's office to report the shooting minutes after Arthur died. And Kyle was waiting when the first deputies arrived and ordered him outside, their guns trained on him as he followed their instructions, walked across the narrow porch and down the steps with his fingers interlocked behind his head. When he reached the ground, he spread-eagled himself on the lawn as the younger deputy demanded; then, with their guns aimed at his head, they approached him and the young one forced his knee into Kyle's back. As he clamped the handcuffs on, the flesh was torn on Kyle's wrist, so that blood ran down his fingers and onto the cheap leather as he was placed into the back of the cruiser.

But Mark hadn't seen any of this. He had just heard about Arthur's death when O Boy and a deputy pulled into Teeve's drive, siren wailing, lights flashing, O Boy telling Mark to come with him.

On the drive to Lakewood Garden, the radio crackled with static, but Mark could occasionally hear a woman's voice, causing him to wonder if the dispatcher was Olene Turner, Amax Dawson's old flame.

The overpowering odor of stale cigar smoke that met Mark at the door of Arthur's condo gave him a sour taste at the back of his throat. But it was going to become worse.

The living room was comfortable looking. Not much clutter. Yesterday's paper folded carefully, recent mail stacked orderly, ashtrays emptied and wiped clean.

The kitchen, open to the living room, was small, compact, neat. Bright blue canisters, a dish towel hanging from a hook, a washed coffee cup turned upside down in the dish drainer.

But as he passed down the hallway from the living room to the bedroom, Mark's dread began to build. He followed O Boy past the bathroom—lights on, towels folded neatly on a shelf, shaving equipment lined up near the sink. The room smelled of scented soap.

But as he approached the next doorway, the smell of soap gave way to another smell, a familiar odor Mark had encountered many times in surgery after he'd cut into a dog's abdomen to take out a ruptured spleen, or sliced into a cat to remove a cancerous tumor, or amputated the legs of an old and beloved pet whose hindquarters had been crushed beneath the wheels of a car.

Blood. The smell of warm blood.

Mark had known, of course, that O Boy was taking him to the place where the killing had occurred, but he had certainly *not* expected to see the body.

Apparently Arthur, wearing pajamas, had been in bed when Kyle walked in; the covers of the bed had been disturbed, and a small TV was still on. But the shots that killed Arthur had not come as he was sleeping, had not come from a shotgun at the back of his head. He had not enjoyed the luxury of a quick death, that one final instant of knowing. Then not knowing.

No, that would have been too easy, too swift, to satisfy Kyle.

Having lived a life of sweet compassion, a sometimes drug-induced sense of love for his fellow creatures, Kyle couldn't stand to see suffering. If a fly was struck but not killed by the slap of a swatter, if a wasp was living in agony from the poison of a fogger, Kyle would give them the gift of death.

But that was not his intention when he killed Arthur. No, from the looks of the scene, Arthur had been in bed watching TV when Kyle came into the room with the shotgun. He had then, most likely, confronted Arthur with what he'd learned about Gaylene's ride from jail, a ride that detoured by the cabin and led to her rape and humiliation.

Arthur, certain by then that Kyle was going to pull the trigger, had jumped out of bed to wrestle for the weapon. But he was too late.

Kyle, who'd never handled a shotgun before, fired one round into Arthur's belly. A shot that tore open his flesh, freed his intestines from their confinement of skin, muscle and bone, causing him to cradle his guts in his arms as he slipped off the bed, onto the floor, more or less sitting up, his back resting against the mattress.

Finally, perhaps because Kyle had said all he had come to say, or because of his compassion, he found he couldn't watch Arthur suffer anymore, so he'd ended it

with another blast, this one to Arthur's head, a shot that
had blown away most of his face.

After Mark had retched for the second time, he went to
a hose connected to a faucet at the side of the condo,
washed his face, doused his head, then drank deeply.

"You gonna puke again?" O Boy yelled from across
the yard, where he was leaning against the door of his
patrol car, smoking a cigar from a box of Roi-Tan he'd
found in Arthur's bedside table.

"You finished with me yet?" Mark asked, making sure
to stay upwind of the cigar smoke.

"Hell, no. I want to hear the rest of this fucking story
of yours. It's just now getting good. Let's see. You
hooked up with Lantana Mitchell, then she drove you to
the nuthouse, where you got Kyle all riled up about
Arthur slipping Gaylene a bit of the old sausage. Then
you came back to town, went to the radio station and confronted Arthur, accusing him of raping Gaylene."

O Boy spit, took another drag on the cigar. "How am I
doing so far, Nicky Jack? I got all the facts straight here?"

Mark said nothing.

"Now, let's assume that Arthur and Gaylene played a
little in and out, whether she wanted to or not. Either way,
if he was your daddy, you just got him killed. Now, tell
me something. How does that make you feel?"

Mark choked back the bile he tasted at the back of his
throat, fighting not to throw up again, which was exactly
what O Boy was going for.

"What I can't understand is why. You came here, so
you said, to find your mama, but you discovered she was
dead. Then you went to a hell of a lot of trouble to find

out who your daddy is. But once you thought you'd figured it out, you set him up to die."

"I didn't set up a goddamn thing, and you know it,"
Mark said. "Kyle was locked in that hospital, under
guard. How could I know he'd get loose, kill Arthur? And
by the way, how did Kyle get out?"

"That's my job to find out. Not yours. But let's get
back to the business of Arthur picking Gaylene up at the
jail just so we'll be clear on that. In case you didn't know
it, he was doing her a favor; and so was I. She was drunk
out of her mind when I stopped her on the highway.
Wonder she didn't kill somebody. So I had the car towed,
gave Rowena a ride home and took Gaylene to jail.

"But a few cups of coffee and an hour or so later, she
had the jailer call me back to her cell. She was still in bad
shape, but aware enough to know she was in trouble. She
cried, said if her folks found out, it would kill them.

"Well, I couldn't see much to be gained by holding her
over for arraignment, charging her with DUI. She'd never
been in trouble before, so when she asked me to call
Arthur, see if he'd pick her up, take her to Rowena's, I
said sure. Why not? She worked for him, and I figured he
wouldn't mind helping the kid out. He showed up fifteen,
twenty minutes later and we let her go with him.

"If anything happened between the two of them after
they left the jail, I never heard about it. But Gaylene had
a problem keeping her drawers pulled up, so it's not
beyond reason. He might've been porking her all along.
'Course, you probably don't want to hear that, you being
so bound and determined to prove she was your mama.
Now, anything else you want to know?"

"Yeah. I want to know who killed her. And I don't buy
that Joe Dawson story. Not for a minute."

"Oh, is that right? Well, Mr. Detective," O Boy said, "I would certainly be happy to deputize you, put you on the case, but unfortunately that case was closed. Almost thirty years ago. Joe Dawson killed Gaylene Harjo," he said. "End of story."

"No, not quite the end."

"Really? Then where do we go next?"

"How about California," Mark said.

"What the hell you talking about?"

"If Dawson killed her, then how did I get to California? Who took me? Who arranged for my adoption?"

"I wouldn't know a thing about that."

"No, I don't suppose you would, since you accused Joe Dawson of not one, but two killings. You even had most of the people around here believing he buried me someplace on his own land."

"And how many believe *you*? Huh?" O Boy asked. "How many believe you're really Nick Harjo and not just a fucking punk trying to get some publicity that might earn you some big bucks for one of them TV movies? Or maybe a book."

"It was a woman who showed up at the lawyer's office in Los Angeles," Mark said. "She had a baby in her arms and my birth certificate in her purse. Said her name was Gaylene Harjo. But that would have been quite a trick, wouldn't it, since my mother was already dead right here in DeClare."

O Boy pushed away from the patrol car, crushed the cigar beneath his boot and stomped across the narrow strip of grass that separated Arthur's condo from the one next to it, the area where two of his deputies were studying their shoe tops.

"You boys don't have no goddamn work to do? No

reports to file? No follow-ups to those burglaries? If not, then maybe you better be thinking about applying for unemployment 'cause your county paychecks might not be coming in next month."

The deputies got into a vehicle and created an exit from the condo that would have made a good scene in a bad movie.

"You got any proof of what you just said about some woman claiming to be Gaylene?"

"I do."

"Then you best tell me what you know or I'll charge you with withholding evidence."

"How could I withhold evidence in a case that was closed thirty years ago?"

"Listen here, you son of a bitch, you don't know what you're getting yourself into."

"It's a little late for you to be threatening me, Sheriff Daniels. Way too late. Because I'm already into it."

O Boy said, "And you think I'm not? That's my brother in there."

Mark reached Teeve's after two, but even at that late hour, he'd had to shoulder his way past the crowd gathered in front of her house. All but a couple of reporters could tell he was not in the mood to chat, but finally even the two of them backed off when they sensed he was furious, confused and exhausted.

O Boy had driven away from Arthur's condo alone, leaving Mark to walk, but he'd hitched a ride with a couple returning home from a late night of bingo at the VFW.

Ivy, who'd been waiting up, ran to the back door when she heard him knock, yanked him inside and into her embrace.

"Are you okay?" she asked.

"No. I'm not okay."

"Here, sit down."

She pulled out a chair for him at the kitchen table.

"Can I fix you something to eat?" she asked. "We have some split pea soup or some leftover meat loaf and—"

Before she finished her list of possibilities, Mark was heading for the bathroom with the dry heaves.

When he returned to the table, Ivy had fixed him a cup of hot tea, but he pushed it away.

"Where did O Boy take you?" Ivy asked. "I went to the courthouse, even made them take me down to the jail. Thought they might be hiding you, but—"

"Jail? No, that would have seemed like a luxury spa compared to what I saw. He took me to Arthur's condo."

"Oh, my God. You mean you saw . . ."

"You don't want to know what I saw. Trust me. It was horrible. Kyle must have been out of his head. And I caused it, Ivy. If I hadn't gone to see Kyle today, hadn't planted the idea in his head that Arthur was the one who got Gaylene pregnant . . ."

"You can't take responsibility for that. You couldn't have known what Kyle was going to do."

"But here's the thing. I don't even know if it's true that Arthur got her pregnant. For all I know, it could have been O Boy, one of the deputies, a boyfriend, a stranger from the bar."

"You can't let guilt kick your ass, Mark."

"Listen, I know you want to help, but I don't really feel like talking about this tonight. I'm beat."

"Sure you are."

"I'd like to take a shower, then try to get a few hours' sleep."

"Okay," Ivy said. "But if you need anything in the night, what's left of it, don't hesitate to call me. I'm a pretty light sleeper."

Mark stayed in the shower as long as he could stand it, trying not to let the scene from Arthur's bedroom replay in his head. Every time a fragment of that picture nudged its way into his thoughts, he'd turn the water hotter until, when he finally stepped out of the stall, his skin was more red than brown.

In the bedroom, Ivy was waiting for him with a glass of warm milk.

"Thought you might need this," she said.

"Thanks." He took a sip, then put the glass on the dresser. After he got in bed, Ivy switched off the table lamp and started for the door.

"Ivy?"

"Yes?"

"Stay with me tonight. Please."

Without a word, she crawled in beside him, where he wrapped her in his arms, buried his face in her neck and whispered her name.

January 6, 1970

Dear Diary,

We had a big surprise today. My brother Navy came home to stay. And guess what he brought with him? A wife named Teeve and a baby girl they call Ivy. Mom didn't even know Navy was married, much less that he had a daughter.

Aunt Teeve is nice, too. She's real pretty and perky. She reminds me of Julie Andrews except she doesn't have an English accent.

They're staying with us until they can find a place of their own, but I hope they stay for a long time even if I do have to sleep on the couch. They put Ivy's crib here in the living room so when she wakes up at night, when she's afraid or cold or hungry or wet, I'm the first one she sees.

Spider Woman

February 27, 1970

Dear Diary,

I scored thirty-four points tonight in our game against Catoosa. Coach said there were two scouts in the bleachers who'd come to watch me play. I'm pretty sure I'm going to get a basketball scholarship so I can go to college.

I haven't told Mom and Daddy, but I'm going to major in art. Mom wants me to get a degree in education so I can get a teaching job here in DeClare. Daddy wants me to study accounting at a junior college so I can finish in two years.

But I'm not going to be an accountant or a teacher, and I'm not going to stay in DeClare. That's for sure!

Spider Woman

Chapter Thirty-one

Teeve was still awake when Mark came in, even though she'd been in bed for hours. She thought about getting up, but when she heard Ivy meet him at the back door, she decided to stay in bed. She couldn't think of one thing she could say to Mark to make him feel better, because she felt so bad herself. All her empathy and compassion had seemed to evaporate along with the dreams of her grandchild.

When she finally crawled out of bed at six, she felt more tired than when she'd crawled in last night. She pulled on her bathrobe, thinking of all she should take care of today, making a mental list that would erase itself before she got out the door.

In the past two days, she'd failed to make her bank deposit; bought groceries, but left them forgotten in the trunk of her car, spoiling three pounds of sliced turkey, three pounds of ham and half a dozen heads of lettuce.

She'd lost her set of keys to the pool hall; given ten dollars too much change to one of her customers; slammed her thumb in the door of the fridge, causing her thumbnail to turn black; and dropped a tray of twenty tea glasses, breaking every one. But the biggest change, according to the domino boys, was that she'd gone strangely quiet.

Lonnie, the lone Republican in the foursome, could always get a rise out of Teeve, a devout Democrat, by repeating some half-assed opinion he'd heard Rush Limbaugh make on the radio. Lonnie was one of those know-it-all do-nothing Republicans who didn't know the issues, didn't contribute money or time to the party, didn't put campaign signs in his yard. He didn't even vote.

All he did was offer up Rush propaganda. Once Teeve had bought him a bumper sticker that said MY DOGMA CAN WHIP YOUR DOGMA, but the joke was wasted on Lonnie, who didn't know the meaning of "dogma."

But Lonnie wasn't on Teeve's mind as she padded into the kitchen, dreading the chores she faced this morning: putting together her salad spreads, getting cookies in the oven and making her famous peanut-butter pies.

Before she turned on the kitchen light and started up the mixer, the blender and the meat grinder, she slipped back quietly to Ivy's bedroom to close the door, hoping the racket in the kitchen wouldn't wake Mark. He obviously needed his sleep.

At first, as she glanced toward the bed, she couldn't make out for sure what she was seeing—in part because of the dark hour of the morning, but mostly because of the incongruity of what she *thought* she saw. It looked like *two* people were sharing the bed.

Teeve switched on a small night lamp in the hall to get a better look. And that's when she discovered her daughter in bed with Nicky Jack Harjo, both sleeping soundly.

He was spooned in right behind Ivy, her head resting on one arm, the other draped across her waist, his hand settled protectively on her swollen belly.

Teeve gave herself a moment to take it all in, but she wasn't about to second-guess what was going on. Whatever it was, she felt good about it. And as she backed silently away, turning off the light as she went, her heart felt lighter.

When she stepped into her kitchen, she decided to hell with chicken salad, pimento cheese and those damn peanut-butter pies. The world would just have to get along without them today.

In her bedroom, she dressed quickly, went to the bathroom to brush her teeth, skipped makeup and ran her fingers through her hair.

She was going out to breakfast.

At nine, the doorbell rang, but Ivy and Mark slept on, didn't even flinch. After Lantana Mitchell tried the bell again, Mark reshifted one leg, the only sign that his sleep had registered a sound. Lantana tried knocking but got no better results, so she worked her way around Teeve's house, peering into windows when she could. In one, she saw Mark and a woman in a bed, still and motionless. Her first thought, after all that had happened in the past few hours, was that they were dead.

At the edge of panic, she pounded on the glass with her shoe until Mark finally roused, slipped his arms slowly and gently from around Ivy, then climbed out of bed in his briefs and motioned Lantana toward the patio door.

"Morning," he said as he led her inside.

"Sorry to wake you," Lantana whispered.

"We had a late night," Mark said, still groggy from sleep.

"Yeah, I heard about Arthur."

Ivy, finally brought around by the conversation, got up and wandered into the den.

"Lantana, this is my cousin, Ivy Harjo."

Ivy, not at all concerned that her T-shirt and underpants revealed her nearly full-term pregnancy, said, "Well, we're not quite cousins. I mean, not in the strictest sense."

"Hi. Glad to meet you," Lantana said, trying to seem uncurious by the encounter. "Looks like congratulations are in order."

"Oh, you mean the baby. Thanks. But Mark's not the father."

"Well, not in the strictest sense," he said, drawing a most puzzled look from Ivy.

"I see," Lantana said, though she didn't see at all.

"Why don't we fix you a cup of coffee," Ivy suggested, readjusting her underwear.

"No!" Then, less insistently, she added, "No, thank you. I can't stay. I came by for a couple of reasons, but then I have to run. Mark, I've set up an appointment with you to meet Lige Haney today. You might remember my mentioning him to you yesterday. He has some information I believe you'd be interested in hearing."

"Sure. I'd like to talk to him."

"He'll be expecting you at his home at eleven this morning. Can you make it?"

"I'll be there."

"Here's his address. Now," she said, the change in her

tone noticeable, "this was faxed to me at the motel ten minutes ago."

Lantana offered Mark a business-size manila envelope. "I think Harold worked on this all night."

Mark and Lantana locked eyes while the envelope changed hands. He knew what was inside, so he studied her face for some clue as to what the DNA test had revealed, but her expression remained unchanged.

He removed several sheets of paper from the envelope, shuffled through some graphs, several studies and a cover letter, which he tried to read but couldn't because his hands were trembling so that the text wouldn't hold still.

"I, uh, I'm not sure that . . ." He was at a loss. "Maybe you should . . ."

"It means there's a 99.9 percent chance that Arthur McFadden was your father."

Mark wiped his mouth with the back of his hand, then sat on the couch as if he suddenly found himself too weak to stand.

"Arthur McFadden," he said.

Ivy scooted in beside him, took his hand and held it inside both of hers.

"I really don't know what to say to you, Mark," Lantana said. "'Sorry' doesn't seem appropriate somehow."

"You don't know what to say? Well, let me tell you, I don't know what to feel."

While Ivy took a shower and washed her hair, Mark dressed, started coffee, poured orange juice and put bread in the toaster.

When she came back to the kitchen, dressed in slacks

and a loose cotton blouse, Mark said, "You were awfully kind to stay with me, Ivy."

"Hope you slept well," she said.

"Very well."

Ivy smiled, leaned over and kissed him on the lips, a kiss that started as a sweet gesture, a casual kiss between casual friends. But it changed when he took her head in his hands, her wet hair curling around his fingers, and the kiss became something more. Much more.

When they parted, he said, "I kissed my cousin that way once."

"Mark . . ."

"Don't say anything, Ivy. Please. Not yet. Just know that I care for you. And your baby."

The woman who answered the door couldn't have weighed ninety pounds. She was totally bald but wore her head uncovered; had an infinity of wrinkles carved gently into her face; and her coloring ran somewhere between overripe cucumber flesh and stale cottage cheese.

Mark didn't have to be told this woman was fighting a tough battle against a nasty opponent: cancer.

Still, she was lovely. She had deep-set brown eyes that looked as rich and strong as polished walnut; her full, unpainted lips held the tint of pale raspberries; and her delicate bone structure emphasized high cheeks and an Audrey Hepburn chin.

"Hello," she said as she offered a warm, firm hand-shake. "I'm Clara, Lige's friend, lover and wife, pretty much in that order, but I'm working hard to put lover in the number one position."

"I appreciate your letting me come by today, Mrs. Haney."

"We've been anxious to meet you. Please. Come in."

Mark followed her down a short hallway, where she whispered, "Lige is probably asleep, but when I wake him, he'll say he was just resting his eyes, which is kind of funny when you think about it."

The room they entered had more books than it was built for, even though bookcases, from floor to ceiling, covered three walls. The books that wouldn't fit in the filled cases were stacked on the floor, the coffee table, the mantel, and in large baskets scattered here and there.

"Lige," Clara said to the small man sleeping in the over-stuffed chintz chair, "our guest has arrived."

"Of course he has," Lige said, straightening. "I heard him at the front door."

"Oh, I thought you might be sleeping."

"No, no. Just resting my eyes. Glad to meet you, Mr. Harjo," he said, offering a hand.

"Please, just call me Mark."

"I'm not surprised that you use the name you've been accustomed to for so many years. New realities need time to take root, don't they," Lige said. "Sit down over there, Mark, where I can see you."

"Thank you, sir."

"Lige. Just plain old Lige and Clara. And this is Phantom."

At hearing her name, Phantom rose from beside Lige's chair, waiting patiently for a command.

"We have company, Phantom," Lige said. "Where are your manners?"

The dog wandered over to Mark, sat on her haunches

and offered a paw, which Mark shook. "How do you do, Phantom," he said.

Her duty complete, Phantom returned to her "spot" and reclined again by Lige's side.

Lige still had most of his hair, silver and as shiny as Christmas tree icicles; his sightless eyes were covered by dark glasses; and he wore a mustache and goatee, which Mark guessed were tended by Clara.

"You know, Mark," Clara said, "you're our number one celebrity around here."

"Certainly seems that way sometimes. Can't say I enjoy it, though."

"I noticed when I let you in that you'd been followed by several vehicles."

"Yes, I have an entourage wherever I go now."

"May I get you some coffee?" Clara asked.

"Please don't go to any trouble for me."

"Actually, we enjoy a cup every morning about this time. We like it with just a hint of Irish cream in it. Quite a lovely drink. Join us."

"All right. I think I will."

"Wonderful."

When Clara left the room, Lige smiled and began to recite softly, almost to himself.

Be with me, darling, early and late. Smash glasses—
I will study wry music for your sake.
For should your hands drop white and empty
All the toys of the world would break.

"That's beautiful," Mark said. "Did you write it?"

"No, but how I wish I had. John Frederick Nims. The title is 'Love Poem.' So, Nick, we haven't had such goings-on in DeClare since you were taken from us. And now, you walk out of our past and into our lives once again."

Clara, returning with a tray holding three mugs and a plate of brownies, said, "Lige, dear, this handsome young man has asked us to call him Mark."

"Oh, did I slip up?"

"No problem," Mark said.

Clara handed Lige a mug, then placed the tray atop a pile of books in braille on the coffee table. "Help yourself, Mark. I should tell you that I added a pinch or two of pot to the brownies, a trend I missed in the sixties, so I'm just now catching up."

Mark took a mug of coffee, sipped at it, then realized it was a cup of cream liqueur with perhaps a couple of tablespoons of coffee added.

Lige held his mug aloft, waited for Clara and Mark to heft theirs, then said, "'*The Joy that isn't shared, I've heard, dies young.*' Here's to you, Anne Sexton."

"Lige can't eat, drink or go to the john without quoting poetry," Clara said. "Well, I think I'll retire to my room to do some reading and let you two take care of your business." She wrapped two of the "spiced" brownies in a napkin, grabbed her coffee mug and started for the door. "If I don't see you before you leave today, Mark, I hope I'll see you tomorrow."

"Thank you," Mark said, standing. After she'd gone, he added, "She's a lovely woman."

"Yes. She is."

The room was quiet for such a long moment that Phantom raised her head to check things out.

Finally, to break the awkward stillness, Mark said,

"Lantana Mitchell told me you might have some information that would be important to me."

"Yes, perhaps I do." Lige reached to a table beside his chair and picked up a newspaper, yellowed with age. "This is an article I wrote in 1972. It was to be a three-part feature story about Kippy Daniels. I imagine you know something of his background, don't you?"

"A bit. Teeve and Ivy have filled me in on some of his history. I know that his mother went to school with him almost every day from first through twelfth grade."

"And so much more. She did so much more for that boy. She made him a Boy Scout, she even became a den mother. She helped him with his 4-H projects; taught him to ride a horse; to make change. She took him to dance classes; gave him art lessons.

"In other words, she made him a world he could fit into. A world that would accept him. And he was accepted by almost everyone but his own father. I think O Boy has always been ashamed of Kippy, a resentment he takes out on Carrie. But apparently that's a trade-off she has accepted. Decided she'd rather take her lumps from O Boy than live without her son."

"What do you mean," Mark asked, "live without him?"

"It's no secret that when Oliver found out about the boy's impairment, he wanted to put the child in a home. I guess he all but beat Carrie to death when she refused. But refuse she did. And the boy flourished because of her and her alone.

"Anyway, just before this, the first in the series of articles to be published, Hap Duchamp set up the Kippy Daniels Trust Fund at the bank, Hap's bank then. You see, Kippy needed surgery. He had a congenital heart disease that goes hand in hand with Down syndrome children.

"Without the surgery, Kippy wasn't going to make it, but the operation was expensive. Of course, Carrie didn't have any money. And O Boy was a deputy, making just enough to get by; Carrie was taking in ironing, cleaning houses, baking and delivering pies and cakes. She worked here for Clara once a week. She'd do any kind of work she could get as long as it was after school or on weekends because she spent Monday through Friday in class with Kippy.

"So Hap and Clara and I came up with the idea of the fund, and Hap kicked it off by contributing ten thousand dollars."

"Wow."

"Oh, Hap's the best kind of man. Decent, generous, kind. He's gay, you know, but if we had more men like Hap Duchamp, this would be a better world."

"So how much money was raised?"

"None. The day the article came out, I got a visit from O Boy. He was enraged. Out of control. Said I'd better not print another word about his 'geek kid.' That's what he called Kippy, his 'geek kid.'

"Threatened to sue me, the newspaper, the bank and the city. Implied physical threats as well. Said he didn't need charity and Kippy didn't need surgery. Blamed the whole 'mess' on Carrie, then went home and beat hell out of her."

"So what about Kippy's surgery?"

"Here's the strange thing about that. A few weeks after O Boy's blowup, Carrie called Clara, told her she wouldn't be able to clean for her the next week or do her ironing. Said she and Kippy were going to Arkansas to see her daddy. Carrie's parents were divorced, had been for a number of years, but Carrie had hinted that her father was well-off.

"Well, she left, came back a few days later and took Kippy to Tulsa for his heart surgery. I heard she paid the doctor and the hospital in cash.

"Any idea where she got the money?"

"I had assumed she got it from her father in Arkansas. But later I learned something weird. Very weird."

"Weird? In what way?"

"Clara and I went to a little town, Beebe, Arkansas, to visit an old friend who taught at a college there. Found out while we were there that Carrie's dad had died in 1969."

"So she lied about going to see her father. And the money for the surgery?"

"I don't know where it came from. But she paid for Kippy's surgery five days after Gaylene was murdered."

April 2, 1970

Dear Diary,

I'm about to finish my painting of the two faces of the Indian woman. I don't know yet what I'm going to call it, but I think I'll give it to Mr. Duchamp.

I went to lunch today with Kyle Leander. We had fried chicken at the Hen House. I know Kyle is doing drugs again. I can tell. And he's only been out of rehab for about a month this time.

I've been thinking that after I finish college, I should live in New York City. It's a place where artists have a good chance to show their work. When I asked Row if she'd go with me, she said she and Junior Warner might get married when school's out. Well, if that happens, I'll go to New York by myself. I'm not afraid. Not at all. But when Oscar gets out of the Marines, maybe he'll come to New York, too.

Spider Woman

Chapter Thirty-two

Mark arrived at the bait shop in the middle of the afternoon, which turned out to be a good time since there was only one couple, a middle-aged man and woman, buying a few dozen minnows, some hooks and soft drinks. When Carrie saw Mark come in, she turned to her work, obviously not thrilled to see him.

As soon as the couple left, she started mopping up the floor where water had sloshed over the side of the minnow bucket.

"How're you doing, Carrie?" Mark asked.

"Thought I asked you not to come back. Told you your coming here caused me problems. Either you didn't hear me or you don't care if I get in trouble."

"I'll try not to take up too much of your time."

"It's not my time I'm worried about, but I'd appreciate it if you'd clear out of here before O Boy comes driving up."

"At this hour of the day? I figured he'd be in his office or—"

"You can never tell with him when he'll show up.

Sometimes it's four in the morning; other times, like now. So I wish you'd just leave before—"

"Kippy had some serious surgery when he was a kid, didn't he?"

"Yeah," Carrie said, her suspicion already set in motion. "Why? Why do you want to know about that?"

"I heard it was pretty damn expensive."

"So?"

"Carrie, would you mind if I asked you where you got the money?"

"Yes, I'd mind. That's none of your business."

"You told Lige and Clara Haney you went to Arkansas to visit your dad. They thought you got the money from him, but as it turned out, your father had been dead since 1969. So I'm wondering why you told that story."

"I don't know what you're talking about."

"I think you do. And I think I know what happened."

"Do you? Then you must be pretty darned smart. Or maybe you just think you're smart."

"I believe O Boy killed Gaylene, then sent you to California with me for a prearranged adoption that would pay you twenty thousand dollars."

"Right," Carrie said with a wry smile. "I can just see O Boy handing over that kind of money to a hospital. You don't know him very well, do you."

"No. But if Kippy were my son—"

"Well, he's not, so don't try to second-guess what you'd do if he was yours because there's no way for you to know what it's like to raise a son like Kippy who has a father like O Boy."

"Then why don't you tell me."

"I'm not telling you nothing. Now, I've got work to do." Carrie lifted a case of cigarettes from the floor to the counter and began stocking the rack behind the register.

Mark said, "If I could just ask one more question—"

"You can't. So you might as well take off. I don't have nothing more to say to you."

"Afternoon, Kippy," Mark called out as he skirted the edge of the pond to where Kippy was fishing.

"Hey, know what I caught? Come see."

Kippy dropped his pole and pulled his fish basket from the water to show off three good-size perch.

"Good catch!" Mark said.

"I lost one. A catfish, I think. 'Bout this long." Kippy held his arms as far apart as they would reach. "He put up a damn good fight."

"I'll bet he did."

"You gonna fish?"

"No, not today."

"Then . . . I can't remember your name."

"Joe," Mark said.

"Then why did you come to the pond, Joe?"

"I wanted to talk to you."

"Okay, but if that catfish comes back, I can't listen to you 'cause he'll be putting up a damn good fight."

"Kippy, do you remember a baby boy who lived close to you when you were little? His name was Nicky Jack. Nicky Jack Harjo."

Kippy's face lit up. "He was my best friend. Him and his mama lived across the creek, back of us. I used to go over and see him. Sometimes his mama would let me watch her give him a bath or let me hold him while he took his bottle. And sometimes, when it was raining, she'd read us *The Cat in the Hat*. Do you know *The Cat in the Hat*?"

Mark smiled and said, "I sure do."

"I loved *The Cat in the Hat*. So did Nicky Jack. He was too little to talk, but he always laughed when his mama read that story."

"Do you know where Nicky Jack is now?"

"Me and my mama took him to the land of milk and honey. Or honey and milk. I can't remember."

"Where is the land of milk and honey?" Mark asked.

"I don't know, but my mama said it's a place like heaven."

"It is, Kippy," Carrie said. "Just like heaven." She'd come over the fence and through the weeds without making a sound.

"Mama. Joe knows *The Cat in the Hat*."

"That's nice."

"And look what I caught." Kippy showed her the perch in his basket. "I lost a catfish 'bout this long," he said, giving his arms another good stretch. "He put up a damn good fight."

"He must've been awfully strong."

"What're you doing here, Mama? You gonna fish?"

"No, I came to get you. It's almost time for supper."

"We having something I like?"

"Sure are. Weenies with ketchup, macaroni and cheese and green beans."

"Yay," Kippy said.

"You go on to the house and wash up while I talk to Joe for a few minutes."

"Okay. Bye, Joe. Next time it rains will you come over and read *The Cat in the Hat* to me?"

"I'll try, Kippy. I'll sure try."

Carrie and Mark watched until Kippy topped the hill, carrying his fishing pole and basket of perch. After he disappeared, she said, "I've had so many good years with him." She sat in the soft mud at the edge of the pond. "Wouldn't have had many more, though. Actually, he outlived his time. Most Down syndrome adults don't live much past thirty."

Mark sat down beside her as she looked across the pond, staring at nothing—something only she could see.

"Kippy went over to the trailer one day," she said. "Gaylene was asleep back in the bedroom, but you weren't. You were in your playpen in the living room. Kippy decided to take you to the creek and give you a bath, the way he'd watched Gaylene bathe you at the kitchen sink.

"So he took off all your clothes and all his, then waded in with you in his arms. But the water was cold and you started to cry. That's when Gaylene, crazy with fear after discovering you were gone, found the two of you naked in the creek.

"You were screaming and Gaylene was screaming and Kippy was so scared, he started screaming, too.

"When I heard the commotion, I run to the creek, found the three of you there, sent Kippy home and tried to talk to Gaylene. She seemed sure that Kippy had done something bad to you, something besides dunking you in cold water, but I talked to her, tried to explain that Kippy only wanted to give you a bath. Did my best to settle her down.

"Finally, she said she believed me, promised not to tell anyone, but I wasn't sure, so I followed her back to the trailer, still hoping to convince her not to talk about what had happened. I knew if she ever told anybody, the word would get out that Kippy was dangerous and they'd take him away from me. Put him in a home for the rest of his life."

Carrie began to shiver though the temperature was close to a hundred.

"She promised she wouldn't say anything, but I couldn't take the chance. Couldn't let them take away my boy.

"I don't remember picking up the knife. Honestly, I don't. Don't remember stabbing her. But when I got home, I had blood in my hair, on my clothes, on my hands. And on you."

"On me?"

"I'd brought you home with me."

"Why?"

"I don't know. I didn't have a plan. I just knew I couldn't leave you there. Not with her like that. Besides, I didn't know how long before someone would find you. There could have been a fire, or . . ."

When Carrie stopped talking, Mark said, "You don't have to go on with this if you don't want to."

"So there I was," she said, "holding a terrified baby, both of us covered in your mother's blood. I got in the shower with you in my arms. I couldn't let Kippy see us like that.

"Then I remembered a story I'd read in the *Enquirer* about people in California, rich people who were willing to pay a lot of money to adopt children.

"I still had that magazine, so I called and got the number of the attorney in the story and I phoned his office, pretending to be Gaylene Harjo. Three days later I was on a plane with you, a plane to L.A.

"When I got back to DeClare, I found out Oliver had blamed the murder on Joe Dawson." Carrie brushed away a tear with the back of her hand. "So I used the adoption money for Kippy's heart surgery."

"Did O Boy know you'd killed Gaylene?"

"Yeah. He knew. I kept you at our house until I took you to California. I didn't tell him about the money until after Kippy's operation, though, 'cause I knew Oliver would take it away from me."

"Carrie, did O Boy kill Joe Dawson?"

"We never talked about it, but I think he did. He's a mean bastard."

"He beats you, doesn't he."

Carrie glanced at Mark, then looked away. "But not Kippy. Not once."

"Why did you stay with him? Why did you take that kind of abuse?"

"Each time he'd say he was sorry, say he was gonna change. And I believed him, at least for the first few years. By then, I knew if I left, he'd kill me and put Kippy in a home. So I stayed."

"But didn't you ever think about—"

"Oliver had so much hurt in him. He had to deal with it somehow, I guess, and taking it out on me was the most easiest way."

"What kind of hurt?"

"His mother. She was pure evil. You wouldn't believe the things she did to Oliver and Arthur."

When Carrie started to cry, Mark took her hand.

"I know this won't mean anything to you," she said, "but I'm sorry about Gaylene. Not a day goes by that I don't feel bad about what I did to her. And to you. But I couldn't never let them take Kippy away from me. I'd never let that happen."

April 11, 1970

Diary,
   Oscar Horsechief was killed yesterday in Vietnam.

Chapter Thirty-three

When Carrie left Mark on the bank of the pond, he was sitting with his knees raised, his arms wrapped around them, his hands locked in a death grip as if he were trying to hold his body together.

For a while he sought comfort in watching fat, dark clouds drifting overhead. But when he began to see disturbing shapes in them—a knife held by a delicate hand, blood splattered onto a windowpane, a girl's face, her features twisted with fear—he closed his eyes, hoping for total blackness behind his lids as he fought the scenes beginning to play in his head.

For the past week, ever since he'd been to the newspaper office where he read accounts of the murder, read about the wounds on his mother's body, he'd hidden the details. Zipped them up in a mental body bag he'd resolved never to open, never to look at what was held inside.

But now, with Carrie's confession darting around in his mind, sharp images had pierced the body bag, its contents beginning to spill out.

He saw Gaylene running from the creek, cradling a wet, naked baby shivering in her arms.

When she reached the trailer, she dried, diapered and dressed him in soft blue pajamas with yellow ducks as she calmed him with a sweet, reassuring voice, telling him he was all right, safe now with her, because she would die before she let anything bad happen to him.

Then she carried him to the kitchen, where she put his bottle on to warm. While she waited, she kissed his head, his chubby hands, his face, as she rocked him gently from side to side.

She turned toward the door as Carrie, wild-eyed and panting, opened it and came inside, her voice quivering as she explained once again that Kippy had not meant to harm Nicky Jack, that he only wanted to bathe him in the creek.

In response, Gaylene had offered reassurance, promised again never to speak of what had happened.

Then Carrie, obviously relieved, had reached for the baby, but Gaylene stepped back, tightened her hold on her child, a protective move that Carrie interpreted as an ominous act.

As Gaylene turned and took the baby's bottle from the pan warming on the stove, she didn't see Carrie pick up the paring knife from the kitchen counter, didn't see the first thrust, but felt the pain as the sharp blade pierced her shoulder.

She let the bottle slip from her hand, heard it smash on the floor, saw her blood splatter against the kitchen window and spray the door of the refrigerator.

At first, she couldn't comprehend what was happening. She'd seen enough movies to know that people got stabbed at night as a storm raged. She knew what was about to take place when a gust of wind blew the flame from candles or when a room was illuminated by a flash of lightning. And she was well aware that when a frightened woman crept down dark basement stairs, the music would swell as the camera moved in for a close-up of a man in the shadows waiting at the bottom.

But such a thing could not happen on a clear, sunny day, not with Momma Dog barking outside at a treed squirrel or with the faint whistle of a freight train passing through town. And certainly nothing dire could take place in the kitchen of her trailer with her baby boy in her arms.

When she saw Carrie lift the knife again, she put out her hand to shield the baby, causing the steel blade to cut away the tip of her little finger. But Carrie's next lunge came too hard and too fast for Gaylene to deflect it, the wound too deep in the side of her neck for her to fight off another blow.

Knowing then that she was going to the floor, she sank to her knees, then slipped forward, making sure to keep the baby beneath her as the final strike of the knife buried the blade in her back, just beneath her ribs.

Mark opened his eyes then but made no effort to hold back his tears. He simply allowed himself to cry, knowing it was finally time to weep for his mother, the girl who had wanted to be an artist.

He had come to this place in Oklahoma to find the mother who had let him go, the mother who had not loved him enough to keep him.

Instead, he'd found the girl who had given up her dreams, but not her baby.

Chapter Thirty-four

Later that day, when Mark arrived back at Teeve's, he started to pack his things in a cardboard box he'd found in the garage. When he put his box in the rental car, he noticed both the front and back floorboards were littered with empty Twinkies packages and bottles of Chocolate Soldier. The big surprise for him was that he didn't even care, a sign that Ivy was rubbing off on him. In more ways than one.

"Honey," Teeve said, "are you sure I can't fix you something to eat? At least make you a sack lunch to take with you on the plane?"

"No, Teeve. They'll feed me, but thanks anyway."

"Any laundry you want done?"

"No, I guess I'm all set to go. I'll have to stop at the motel, grab what I left there and settle my bill, then I'm out of here."

"We're going to miss you."

"I'll miss you. And Ivy. Do you know where she is?"

"In the backyard, I think."

"Then I'll catch her back there." He embraced Teeve, kissed her cheek. "You take care of yourself. Ivy, too."

"I will, honey. I promise."

After Mark loaded his box into the trunk of his car, he went around the side of the house to the patio, where he found Ivy. She was staring off into the distance as she rocked in an old aluminum glider splotched with rust. As he watched her, he was reminded of something Kyle had asked him. *Do you know what it's like to love a woman so much that just watching her breathe stops time?*

When she looked up, saw him standing there, she brushed away tears.

"Aren't you going to see me off?" he said as he scooted in beside her.

"No. I don't want you to go, so I'm going to sit out here and pout until the sun goes down or it's time to eat. Whichever comes first."

Ivy tilted her head back, blinking rapidly, trying to keep the tears from falling.

"Ivy?"

"I just don't think you're ready to go back yet."

"Why? Are we having chicken fried steak and gravy? If we are, I'll have to miss my flight."

"You know what I mean."

"That's what men don't understand about women. You say 'you know what I mean' when we don't have any idea what you mean."

"You've been through a lot here. You found out about your mother. How she lived. How she died. That can't have been easy. Then, you discovered more than you wanted to know about your father and you saw—"

"Ivy, Arthur McFadden caused a baby. That doesn't make him a father. Think about this. You take a ceramics class, you make a . . . I don't know. A bowl. A little bowl. Now that doesn't make you an artist, does it? Or, let's say you're a kid—nine, ten years old. Your uncle is driving, puts you on his lap and lets you steer the car for a few hundred yards. Now, are you a driver? No.

"Was Arthur McFadden a father? No. He *caused* a baby. Simply contributed an ingredient. When it was finished, it was a baby. He caused it, but it wasn't his. He was just the causer.

"Now, Gaylene *had* a baby. She carried it for nine months, nurtured it, gave it birth. She got up with it at night, nursed it back to health when it was sick. She read to it, sang to it, cried with it, laughed with it, kissed it. Loved it. Was she a mother? Yes. Hell, yes! And she was *my* mother."

Mark looked away, but Ivy could see the muscles working in his jaw as he clenched his teeth. In anger or sadness, she couldn't tell.

"See, this is what I'm talking about. You've got a lot of stuff in your head and you're going to have to deal with it. Work through it."

"And I will," he said.

"How? Who are you going to talk to in California?"

"You, for one. Believe it or not, we have phones way out west, all the way to California."

"Seriously, who's going to help you out there?"

"We have therapists *and* phones. What do you think of that? Psychologists, psychiatrists, stress managers. Why, Ivy, it's Hollywood. We've got bizarros who can make you remember being in the womb. I had a lady once with a poodle she couldn't house-train. She paid five thousand dollars to some weirdo who claimed the dog peed in the house because when he was in the womb, the bitch carrying him had been bitten by a snake in the backyard."

"You just made that up, didn't you."

"Yeah, but it's a good story, isn't it? I mean, it illustrates my point."

"You know, when you need to talk, the best person is the listener sitting across the table from you, someone you know, someone you trust. Someone you have a history with who'll hold your hand. Someone you care about."

"Someone who has a belly that looks like a giant water balloon?"

She smacked him on the shoulder, then put her arms around him and kissed him on the cheek. "I just don't want you to go."

"I have to, Ivy. I've got a clinic back there. And it's in trouble right now."

"And you've got a Jaguar and a house on the beach and a grand piano."

"Right. But somehow none of that seems as important to me as it used to. As it did before I came here."

"Are you really coming back here?"

"Sure. That doctor who's going to deliver your baby might need my help."

"Your help?"

"Hey, I've delivered Rottweilers, wolfhounds, Saint Bernards and Great Danes. A baby? Piece of cake."

"I'm scared."

"No, you're not. You're just tired of being pregnant."

"I'm scared of having this baby. It's going to hurt, and I'm not good with pain."

"Hey, you want to know about pain, let me tell you about my kidney stone. Having a baby is nothing

compared to what I went through. Women go on about
how it hurts to have a baby, but—"

"Smart-ass."

"I'd better go, Ivy. I've got to stop by the motel and
get to Tulsa. My flight's at eight."

"Okay, go on, then," she said. "See if I care."

"I hope you do."

"You just wait and see. You're going to miss me."

"I already do."

"Me too."

They stood, kissed, then walked to the gate, where
they kissed again. Not a "hi, cuz, how you doing" kind
of kiss; not a "haven't seen you in ages" kind of kiss.
This was a passionate kiss between a woman and a man.

When they parted, Mark said, "Ivy, I hope you'll
think long and hard about your decision when this baby
is born. You'd make a terrific mother."

"Mark, commitment isn't my strong suit."

"I know."

"Well, you're one to talk."

"But I think I can change."

"You'd better go or you'll miss your flight."

Mark kissed her on the cheek, then patted her belly.
"I'll see both of you in the delivery room," he said.

"You mean it?"

"Wouldn't say it if I didn't, ma'am. I never lie. Not to
my horses, my cows or my women."

"Oh, God," Ivy said, laughing and crying at the same
time. "You're beginning to sound like a damn Okie."

"So long, Ivy."

"Bye, Nicky Jack."

Epilogue

The christening was held on the back lawn of Hap and Matthew's home on the first Saturday of April, a glorious, sunny day when Lorraine Leann Harjo was nearly six months old. Gaylene's middle name had been Lorraine, and Leann was Teeve's middle name, so the decision to name the baby was an easy one.

Ivy had wanted to have the ceremony in the spring, her favorite season. And for one of the few times in her life, she had insisted on perfection.

Swanson's Funeral Home, which had provided the tent where the DeClare Ladies' Auxiliary had served those who searched for little Nicky Jack Harjo almost thirty years ago, now provided the chairs arranged in a semicircle on the lawn.

The tall camellia- and magnolia-scented candles came from Making Scents, a new venture by the Ladies' Auxiliary, who used the profits to help operate a shelter for abused women.

The Young Democrats, who had bought yellow ribbons

to tie to trees back in 1972, now provided white ribbons for the pines, oaks and elms surrounding the lawn.

The DAR, still in competition with the Auxiliary, set up a table covered with an Irish linen cloth, on which they placed vases of fragrant violets and candytufts as well as a magnificent silver tea service. And, at Martha Bernard Duchamp's insistence, they added a lovely antique bowl, which she filled with a punch heavy with Everclear, a drink both potent and aromatic with the familiar and overpowering aroma of Christmas trees.

Patti Frazier contributed the music to the affair, her accompanist one of Joe Dawson's daughters, who played piano at the Abundant Life Temple. The piano was moved and delivered to the patio free of charge by four of the younger and stronger deacons at the AME Church.

Hap and Matthew were the hosts, of course. Hap met the guests at the front door, then escorted them through the house and onto the back lawn. Matthew spent all his time in the kitchen, wearing a white apron and chef's hat. Despite the misgivings of everyone who'd tasted Matthew's food before, Ivy had picked him as caterer. And he'd surprised them all, outdoing himself with luscious bacon-wrapped broiled mushrooms, cheese puffs, almond-and-cream-cheese canapés, tiny lobster croquettes and spiced nuts. For desserts he prepared hazelnut tortes, cranberry crepes flambé and poppyseed cake.

Three tables were set up on the patio: one for coffee, tea and punch; one for Matthew's culinary creations; and one for presents for Lorraine, most gift-wrapped except for a large rocking horse carved by Jackson and Johnny Standingdeer, a project they'd been working on for more than three months.

The crowd was large, even more Harjos and their friends than had gathered for the family's last funeral, that of Enid's husband, Ben.

Lantana Mitchell showed up, looking younger and more glamorous than many thought she had a right to, but certainly not her plastic surgeon and, for sure, not her agent, who had sold her book for six figures, the title *Back to Life: The Story of Nick Harjo*.

Lantana was wearing a lemon-colored silk suit by Yves Saint Laurent and a diamond paid for by the proceeds of her book. She was accompanied by her new husband, Harold Madrid, responsible for the DNA testing proving that Arthur McFadden was Mark's father.

Three of the domino boys were there, two actually in dress clothes—polyester leisure suits. Lonnie Cruddup had died of pneumonia the previous winter. And Ron John O'Reily, who often didn't know where he was or why he was there, was wearing one of his old uniforms from American Pesticides, the company he'd retired from several years earlier. His dementia had progressed until the last thing he had to hold on to—the game of Shoot the Moon—had evaporated a few months earlier.

Johnny and Jackson Standingdeer had tried for a time to resurrect the game with some younger players but finally gave up. The game was not the same without Lonnie and Ron John.

Amax Dawson and his family were all present, as was Olene Turner and her gentleman friend, but he went largely ignored once Amax arrived.

Rowena Whitekiller had flown in from Chicago with her teenage daughter, Gaylene. Rowena had brought a camera and a bag of film, and she shot every roll.

Of course, not everyone who'd been involved in the

Nick Harjo saga was present, and not all of the news of what had happened to them was pleasant.

On the day Carrie had admitted killing Gaylene, she had joined Kippy at the house, then put him in the car with her inside the closed garage. After she started the engine, she held him in her arms as she read *The Cat in the Hat*. They were both dead of carbon monoxide poisoning before they were found, proof that she meant what she said at the pond: *I couldn't never let them take Kippy away from me. I'd never let that happen.*

O Boy was serving his time on death row at the Oklahoma State Penitentiary in McAlester, for his part in covering up Carrie's crime with the murder of Joe Dawson.

Kyle Leander was in the Oklahoma Eastern State Hospital for the Criminally Insane, but according to those who heard from him, he seemed to be at peace and had become quite fond of the place, as they were "not stingy with Lortab, Demerol and Thorazine."

But neither Carrie nor Kippy, O Boy nor Kyle, was on the mind of Lige Haney, who began the christening service that had taken days to prepare, as it included several verses from the Bible, the Koran and the Tipitaka, the holy book of Buddha; poetry by Maya Angelou and Maxine Hong Kingston; and quotes from essays by Thoreau, Louise Erdrich and the comic strip *Peanuts*, all of which Clara had typed in braille. And today, standing at Lige's side, her silver hair grown long enough to curl softly around her face, she was radiant.

Teeve had made Lorraine's christening clothes, a lovely long gown edged by Swedish lace and embroidered with tiny leaves of ivy along the hem. And she held the baby while Lige sprinkled Lorraine's head with holy water that came from a natural spring and had been blessed in Cherokee by Johnny and Jackson Standingdeer.

When Lorraine felt the drops of water on her face, she looked surprised, then pleased, and, finally, she laughed.

As Lige concluded the service, he said, "Lorraine Leann Harjo, honor thy father, Nick Harjo, and thy mother, Ivy Harjo, which is the First Commandment with promise; that it may be well with thee, and thou mayest live long on the earth."

And everyone drawn together by love on that day and at that moment chorused, "Amen," as Nick and Ivy held tightly to one another and their baby.

About the Author

BILLIE LETTS is the author of numerous highly acclaimed short stories and screenplays, and a former professor at Southeastern Oklahoma State University. Her first novel, *Where the Heart Is*, won the Walker Percy Award, sold more than three million copies, and became a major motion picture. Her second novel, *The Honk and Holler Opening Soon*, was named the first "Oklahoma Reads Oklahoma" selection. Her third novel, SHOOT THE MOON, was both a *New York Times* and *Wall Street Journal* bestseller. Billie Letts lives in Oklahoma with her husband Dennis.

Come home
to the wonderful
world of Billie Letts.

＝

Please turn this page
for a preview of
her latest novel

MADE IN THE U.S.A.

available
wherever books are sold.

Chapter One

Lutie McFee struggled into the too-tight red turtleneck, smoothed it across her ribs, then checked herself out in the mirror of the Wal-Mart dressing room.

She was almost pretty, but still had the not-quite-finished look of a teenager—unlined skin dappled with sand-colored freckles, cheeks not quite shed of baby fat, frizzy hair too wild to be tamed by gel or spray. Her hips were as narrow as a boy's and her feet looked too big for her tiny ankles and spindly legs.

But worst of all, she was convinced—not for the first time that day—that her breasts were never going to grow beyond the two walnut-sized bumps on her chest. The best she could hope for was a Wonder Bra, but doubted even that would perform the miracle she needed.

After she got kicked off the gymnastics team, she was free to eat again—whenever, whatever and as often as she wanted. So she began to satisfy her yearning for chili-cheese-fries, chocolate malts, double-meat hamburgers, coconut cream pie and banana nut muffins slathered with warm butter.

She figured if she'd pile enough weight onto her stick-figure body, she'd eventually be able to replace her training bras with triple As, or maybe even doubles.

But it didn't happen.

She jumped from one hundred and six pounds to one-eleven and remained a size two. But most disappointing of all, the additional five pounds didn't go anywhere near the training bra, though if she used the right kind of socks for stuffing, she could pull off a size A.

One of the consolations for all the hours she spent in the gym before and after school was the shelf in her bedroom crowded with trophies, ribbons and medals all for her balance beam performances. Margie Holcomb, who replaced her, hadn't even earned an "Also Mention Certificate." Not one.

Coach Stebens had fought for her, taking on the entire School Board, but like Lutie, she'd known from the beginning, the day the lie started circulating from classrooms to lockers, from the cafeteria to the parking lot, that it was a lost cause. Why? Because Superintendent Holcomb was Margie Holcomb's grandfather who thought if Lutie lost her place on the gymnastics squad, then she—Margie—would win all those trophies. Of course, that plan didn't work out. Margie was a mediocre gymnast at best; but Lutie was the best ever produced in not just Spearfish, but in all of South Dakota. And many said she had a good chance of going to the Olympics. That's how her first dream of all her dreams was born.

The first time a judge placed the ribbon with the First Place Medal around her neck and her coach handed her a bouquet of roses, she had all she'd ever dreamed of.

RECOGNITION!

But given the number of months since she had been

disqualified and now, the summer before her junior year, the dream of competing in the Olympics had died. Not a painless death either, not the kind that comes quietly in the night, stops the heart gently and takes the next breath away with an unknowing comfort.

No, this death was shocking in its suddenness. Mourned. Buried. Grieved in lonely silence. Gone.

Replaced now with a more realistic goal. No longer a dream, actually, but more of a longing for the kind of attention so many other girls got seemingly without effort. Popular girls with rounded hips and breasts that bounced like water balloons, but with little promise that she was destined to become the next Pamela Anderson, she thought she could be willing to settle for less.

If she could manage to give nature a boost, she would bleach her dark hair until it was the color of honey with streaks of gold. She would get more holes pierced in her ears, and have a pair of kissing lips tattooed on her neck. She might even wear a nose ring.

But until she could find a way to get out of Spearfish, South Dakota, that was not likely to happen.

She took off the turtleneck, folded it into a neat square, then tucked it into the front of her underpants. She'd just rezipped her jeans when someone knocked at the dressing room door.

"This room is taken," she yelled.

"Lutie, let me in."

"I'll be out in a minute, Floy," she said, her voice edged with anger.

"Open the door."

Lutie pulled on her old sweat shirt, bloused it around her hips, then unlocked the door.

Floy Satterfield, at nearly three hundred pounds, filled

the doorway. She had long ago given up on diets, counting instead on having her stomach stapled when she could put the money together. But that was a dim prospect given her four hundred dollar welfare check and the two extra mouths she had to feed.

"I need to go home," Floy said.

"Go? We just got here."

"I ain't feeling good."

"What's wrong now?" Lutie came down hard on the "now."

"Damned indigestion again." Floy fumbled a roll of Tums from her purse and popped two in her mouth. "You go find your brother and meet me out front."

"Well, I don't know where he is."

"He'll be where he always is. Now hurry."

Lutie waited until she could no longer hear the slap of Floy's rubber thongs, then slammed the door. She readjusted her sweat shirt, then satisfied that no one would guess she had a sweater stuffed in her pants, she ran a comb through her hair and checked her mascara.

She stepped out of the fitting room carrying the flannel nightgown and tweed jacket she wouldn't have been caught dead in, but she'd used them to conceal the turtleneck from the dressing room attendant.

Ignoring Floy's demand to hurry, Lutie made her way to the magazine rack where she pulled out a couple of movie magazines, then sat down cross-legged on the floor and began flipping pages. Each time she came across a picture of Brad Pitt, she ripped the page out, folded it so as to avoid creasing Brad's face and slid it into her purse.

Fifteen minutes later she found her brother Fate in the electronics department at the keyboard of a display computer where he was trying to find out who invented shoelaces.

Though he was only eleven, he sometimes seemed to Lutie more like an old man than a child. He wore thick glasses with wire frames; worried about global warming and the endangerment of pandas; and moved like creeping Jesus. He liked plaid shirts, buttermilk, and old clocks. And he had a habit of running his fingers through his hair which she predicted would make him bald before he finished eighth grade.

He spent most of his time reading, watching weird TV shows about lighthouses, Roman baths, prairie dogs, Jack Kerouac and the Khmer Empire—subjects that nobody else would give two hoots about.

And he played games by himself—Trivial Pursuit, Scrabble and Boggle.

He had no friends that she knew of—was never invited to sleepovers or slumber parties, campouts or even birthday parties. And he never invited boys to the places where he and Lutie happened to be living.

He went for long solitary walks at night and in the rain, he often talked in his sleep, but in strange languages she couldn't identify.

Lutie wouldn't be surprised if he grew up to be a shepherd.

"We gotta go," she said.

"I'm not ready yet."

"Floy's waiting on us."

"I just now got on the net, Lutie. Some girl's been hogging it for the last half hour."

"So?"

"I need a few more minutes."

"Suit yourself. But Floy's gonna be pissed. Big time."

As Lutie walked away, she saw several people rushing toward the front of the store, but she was too interested in getting to the cosmetic section to investigate what was going on.

A clerk restocking hand cream eyed her suspiciously as she began pulling tubes of lipstick from the Revlon rack. But when two older teenaged girls came by and started opening bottles at the perfume counter, the clerk's attention was divided.

Lutie found a shade of Lightning Red she liked, palmed the tube and meandered to the other side of the aisle where she slipped the lipstick into her purse.

Suddenly, the intercom blared. "Code Blue. Code Blue at register three."

The announcement sent the clerk hurrying away as Lutie moved on to a shelf of Maybelline make-up. She tried one shade of blush, then another, dabbing color onto her cheeks until her face looked bruised.

Finally, she settled on Purple Twilight, dropped it in her purse, then headed toward the front of the store where she knew Floy would be fuming.

But she wasn't the only one going that way. People were rushing past her and she could see a crowd forming at one of the check-outs.

The intercom crackled with static. "Attention Wal-Mart shoppers, we need a doctor at register three. Uh . . . is there a doctor in the store?"

When a man in a cowboy hat bumped Lutie with his cart, she said, "Hey. Watch where you're going!" but he ignored her.

"What happened, Ida," the man yelled to a skinny woman ahead of him.

"They said some woman dropped dead at the check-out."

"No shit?"

"Come on!"

Lutie had just reached the edge of the gathering crowd when a baby-faced boy wearing a starched blue shirt and a security badge pushed past her.

"Did someone die?" the skinny woman asked him.

"Looks like it."

"You know who it is?"

"Big fat woman's all I know."

Lutie felt a knot of dread building in her chest. She called Floy's name, but with the noise and commotion inside, and a siren blaring outside, she knew Floy couldn't hear her.

She tried to push her way through, but too many people were pushing back, so she circled around, trying to get in from the other side, but no one would budge.

Then she saw a policeman coming through the door.

"Okay," he shouted. "You folks move back and let me through."

The crowd grew quiet as they parted to make room for the policeman who shouldered his way inside the group. Lutie fell in behind him.

And that's when she saw Floy.

She had pitched sideways when she fell, slamming into racks of batteries, disposable lighters, *TV Guide*s and candy, spilling them onto the floor beside her. Her head was twisted at an angle that would have been painful had she been able to feel pain, and her glasses had slipped onto her cheeks. Her mouth was pulled into a perfect O as if she had been about to whistle, and bits of the Tums she had been chewing clung to her bottom lip. And her fingers, adorned with rhinestone rings, still clutched the *National Enquirer* she had just paid for.

The policeman knelt beside her still body and dipped his fingers into the folds of flesh around her neck, probing for a pulse. Then he bent over her and put his cheek next to her opened mouth. Moments later, he straightened, pretending not to notice the urine seeping through the crotch of Floy's blue polyester pants and puddling beneath her buttocks.

He stood and faced the checker behind the register. "You know who she is?" he asked.

The checker shook her head. "I seen her in here before though."

Then he turned to the crowd around him. "Do any of you know this woman?"

Those gathered craned their necks and waited.

"Is anyone here with this woman?" he yelled.

Then softly, her voice hardly more than a whisper, Lutie said, "I am."

Reading Group Guide

A Q & A with Billie Letts

Q. *How do you plot your novels? Do you have the whole story in your mind before you start . . . let the story take on a life of its own . . . or use some other method, such as a storyboard? For example, how and when during the creation of this novel did you come to the decision to have Kyle kill Arthur?*

A. I don't plot my books. I have a rather vague beginning and ending in mind when I start. But so much of what happens between the first chapter and the last is a surprise to me. That's the part of the writing process that intrigues me. And the part that often makes me want to give up writing and become a lumberjack.

I didn't know when I started *Shoot the Moon* who had killed Gaylene Harjo. At first, I thought it was O Boy Daniels. Then I decided it was Arthur McFadden. When the identity of the killer came to me, it was truly a thought of the moment. After that, the rest of the story started falling into place, including Arthur's death.

Q. *A major character, if not the main character, of this novel is Mark Albright, aka Nicky Jack Harjo. Is it difficult as a female writer to find a male sensibility or voice? Is it easier to write from a woman's point of view?*

A. I like writing from a male's point of view. Forney Hull, Moses Whitecotton, Caney Paxton, Bui Khanh—I enjoyed creating each of these characters in my previous novels and I loved them from the moment they came to life in my head.

That wasn't the case, though, with Mark/Nick. He was, in the early part of the book, snobbish and hateful. He was raised by affluent adoptive parents who provided private schools, nannies, travel, wealth—everything that contributed to his acting so superior.

But after I got to know him better, I realized that he was an unhappy loner who needed to be loved. We got along much better after that.

Q. *You seem to prefer a third person point of view in writing your novels. Have you ever written in the first person? Is there a character in this story who most resembles you and speaks with your own voice?*

A. I've tried writing in the first person but you know what the problem is? All those sentences with "I" in them. I just couldn't handle that.

If there is a character in *Shoot the Moon* who most

speaks with my voice, it's Ivy. She sounds quick and funny, but she's no more sure of herself than I am. We're both vulnerable, but we try to hide our insecurity with humor.

Q. *You have created two very nasty villains in this novel in Arthur McFadden and 0 Boy Daniels, his half brother. Was it challenging or just fun to create such "bad guys"?*

A. I don't find it difficult to create the villains, but it's painful to write what they do to "people" I care about. I cried when Roger Brisco inflicted such pain in *Where the Heart Is*. I had nightmares about what Sam Kellam did in *The Honk and Holler Opening Soon*. And many times as I was working on *Shoot the Moon*, I had to walk away from the typewriter because of the pain these two half brothers inflicted on others.

Several years ago, my husband and I were making a long drive to North Carolina. A copy of *Where the Heart Is* on tape had arrived shortly before we left home, so I took it along so we could listen to it as we traveled.

I think we were on the third cassette when I switched it off and began to cry. My husband asked me what was wrong.

"That poor girl," I said. "Novalee. She's just so vulnerable."

"Well, hell," he said. "You made her that way."

Writing is a strange endeavor!

Q. *All your novels have been set in small towns. What is*

there about small-town life that interests and inspires you? Is DeClare, Oklahoma, a real place?

A. Oklahoma is mostly empty country, dotted with towns and small communities, some so small they don't even appear on a map. The total population of the state is roughly three million; Oklahoma City and Tulsa, our largest cities, account for about two-thirds of our population.

Though I was born and raised in Tulsa, I've spent more than half my life in towns of only a few thousand, but it's here, in these off-the-interstate places, towns with two stoplights and one taxi, where real "characters" emerge in a way they don't in cities, towns where these "characters" are more easily known than they are in metropolitan areas.

So these are the places I go to tell my stories: a town with a run-down drive-in café operated by a Vietnam veteran in a wheelchair; a pool hall owned by a woman who makes peanut butter pies, frequented by four old geezers called the "domino boys"; an AME church, an abandoned school bus, and a massive retail store where a Vietnamese man, a Native American woman, and a seventeen-year-old pregnant girl live secretly, hiding out from a world that has offered them little solace.

Is DeClare a real place? Only in my mind and the minds of the readers who might leave the interstate and visit this small town for a few hours someday.

Q. *What gave you the idea to let Gaylene speak "from beyond the grave" in her diary? You had to keep her "voice" that of a young girl. Was that easy or diffi-cult to do?*

A. In the first draft of my manuscript, I had only two entries of Gaylene's diary, which Enid gave to Mark on the day they met. After my editor, Jamie Raab, read that draft, she said, "I'd like to know more about Gaylene. I think you can accomplish that by letting us read more about her through her writing."

Jamie's idea led me to create another twenty-five or thirty entries in just two days, a real record for me as I'm a slow writer. But I could recall my own teen years, could remember too clearly what seemed important to me then—my buckteeth (much too big); the size of my breasts (much too small); boyfriends (how to get them); freckles (how to get rid of them).

By crawling back into my teenage skin, pulling up some old memories, both the pleasant and the painful, I found the "voice" of Gaylene telling me her story.

Q. *In your introduction of all the major characters in the prologue and your summing up of their fates in the epilogue, are you consciously reaching back to the structure of some of the great novels of the nine-teenth century? What prompted you to set up your novel with that beginning and ending device?*

A. If my book is shaped in some way resembling those "great novels," it's not by design, but I'm compli-mented that you would find any comparison of my story to those classics.

In *Shoot the Moon*, I needed to give Mark Albright some distance and some time to adjust to becoming Nick Harjo. And because the characters introduced in the prologue play some part in my story, I thought the readers would want to know what has transpired in the months between Mark's departure and Nick's return.

So, the device of using prologue and epilogue seemed to contribute to the rhythm of the structure of *Shoot the Moon*.

Q. *Where did you get the idea for this novel? Was there a real-life child disappearance that intrigued or haunted you?*

A. In 1968 someone (and I'll probably never know who) apparently planned to abduct my three-year-old son Tracy from a day care center.

We were living in Champaign, Illinois, where my husband was working toward his doctorate; I was teaching in a small town high school thirty miles away.

One afternoon after school, I drove back to Champaign and went to pick Tracy up. The manager of the day care met me at the door to ask why I hadn't come sooner, as I said I would when I'd phoned earlier in the day.

When I told her I hadn't called, she explained that a woman who sounded like me had phoned asking her to have Tracy ready and waiting because we had a family emergency, so I would come for him soon. And given the urgency of the situation, the caller asked her to have him wait outside.

As a result, the manager had dressed Tracy in his coat, hat, gloves, and sent him outside to wait on the swings. Fortunately, after a half hour or so of sitting in the cold, he'd come back inside to thaw out.

Of course, we reported the incident to the police, but nothing ever came to light as to who might have made that call.

Now, some thirty-five years later, each time I read about an abducted child, I relive the fear I felt that day. I don't know how many children were abducted back in 1968, but I believe someone was planning for my little boy to be one of them.

Q. *The title for this novel,* Shoot the Moon, *comes from the domino game played by the old-timers in Teeve's Place. Were the domino players or the game itself something from your own life?*

A. Soon after my first son was born, my husband, Dennis, and I moved to Wagoner, Oklahoma, his hometown, so that he could commute to Northeastern Oklahoma State University while his mother cared for the baby and I worked at the courthouse. Each day when Dennis came back from his classes, he'd go to King's to play Moon, a gambling game played with dominoes. King's, the pool hall, was also called—by the regulars—The Hall of Science, The Office, and The Recreation Hall.

The good Baptists called it The Den of Sin because of the gambling that took place inside.

Females weren't welcome in the Oklahoma pool halls back then, so if I needed to reach Dennis, I would have to call. It took me some weeks to learn that the second the phone rang, the place echoed with a chorus of "I'm not here."

If speaking to my husband was especially important, I had to go downtown and knock on King's window, an act frowned on by the old-timers. So you can imagine what the reaction was when one day I didn't knock, didn't wait on the sidewalk. Instead, I marched into King's trying to look fearless and fiery as I encountered two dozen men, all of whom were speechless. The dark, ugly room was smoky and absolutely silent.

I have never seen Dennis move faster than he did that day as he jumped up from the domino table, escorted me outside and followed me home.

I am happy to report that some of the men present then still remember and rehash the day a woman entered the pool hall.

Q. *What subject area do you gravitate toward when you walk into a bookstore? What books have you been reading lately? Is there any current author whose writing you absolutely love?*

A. I always go first to the fiction section in a library or bookstore. I've recently read *What Night Brings*, by Carla Trujillo; *Last Year's River*, by Allen Morris Jones; *Three Junes*, by Julia Glass; *The No.1 Ladies' Detective Agency*, by Alexander McCall Smith; *The Monk Downstairs*, by Tim Farrington; *Never Change*, by Elizabeth Berg; *A Handful of Dust*, by Evelyn Waugh. I am currently reading *The Amateur Marriage*, by Anne Tyler; and *The Stones of Summer*, by Dow Mossman. Oh, two more I read a few weeks ago, *Peace Like a River*, by Leif Enger; and *The Last Juror*, by John Grisham.

I love the work of Anne Lamott, Howard Mosher, Sandra Cisneros, Pete Dexter, Maya Angelou, Anne Tyler, and Barbara Kingsolver.

Q. *Issues of race are like a background noise in this book, not the obvious trigger of any crises or climax, but always "loading the gun" one might say. What prompted you to make Gaylene a Cherokee?*

A. I guess the most obvious answer is that this story is set in Oklahoma, home to *many* Native Americans. Look at the names of some of our towns: Anadarko, Chickasha, Waynoka, Tahlequah, Checotah, Wapanucka, Tonkawa, Oologah.

In addition, I feel that any time a character is not Caucasian, Anglo-Saxon, and Protestant, a story offers the possibility of added tension. Perhaps you remember some characters from my previous novels: Moses Whitecotton and Galilee Jackson, both African American or Vena Takes Horse, a Crow woman, or Bui Khanh, a Vietnamese Buddhist, all of whom have suffered the effects of racism on some level in my first two novels.

And in this story, Gaylene Harjo and Rowena Whitekiller, Cherokee girls, knew the meaning of bigotry, just as Joe Dawson is the victim of overt racism.

Bigotry and racism reflect the most vile kind of thinking and behavior in our society. My greatest hope is that my stories might lead readers to greater acceptance, tolerance, and compassion for one another.

Q. *Your use of humor shines through in your "quirky" characters, such as the wonderful domino players. How planned is your introduction of a humorous scene? Do you tend to juxtapose a lighter episode with a darker one? Would you categorize your books as comedies or tragedies . . . or something else?*

A. Actually, I don't really plan my scenes. I generally just start writing a chapter with one or two rather vague goals in mind, a couple of events that will move the story forward. If something humorous occurs to me along the way, I'm delighted.

I suppose I'd categorize my books as "slice of life" novels . . . what happens to my characters seems to me to be the result of living in the chaos of the real world.

Q. *Unmarried, single mothers have now appeared in all your books. This book features two such young women, Gaylene and Ivy—and tangentially introduces a third, Lantana. Previously, you have said you put your characters in situations where they must make choices about bringing another life into the world. But since your characters are your creation, aren't you, the author, really making their choices when they opt for abortion, adoption, or keeping their babies? Do you think you will continue to use this issue in your next book?*

A. Yes, more than likely I will. Why? As I've said before, the greatest decision a woman must make in her life is whether or not to give birth. And if she chooses to have a baby, her next decision is whether to keep the child or put it up for adoption. As you pointed out, I have made those choices for many of the females in my novels when they discover they're pregnant.

As a fiction writer, my choice depends on the character's story line. For example, if Novalee Nation had not been pregnant, I would have written a very different book. The same can be said for Vena Takes Horse, Ivy, and other characters I've created.

As a woman, I'm so glad I made the decision to have and keep my children. But my decision is not the right decision for *all* women because of a number of circumstances. Therefore, I respect and will fight for a woman's right to choose. And in future books I write, I will continue to explore the choices women are often forced to make.

Discussion Questions

1. In her novels, Billie Lefts beautifully captures the personalities in Oklahoma's small towns. Do you think DeClare, Oklahoma, could be "Any Town, USA" or is it uniquely a small town in the state of Oklahoma?

2. Key themes in this novel deal with the question of identity and self-knowledge. Mark Albright (Nicky Jack Harjo) doesn't know who he is. What does he learn about himself during the course of the story? Does he change in any fundamental way from the beginning to the end of the book?

3. Some philosophies say that who we are is a question of genes. Others that we are formed by our upbringing, experiences, and culture. Does nature or nurture have a bigger impact on the characters in this novel?

4. Do you find the love relationship between Ivy and Mark/Nicky Jack believable? Why or why not?

5. We get to know Gaylene, posthumously, through what other people say about her and through her diaries. Are the two views of her similar or different? Why does she call herself "Spider Woman"?

6. What life lessons does Gaylene encounter through the crucial years she is writing in her diary? Does she change as a result of them?

7. What importance do you think race has in this novel: not much, some, or a great amount? What are some examples of racial discrimination faced by characters? Mark/Nicky Jack doesn't know he is part Cherokee. Is it important that he does know?

8. The book also raises some troubling issues faced by adopted children. What are they? Do you think an adopted child should be given his birth parents' identities? Why or why not?

9. Mark/Nicky Jack talks about having a careful plan for his life, and then fate dramatically changes that plan. He points out that Ivy has no plan at all, and she's drifting through life. What are the pros and cons of each character's approach to life? What is your own approach?

10. What do you make of the domino players? Why are they in the story? What do they contribute besides the title?

11. A frequent situation in the novels of Billie Lefts is the dilemma faced by an unmarried pregnant woman about the child she carries. In this book, what choice does each of the unmarried pregnant women make with regard to her unborn child, and what are the consequences of that choice? Do you think each woman makes the best choice for her?

12. Because this is fiction, the author can create any ending she wishes for her characters. Do you agree with the fate she gives to each of the major characters? In particular, how do you feel about what happened to Carrie and her son Kippy? Are you convinced she would have taken his life along with her own?

13. Who would you say is the happiest or most "together" character or characters in this book? Why? Does "shooting the moon" make for happiness?

14. If there is someday a sequel about Mark/Nicky Jack and Ivy, what do you think might happen to them? Do you think their relationship will last?

Billie Letts on . . . The Call That Changed My Life

"Billie?" she said when I answered the phone.

"Yes."

"Hi. This is Oprah Winfrey."

I couldn't speak.

"Congratulations," she said. "I've selected your book, *Where the Heart Is*, for my book club."

I still couldn't speak.

"Hello?" she said, checking to see if I was still on the line.

I knew I had to say something, anything, but all that came to my mind was the timing of her call.

"It's a wonder you caught me at home," I said. "You see, my husband and I have been staying with our son in California for a few months while I've been working on a screenplay, but I got worried about our dogs here even though the dog catcher feeds and waters them every day and I know he takes good care of them; I'm afraid that someone might come into the yard and leave the gate unlocked and the dogs, they're named Doug and Sweetie, might get out and get hit by a car, or someone could take them to sell to labs that use dogs for experiments, which happens more than people might think, but I doubt anyone would steal them to keep because they're mixed-breed strays, and by the way, Doug came from Chicago, a street dog that was tied to a fence in an alley during a freezing rain, so my son's girl friend . . ."

If Oprah hadn't laughed, I would have told her how Doug and Sweetie got their names, listed all their favorite foods, mentioned that Doug was a jumper and Sweetie was . . .

I had watched several of Oprah's dinner parties where the book discussions took place. Sometimes they were held in the author's home or in a lovely New England inn, or even at Oprah's home. And the dinners were almost always prepared by her personal chef—gourmet meals served on delicate china, the table covered by fine linen, a centerpiece of cut flowers.

My dinner party was held in the snack bar of a Wal-Mart just outside Chicago.

Oprah wasn't there when my husband and I arrived, but Martha Williams, Darlene Stark, Gail Christian, and Mary Ann Perri, the four women who had been chosen to discuss my book, were. We quickly formed a bond prompted in part by the anxiety of being on television and saying something stupid, and in part by our excitement at meeting Oprah.

When she did arrive, the five of us were standing together as if we were in a receiving line. Oprah went from one woman to the other, shaking hands as she introduced herself. I was rather puzzled when she passed me by and went to one of the tables in the snack bar where her hair and makeup people were waiting.

I believe it was Martha who whispered to me, "Billie, doesn't she know who you are?"

"No, we've never met."

Seconds later, Jill Adams, the producer of the show spoke to Oprah and pointed to me.

Oprah, smiling, called to me across the room. "Hey, Billie," she said, "I thought you worked for Wal-Mart."

So much for celebrity.

Our instructions were simple enough: follow Oprah to the counter where the food was laid out—corn dogs, chicken nuggets, burgers, typical Wal-Mart fare—then follow her back to the table and take the seats we'd been assigned.

The snack bar had been cordoned off from the rest of the store, but at the end of each aisle shoppers had gathered to get a glimpse of Oprah. Inside our area there looked to be a hundred people—the film crew, Wal-Mart executives, and many members of Oprah's staff. And cameras, oh, so many cameras pointed at us and so many microphones hanging over our heads.

All five of us, the readers and myself, were petrified when we heard someone shout, "Cameras rolling," but Oprah was relaxed and friendly as we took our seats at the dining table. We all watched her and followed her lead. When she put her napkin in her lap, we did the same. When she took a sip of water, we took a sip of water. I think we may have made some small talk as we prepared to eat, but when Oprah turned to me and said, "Billie, would you say the blessing?" all talk ceased. Absolute silence.

I froze. I thought my heart would stop. I even thought about faking a fainting spell. But there was nothing to do but pray in front of those cameras to an audience of millions.

"Of course," I said, my voice quivering.

We bowed our heads and I prayed.

Afterward, I asked my husband what I'd said as I couldn't recall one word.

"You did fine," he said, "Just fine. But it was the shortest blessing I've ever heard."

When the meal began, so did the discussion of my book. Now, Oprah could eat, think, and talk at the same time, and do it all with grace, but the rest of us looked like frightened kids sent to the principal's office for misbehaving.

We were, of course, intimidated by the cameras, awed by being in the company of Oprah Winfrey, and terrified at the prospect of eating. What if we had chicken in our mouths when she asked a question? What if we had mustard or ketchup smeared on our chins or dropped food in our laps or got lettuce stuck between our teeth?

So while Oprah ate, the rest of us watched her and tried to offer intelligent responses to her questions, tried to contribute what we could to the discussion.

Once, I tried to take a drink of my tea because my mouth was so dry my upper lip was sticking to my teeth, but my hand was shaking so badly that tea sloshed out of my glass and into my plate.

When the meal ended and the discussion came to a close, my plate was as full as it had been when we started, only now my salad, chicken, and fries were islands in a sea of tea.

* * *

Certainly, the mileposts in many of our lives are similar—the births of children, the deaths of those we love, family ties and friends. All are life-altering.

But in my life, following those events, nothing has been more significant than Oprah's selection of *Where the Heart Is*. The book has been read around the world by millions of people, and while I am pleased with my story, and thankful to my agent and Warner Books, Oprah is the reason for most of those readers.

She has altered the reading habits of multitudes. She has reinvigorated an interest in books that many seemed to have lost. But more than her influence on readers, she has become a kind of lightning rod of passion for many of us to have more satisfying lives, lives in which we can think better of ourselves.

Oprah is one of my heroes. Not because she chose my novel for her book club, but because she works in a myriad of ways to make our world a better place.

Long before that phone call came, before that voice said, "Hi. This is Oprah Winfrey," I had already learned to like her, to trust her . . . just the way we feel about friends.

VISIT US ONLINE
@ WWW.HACHETTEBOOKGROUPUSA.COM.

AT THE HACHETTE BOOK GROUP USA WEB SITE YOU'LL FIND:

CHAPTER EXCERPTS FROM SELECTED NEW RELEASES
•
ORIGINAL AUTHOR AND EDITOR ARTICLES
•
AUDIO EXCERPTS
•
BESTSELLER NEWS
•
ELECTRONIC NEWSLETTERS
•
AUTHOR TOUR INFORMATION
•
CONTESTS, QUIZZES, AND POLLS
•
FUN, QUIRKY RECOMMENDATION CENTER
•
PLUS MUCH MORE!

BOOKMARK HACHETTE BOOK GROUP USA
@ WWW.HACHETTEBOOKGROUPUSA.COM.

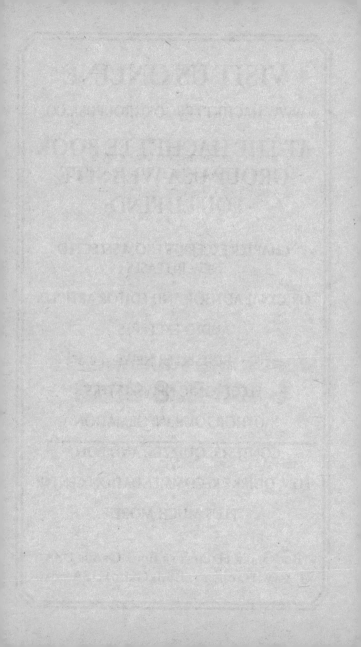

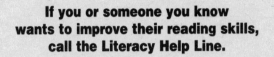